THE BLUE
IS WHERE
GOD LIVES

THE BLUE
IS WHERE
GOD LIVES

A NOVEL

SHARON SOCHIL
WASHINGTON, PhD

THE OVERLOOK PRESS
New York, NY

Library of Congress Control Number: 2022947228

ISBN: 978-1-4197-6710-4
eISBN: 978-1-64700-964-9

Printed and bound in the United States

1 3 5 7 9 10 8 6 4 2

Abrams books are available at special discounts when
purchased in quantity for premiums and promotions as
well as fundraising or educational use. Special editions
can also be created to specification. For details, contact
specialsales@abramsbooks.com or the address below.

ABRAMS The Art of Books
195 Broadway, New York, NY 10007
abramsbooks.com

To Richard Peña, who said, when everyone else said the opposite:
"You should write. You're a really good writer."

PRE(R)AMBLE

THEY SAY IT CAME FROM the ships. Living in the cracks of the planks. A memory inhibitor. Something designed to erase yourself. Sleeping on pillows made of ash. Dripping from the dicks of men the color of clouds and seeping into the material consciousness of our sleep. We didn't really understand the severity of the situation. Language had been rerouted. Killings were rampant. We caught it. Ended up acting just like them.

Those of us lining both sides of the ancient Gambia River became West Africans. West Africans became Geechee. Geechee became Black—a condition that created White people.

Black folks lost themselves when they moved up north. And memories had the pleasure of being rescored in the palm of a new music and new tongues speaking wildly, pulled from the cracks of Creation like a demon with curses to pass out weekly on one of their most favorite holidays—Sunday. We cursed that day, making it so that if *we* worked on that day, *they—the cloud-colored people—*would end up no longer able to speak in tongues. An exorcism of almost six million Black folks left the open space of southern American landscapes that overwhelmed with dreams of red, yellow, orange, and blue—a sky so blue it makes you want to curl up and immerse yourself in it, and so wide dumbass motherfuckers thought they could touch it. Fools were always jumping off roofs trying to touch it. When southerners got up north, they found buildings so tall that they hid the sky. People from the south couldn't get their balance, and they never did get their balance back. Ran some of them plum crazy, as the old folks used to say—*plum crazy*.

The axe-wielding woman was one of them old Geechee people who moved north and went plum crazy.

She held that axe to her grandson's head, spewing threats that at first nobody took seriously, even though she had already made good on that fuckin' promise. In Houston, Blue was kept in suspense for two hours before they told her the truth. It would have been more humane if they had just told her the truth from the beginning.

This axe-wielding woman had unobtainable hopes about her actions. She hoped they would not be misinterpreted as a desperate act but as a radical gesture demanding that life should change and that things should end as they were. But this was no glorious call for revolution; it was the result of a fragmented self—and fragmented selves were so common by then that she barely drew a crowd, even though she had already started hacking into the boy's mother.

Eventually, when it was over, she was described as having *no memory* of the past two hours. Meanwhile, Blue was flooded with memories. Memories that belonged to that axe-wielding lunatic. And other memories that popped in and out of Blue's mind like a jigsaw time line, making no sense at all. You'll see what I'm talking about. Houston. To Detroit. South migrating north. Then the reverse. New York. To Houston. Then on down to the coast, where Texas and Mexico meet in the desert. The Detroit family. The East Texas Rose family. Moving on a nomadic time line also known as the diaspora, like motherless ants with no antennae. Unplanned re-*memberings* that work like severed limbs looking for a way to appendage themselves back to me.

Because I changed too. I'm no different. But I did try to hold on to some elements of myself. Despite my efforts, the umbrella and the little white gloves overtook me. And as unfortunate as it was, those two hours did give me some time to start revealing myself, and the living history that has colonized me, initially perceived to be a *Lie*. But we do work that out later.

As you may have guessed by now, I was there in Detroit, in proximity to Texas. When the blood gurgled from the mouth of Blue's daughter, Tsitra, as her breath snagged in her throat, as her spirit struggled to slip away. Faint as it was, Tsitra held on to her life. Her body still working to pulsate streams of blood running onto the floor. Her dark skin turned purple from the bruising. Tsitra, lying on her right side, *could see us*. Lying there caked in her blood, *she could see us*. The axe-wielding woman holding Tsitra's son in one hand and the Georgia-made axe in the other. *She could see us*. The baby not even crying at all. *She could see us*. Looking up at his grandmother through the biggest, blackest most innocent eyes you've ever seen. *She could see us*. Sitting on the floor next to her. *She could see us*. Comforting her. *She could see us.* Stroking her left cheek with the caress of a hand. *She could see us.* While his grandmother ranted and raved, *she could see us.*

These two hours required me to rely on re-*memberings* rather than history because I know I cannot, should not, trust recorded history to help Blue navigate this tragedy. It would be absolutely dim-witted of me to rely on Oscar Wilde or Thomas Jefferson or Emerson for the history that will enlighten Blue on these matters. The memory would have to metamorphose itself into metaphorical and imagistic associations. Otherwise it would enter into this crack as it initially did—perceived to be a *Lie.*

For entry into this moment of horrifying knowings, it is important for me not to reveal, that is, reinforce, an already established reality that you and I agree upon beforehand. Authentic characteristics mindful of and rebellious toward the expectations and impositions of my relationship with Blue would encourage an understanding of history versus remembering, and remembering versus re-*membering*. Re-*membering* as in reconnecting memory as in re-appending limbs of the body, the family, the population of the past.

It was the struggle, the pitched battle between remembering and forgetting, that became the device for breaking free that which pits Blue against herself. It was the device that I came to attend to. The monumental tragedy of this moment opened a wormhole that breached the insane rationality of colonization and set us on a path to regeneration through numbers. Or, more specifically, through time.

And the effort to both remember and not know became the structure of our relationship.

1

WHEN THE CALL CAME IN, Blue was just about to leave the house. She'd been studying her to-do list in her reminder app when the buzz startled her, and she dropped her phone. A smile tugged at the corners of her lips when she saw her son's name light up the screen as she bent down to pick it up. Standing back up, she moved through an energy that made her light-headed. The elements around her moved slower against the speed of sunlight cutting across her fourth-floor bedroom. From the corner of her eye, a streak of something slipped past her. She ignored the disorienting swirls, the sense of fragmented time; it was not uncommon for things to move slowly in Houston. The day had begun like any other summer day in South Texas. Sunny. Hot. Still. The humidity made nature just sit for a while, inside of air so thick it slowed down the rotation of the earth around the sun. The plants. The trees. The dirt. The animals. The sky. All of it still, even though in motion. Just sitting for a while, dripping like the sweat off a fat man eating pork.

"Momma. Are you sitting down?"

"No. Why?"

"I think you need to sit down."

"Why?"

"I need to tell you something. And you need to sit down."

"Just tell me what it is . . ."

"Are you sitting down?"

Blue never understood why people asked that question. Delivering news that would rip your heart out was just as bad standing as sitting. "You're scaring me. What is it?"

"I think Tsitra has been killed."

There it was. He dropped the information into her lap, which could not hold it because she was standing. The information fell to the floor, and the weight of it dragged her down with it. On her way down, she began to hear a sound like an echo left behind by one of them old slaves who would rather kill their children than see them become a slave. Who would just do it! Just kill their own babies. In a fit of mercy. And then cry about it for centuries inside caves named after tragedies.

Thirty-eight minutes later, when her son came over to check on her, she was still on the floor where she had dropped. Sitting on her knees and the backs of her heels in a daze. He helped her to her bed. "We're not sure she's dead. The police are outside the house, trying to get to her inside," he said, in barely a whisper.

The woman holding Tsitra and her two-year-old son hostage wielded an axe she brought with her from Georgia, promising to cut off her grandson's head unless everyone did exactly as she instructed.

"Back up! Back up! Get away from this house! Do not come in here!"

The two-hour wait for an update on the horror evolving thirteen hundred miles away in Detroit unfolded like the petals of a night flower at sunset. One petal opened, then another and another and another, until the spiral of a *sunflower* revealed itself in the center of an ironic nocturnal night bloom set against the reflective light of the sun. Coerced by what seemed like the strange randomness of the spiral, memory began to undo itself and she slipped into the beginning stages of a stillness that unraveled her nerves. Stillness was something that had always unnerved her. The first time she had been asked to sit still at fifteen, she had deliberately refused. The idea of no movement at all, to be constrained in such a way, was a direct attack on her freedom to be herself, to live her own life. It was as unnatural to her as death itself.

Blue waited by phone for an update from Detroit, as did a growing crowd outside the dilapidated two-story duplex at the end of Automobile Industry Lane, a long road that ran from the Ford factory in neighboring Dearborn to downtown Detroit and snaked through the city like a river to a dead end at the corner of Garrett Morgan Road on the south side of Detroit.

The initial small crowd, which can be attributed to an insensitivity developed out of an overwhelming number of murders in Detroit, gave way to a larger crowd as more police, paramedics, and firefighters arrived, and the neighbors started spreading the word of who was being held hostage. Tsitra was popular across the city of Detroit. With a heart for the mistreated and a ravenous taste for nightlife, Tsitra was known to both the struggling poor of Detroit and to the Motown wannabe moguls—like her boyfriend, whose mother had already begun hacking into Tsitra's body with one hand while cradling her grandson with the other.

A man in the crowd, charging the house, had to be restrained by three others. "That's my daughter!" he screamed. "I have to get through! Let go of me!"

Also in the crowd, later reported by the Detroit clan of nieces, nephews, and cousins who talked incessantly about the scene outside the falling-down house, were two peculiar otherworldly women. They were described as ghosts. Barely visible, almost sunspots, only a few people caught glimpses of them. Upon being noticed, the women shifted. One woman wore a long flowing white muslin dress that draped her figure with a flattering high Empire-style waistline. She carried a frilly matching umbrella in her glove-covered hand, slightly above her wide-brimmed, matching lace-wrapped hat. The other woman, dressed just as exquisitely, wore a long beige-and-brown dress with a drop waist, hundreds of small buttons running from her waist to the top of her neckline. Her skirt swept the ground as she walked, and it opened to the front to reveal trousers and snakeskin cowboy boots. Her hat was more utilitarian but matched the outfit perfectly nonetheless.

Inside the house were faint cries of "Please. Please. Somebody help me."

The Detroit police had sectioned off the scene with a yellow rope instead of the traditional crime scene's yellow tape. The police chief had innovatively come up with this rope idea because the city was bankrupt and couldn't afford to buy enough tape to keep up with all the murders and other crimes. The rope could be used repeatedly.

Unable to listen to the guttural moaning that pierced right through the clamoring gossip of the crowd anymore, Tsitra's father broke away from the three men holding him and past the rope into a mob of police, who inexplicably turned their guns on him. The police sergeant in charge stepped in between the guns of her subordinates, who were both Black and White, and stopped the man with a simple look of compassion. Where the strength of three men and the prospect of a hail of bullets had failed, the reasoning of a single Black woman prevailed. Tsitra's father, who went by the name of Guitar, fell to his knees, unable to stand any longer, and let out a wail that broke the sergeant's heart. He was overcome by losing Tsitra, his favorite child—the one he had tried to convince his then wife to abort. He always regretted that. He had fallen in love with his daughter as soon as he saw her.

Memory continued to run across Blue's mind, like a vertical conveyor belt moving a steady flow of information in an upward movement, like a moving image story running through a vintage movie projector.

She pictured the dilapidated house at center stage and all the crumbling two-story Tudor houses of Detroit that could be purchased for ten thousand dollars or less. Those with enough ambition to buy one were often left stuck in those decrepit conditions; the renovation costs were too high. Two streets over was Guitar's two-story house, filled with objects he had hoarded and intended to restore.

Tsitra had followed in the footsteps of her father. His people took horror-inducing and exhausting cross-country trips by car and train to their new lives in colonies that grew into ghettos with only treacherous choices. Tsitra, a prodigy of sorts, started college at sixteen. But after meeting her boyfriend in a club—she got in with a fake ID—she exchanged her studies at University of Michigan and the ambition of becoming a lawyer for a modeling career and a baby. Tall and pencil thin, Tsitra was like a mannequin when clothes draped her dark skin body. It made her modeling career a real possibility—but too slim in a city full of hustlers.

The police were trying to negotiate with the axe-wielding woman. Echoing the fading cries from inside the house, Guitar pleaded with the police to just shoot the bitch.

"Why are you trying to negotiate with a crazy woman?!" Guitar yelled.

A woman in the crowd shouted, "So you'll turn your guns on a grieving father, but you just let that crazy bitch hold a young child hostage?"

"Why not just shoot her?" Guitar turned to reasoning with the police, since pleading wasn't working.

"Sir, please just back up behind the rope," a White police officer responded.

"What would be the problem with shooting her?"

The police officer just looked at Guitar, his eyes betraying his confusion with Guitar's question.

"You don't really care about what's going on here," Guitar said with such matter-of-factness. "I know it. They know it," he said, gesturing toward the crowd. "You know it." The police had never put much value on Black life in this country, and certainly not in Detroit, Michigan, a decaying city full of Black people. "So why now? Why her? Why save the one African American who should just be shot?"

The police officer fiddled with his cap and looked at one of his colleagues for support as he walked away from Guitar.

As the scene in the house deteriorated further, someone in the crowd, which had grown to be a horde, said to the family, "You better call Zion."

Zion got the call.

Four years ago, Zion had left his sister Tsitra and followed his mother back to the South, to Houston, where she settled after completing her graduate degree in New York City. He was studying engineering at a prestigious Texas university and was on his way home from class when the Detroit call came. He reluctantly decided to wait for an update from Detroit at his mother's house. But before leaving her alone in her bedroom, Zion stopped to ask one last question before he squirreled away in a bedroom two floors down. "How in the heck did you end up with my dad?" This question—with complex arteries hidden in the simplicity of its presentation—had been the subject of many reflective therapy sessions for his mother.

Right on cue, in a room washed in the sun, a story moved at the speed of its light through her consciousness. It was the story of her ancestors: Blue's great-great-grandparents George Washington Rose and Elizabeth Beacon Rose, who had fought alongside General François-Dominique Toussaint-Louverture in the 1791 Haitian Revolution. Unfortunately, the Haitian victory ended with a twist for the Roses. Benoit Joseph André Rigaud, who was also a leading general in Haiti, took George and Elizabeth captive and sold them to a land baron in East Texas, so named Mr. Barron. Blue felt it must be important to connect to what you know in order to ground yourself before all hell breaks loose.

George, a brilliant, well-educated, handsome, and charming military leader, became Mr. Barron's confidant and led his army to defeat the British in the American colonies, a war that had already claimed all the Barron sons before George arrived. Mrs. Barron had died in childbirth with the last son. With no heirs, old man Barron deeded his property, which included land, soldiers, and enslaved peoples, to George. Barron went into town for what he considered to be his final farewell, as he too was dying from his war injuries. While in town, a young mulatto woman passing for White trapped him into a wedding ceremony. He came back to the plantation with a new heir. The mulatto woman was hateful. But, to be fair, her hate had been shaped by her life. Sold from one owner to the next for years until she ran away—and the first person she ran into thought she was White. The very next day, after her introduction to the Barron plantation, the mulatto, without hesitation, announced to the house staff that all of them would be serendipitously sold immediately upon the death of the lord of the manor. Having vowed never to be sold again, to choose death instead, each person began to envision a noose creeping up and around their necks. *The first instant as the itchy strains of rope roll across the head and down the back of the neck.*

The chills that emerge from underneath the skin of a naked body as apprehensions rise to interlock with the threads. The next second when body temperature elevates to the point of liquid running slyly down the body like cooling mercury on a bronze anvil covered in soft flesh. Then the drop of the braided cord onto the base of the neck where it connects to the shoulders, in that crevice where separation is assured and breakage occurs. Then the budding of strange fruit sprouting from the poplar trees.

"A bold move," George said to Elizabeth.

"She's young. Foolish and naïve," Elizabeth said.

George sat in full military dress at the bedside of Mr. Barron, holding his hand. As it became clear that the end was imminent, George called Elizabeth and the new Mrs. Barron, only five days into her sudden marriage, into the bedroom to say goodbye. Three minutes later, Mr. Barron exhaled for the very last time. At that moment, George stood up from kneeling at Mr. Barron's bedside, walked over to Mrs. Barron, who was a full head shorter than him, and calmly snapped her neck.

George laid her body in the bed next to her husband. Elizabeth redressed the body in an elegant frilly dress, respectful ladies' clothing, something the new Mrs. Barron had never worn in life. Then the pair called in the rest of the staff to pay their respects. Relieved to find that Mrs. Barron had also joined her new husband in the next life, they pulled in a long breath and released it slowly like dragging on a long-awaited and cherished cigarette. Their home was safe. George took ownership of fourteen hundred acres of rich East Texas land and, along with it, the kind of influence that only light-colored skin and money could get you in 1804.

George deeded a hundred acres to each of his eleven children. The remaining three hundred acres were to be devoted to public spaces. The East Texas land passed down for more than a century, constructing the social expectations of the family, until an unexpected tear occurred, a disruption that tore a part of the family away from the inheritance.

Zion rushed into Blue's bedroom, stumbling through the door. Blue was snatched away from the *Lie*'s tale. The pulling left her groggy and disoriented. After two agonizing hours of imagining strange fruit swinging from poplar trees, Zion got the second call from Detroit. It was July 12, 2006, late in the afternoon. One more hour and *the boy* would have turned two years old—officially at 4:44 p.m. on that day. Not in history and not in future. He was an apparition of sorts. Tsitra was eighteen. Whispers seeped through the chaos like a string of thread being pulled through a hem by a needle: $1 + 8 = 9$. Nine, the number of spiritual awakening and a hint that it was time to end a phase, with the promise that the "new" would make its way onto the scene, generally with ferocious violence. Nine entities are lightworkers waiting in dark spaces for their human assignments to arrive. From that point on, eighteen became an important number for Blue, who existed in the silence of the center of a strange sunflower that bloomed in darkness. Feeling unable to even move her limbs, finally, like a summer day in Houston, Texas, Blue sat still.

2

THE STILLNESS LASTED EIGHTEEN MONTHS. One month for each year erased in the loss of her daughter. By the end, Blue was broke again.

Blue's dance with poverty was a pattern she struggled to disrupt, like throwing a stick in the wheels of a roller coaster that had highs—the time she bought a new town house in downtown Houston—followed by steep declines so low that sometimes she had no food in that town house. After she buried her daughter and *the boy* in Detroit, she gave up on trying to win against something that seemed so clearly fated. If memory had served her right, the best she could hope for was a miracle against a poverty delivered through a race-based caste system unique to a nation that was beginning to shape itself at the same time the word "race" was born in 1505.

The bank had given Blue one hundred and eighty days to solve her problem or they would solve it for her: they would take her house. It didn't even occur to her to just sell the damn thing. Instead, she went south, to The Ranch, a little-known silent retreat center in the Texas desert run by a Catholic order that was branded more than a hundred years ago as ruthless assassins in defense of the poor. It was started in 1798 by this exiled order from Rome when the founder had traveled to the shores of the newly forming American colonies with a group of dark-skinned peoples who had been captured, sold, and brutalized during the Middle Passage.

Blue had gone in observance of the upcoming second anniversary of the event that had ripped opened a breach triggering a journey into parallel explorations. She would stay for seven days. Seven is the number for obstacles overcome and success realized. She had hoped the seven days would be like those in the Book of Genesis. Seven days of creation.

On the five-hour drive south from Houston to The Ranch, everything opened up to her like a blue sky that hovers above a creation experience. Before she left Houston, she had a dream about inventions hovering in the atmosphere of her bedroom: the blueprints of each one sparkled with shimmering light. But she couldn't see any details. She believed that the answer to her historical financial struggle could be in one or all of those inventions. But her inventiveness had been hijacked by grief for nearly two years. Now, as she drove along the highway, a ceiling lifted, and she felt free to explore ideas again. And as she imagined the real and the possible, she stumbled across something important about how time works. It doesn't move; we do. Blue was driving alongside the year 1848.

As the highway drew closer to the Gulf coast, just seven miles from her destination, it turned into a two-lane road that rolled into a small town that felt strangely familiar. *I've been here before. But I've never been here before.* She looked out the window of her car and saw a big white house sitting at the corner of the two main roads that ran through the town. Suddenly she was sure and she said out loud, to no one in particular, "I. Have. Been. Here. Before."

Twelve minutes later, a small sign that would no longer be visible when the sun went down informed Blue she had arrived. She took a quick left onto a dirt road and drove three more miles to The Ranch. The sun was setting and the sky dripped reds, oranges, and yellows and streaks of navy blue onto the horizon. Another seven minutes and Blue finally pulled onto the grounds of The Ranch underneath a blanket of purple and blood orange.

Small wood cabins peppered the grounds, starting about fifty yards from the Big House, which looked like the Barkley family mansion on the old TV series *The Big Valley*, a show Blue had watched many times with her father, who had a fascination with Westerns. Given the complete absence, or humiliation, that the television genre bestowed upon Black people, Blue suddenly realized that her daddy's preoccupation was odd. Blue half expected Victoria Barkley to greet her on the gravel drive that ran all the way up to the door.

Out of the car, Blue ran her eyes across the grounds of the old Kenedy estate (Kenedy with one *n*). She inhaled a long deep breath that smelled—ironically, she thought—like lilac. *Lilacs don't grow in the desert, do they?* After savoring the scent, she released it slowly, before taking the few steps needed to get to the house. Once she reached the doorway, she stopped again, because to her left, as she walked through the door, she noticed, and so ran her fingers across, a historical plaque posted on the side of the entranceway that read: BUILT IN 1848. Her mind turned it over and over and over. She followed signs to the admin office down a flight of old wooden stairs to a basement, which led to a room paved over with linoleum and lit above with fluorescents. Blue was greeted by a woman who radiated contradictions. She looked like she got pleasure from the fact that she had no pleasure at all. As if having no pleasure was her way of being sure she was pleasing God. Blue realized she was really no different than this administrator who also served as the house librarian. *Why do we think God gets jollies from us being miserable?*

"Hello, I'm Blue," she said, to stop herself from spiraling in front of the stranger.

The admin librarian drove Blue around the four-hundred-acre property in a golf cart, showing her where all the practical things she would need could be found, as well as the walking trails. As they approached the beginning of the longest walking trail, the one that led down to the ocean, a swarm of baby-blue butterflies flew around Blue like a wedding veil. Their wings, so tiny, fluttered in harmony, and Blue closed her eyes to connect to the sound of their flight. She heard a whisper say: *Can't you see? Where I'm from, the color is blue.*

The admin librarian took Blue to her cabin. It was clean. Functional. Basic. It was perfect. A few other people who had also come to The Ranch for solitude walked across the grounds like zombies in devotion. They came to get away from irreverent curiosities that were driving them nuts. Some people came to pray. Some to write. Some to do nothing. But it was only a few people. No more than ten. Because it was the hottest time of the year to be in the desert—the second week of July, in 2008.

Blue unpacked her luggage and settled into her cabin before she decided to explore the grounds further. Facing east, she found the veranda of the Big House. Where Blue grew up, it was called a porch, and in fact it reminded her of the porch of her childhood home in West Dallas, except it was about five times bigger. She decided she would call this veranda the Porch. She sat on the Porch in a rocking chair. The wind coming off the Gulf of Mexico, only three miles away, was so strong that Blue felt like it could lift her up and hover her above the ground. She reclined into the rocking chair and allowed the wind to carry her back to her drive from Houston. She had felt the same familiar presence when she drove past the quarry, as though she were moving through a bubble made of unseen fingers running slowly across her gut.

Blue looked out across the grounds just as a momma deer and her baby doe ambled by. The two of them stopped for a second to greet her. Blue nodded back and looked out at the horizon. It looked as if she were looking at the ocean, but it was really the sky. Earlier, when she'd rolled through town slowly, she'd felt as if she were looking through the no-glass window of an extravagant horse-drawn carriage while simultaneously looking through the window glass of her luxury car. She had come to refer to occurrences like these as *Wonderland* moments.

To extricate herself from this *looking-glass world*, Blue abruptly stood straight up, as if shifting the position of her body would disturb the energy enough for her to get away from it.

The east wind overpowered Blue with traces of experiences that made her feel as though she'd come home and yet like she had lost that home at some point in the past. It was a mix of happiness and sadness, like a gumbo gone wrong.

She thought, *I'll go up to the lookout tower of the Big House and get a better view. Later, I'll go to the chapel for the sunset meditation and reading of the Lord's Prayer.*

She walked onto the first floor of the Big House, which was one flight of stairs up and led into the grand room, and then up another wide wooden staircase carved by hand and made her way onto the second floor, where all ten bedrooms were empty. The door of the bedroom at the end of the hallway was unlatched, unlike the others. The unlatched door quietly banged against the doorway as it was pushed opened by the wind and allowed to close when the wind refused to hold it open any longer. Blue ignored the banging invitation and went up two more floors, climbing an iron ladder staircase, and walked through the atrium where a chair sat in front of an altar, then out onto the concrete lookout tower. She felt compelled to go left when she pushed past the double glass doors. She made her way around the tower to see across The Ranch, and the entire valley, in every direction. North. South. West. East. All four. *Four is the number for home.* But just as she turned the corner to the east, she hit a wall.

The wall was malleable. Made of emotions. History. And her own memories of living on this property she had never been to before. It was a time so wonderful that when she re-*membered* it, when she rejoined the memory back to her body, like reattaching a limb, the memory doubled her over in longing.

She took two steps further east, and another presence arrested her. She held on to herself as she seemed to take flight back to East Texas, where her daddy had been run out of town. Blue's family never learned the details of the incident that forced their father away from his home, his land, and his inheritance. When her father was sent away, he was severed from the family's wealth and history. The umbilical cord was effectively cut, and Blue's father carried this severed, exiled life into his new family. His youngest child, Blue, experienced the brunt of it when he died. What had been difficult in life was brutal in his death. Not only was there poverty; there was also the entanglement of irreverent unbodied babies trying to be reincarnated.

Blue remembered so deeply, it made her core ache for a history buried in the soft tissue of that memory, which had now somehow found its way into her head.

How could I remember experiences from the past on returning to a place I've never been to before and yet not have known what was about to happen on that day when Zion called?

And morning passed.
Evening came.
Marking the first day.
And the Spirit of God was hovering over the land.

3

EARLY ON THE EVENING OF Friday, July 12, 1848, patrons
of an infamous weekly French Quarter salon party alight
from their carriages. The event is held at a town house on
Toulouse Street, where time misbehaves. It's decorated in
a new design that won't become popular for another fifty
years, a highly ornamental, elaborate style in which geometric forms and vibrant floral motifs come together for bold,
ostentatious architecture.

The interior is as ornate as the exterior, draped in exquisite
materials, custom furnishings, and hand-painted wall treat-
ments. Romantic flair combines with dynamism and movement, asymmetrical lines and large open spaces. Guests enter
the wide ornamental doors and follow the angled straight line
of a long hallway with a floor made of colorful pieces of broken
ceramics. The hallway's walls have a pearl railing that starts
at the entrance and runs the length of a short city block to the
back of the house. Off the hallway on the first floor are only

three rooms, but there are twenty-five rooms on the second floor, one room on the third floor, and an unknown number on the fourth floor. This floor is off-limits. Locked iron bars adorn the entrance to the fourth floor from the stairway. None of these guests have ever seen it. There is another floor that no one knows exists. A basement floor.

The first-floor hallway opens into the Great Red Room. Tonight, music floats from the back of the house, near the Blue Garden, a lush courtyard that backs up to the Mississippi River. At least once a month, an entire corps of light hangers strings several hundred blue lights inside the hedges, flowers, and trees. The white-turned-blue roses are a central feature of the Blue Garden. The lights continue along the sides of the glass roof, spilling onto the white pearl railing of the hallway and dropping their light into the Great Red Room, turning it purple. The music wafts from the Great Red Room into the Blue Garden to charm the lazy haze of people sitting lavishly on furniture made of Italian leather and Indian silk. The music also travels in the opposite direction down the long hallway to greet visitors as they step into a cocoon of purple. A man at the piano, dressed in full tails, plays a music new to everyone—strong, prominent meter, improvisation, distinctive tone colors, and syncopated rhythmic patterns—that flows through the room, dripping over the bodies of its listeners like gravy over a warm biscuit.

Palmer Rose has come to the party in search of Benoit Joseph André Rigaud, the Francophone general who sold his parents into American slavery. Palmer left East Texas driven by a sensation of being haunted by a history threatening to capture his future. He was in Virginia when he received word from home that Rigaud often shows up to these parties in New Orleans, parties you don't need an invitation to enter. The door is not guarded, and all manner of strangers just walk right in.

Traveling with Palmer is Xhosa Angolese, an enslaved West African man on the plantation of Palmer's family. He and Palmer grew up together and it was he who brought word of Rigaud's whereabouts. Palmer and Xhosa enter the long purple hallway. The blue light from the windows is as asphyxiating as it is intoxicating. Palmer feels like he is walking into a spell. Xhosa nearly refuses to go any farther, but the pull of a portal somewhere in the house compels him to keep going. Palmer is in a tuxedo, a new invention that won't become widespread for another eighteen years, picked up by his mother while on a visit to see Queen Victoria of England. The queen was quite curious about the slavery question in the former colonies, and since the Roses, a prominent Black family, are the owner of hundreds of enslaved peoples, the queen was eager to question Mrs. Rose. Palmer's hat and cane are in one hand and his cape thrown over the other. Xhosa, though dressed well enough, is not in a tuxedo. He carries his hat in one hand while stroking the pearls adorning the railing all the way down the hall with the other.

"What are you doing?" Palmer asks Xhosa.

"Feeling the energy," Xhosa says.

"And?"

"It's wild and dangerous, but it's our only way forward."

"Forward?" Palmer asks.

"You want to find Rigaud, don't you? Well, this is the way."

"Yeah. Rigaud," Palmer says aloud, more as an exhalation than a response to Xhosa's question.

"Have you changed your mind?" Xhosa asks, noticing the lack of enthusiasm in Palmer's response.

"I have not," Palmer says with confidence.

They reach a doorway, with twenty-four-foot double doors made of solid bronze. Coming from within are noises of passion, laughter, and abandon. Palmer peeks in. There are three women surrounding one man in the corner of a Roman-style pool-sized bath. In another corner are three men surrounding one woman. There are other couples, trios, and quartet pairings of men with men, women with women, and women with men. Palmer pushes the door open, and an enormous man nearly the size of the entryway that he guards stops the door and asks for an invitation.

"I was told that I didn't need an invitation," Palmer says.

"Only for this room," the man answers. "The rest of the house is open."

"What is this room?"

"The Temple Room. The Roman Bath Room."

"How do I get an invitation?"

"If you were going to get one, you would have it by now."

Palmer and Xhosa continue down the hall. "I saw Rigaud in the corner of that bath," Palmer says to Xhosa. "It would have been so easy to slit his throat in such a room."

"Right. If that big motherfucker wasn't at the door."

Inside the Great Red Room an open bar displays spirits from places unknown to most of the guests, with names

like Dal Forno Romano Amarone della Valpolicella, Château
Latour, Grand Vin, and Tanzania Rouge. The buffet tables
hold all manner of delectables from every corner of the known
worlds: Ghanaian fish, Egyptian fava beans, Cape Town rel-
ishes, Greek yogurts and pastitsio, West Indian roti, French
pastries, Italian pastas, Ethiopian spiced meats.

Palmer and Xhosa enter the Great Red Room. The women
in the room wear long, straight dresses that cling to their slender frames and sweep the floor behind them. The dresses are
transparent and flicker in whatever light is nearby. Large stones
drip from their necks and wrap around their thin fingers and
wrists. Palmer's eyes scan the room, running across the various faces like fingers running across piano keys. In the corner
of the room, near the doorway to the back courtyard, Palmer
unexpectedly sees a woman he knows.

The blue, red, and white lights grow brighter as the sky
prepares for the moon to make its appearance. Suddenly the
sun drops and the sky flattens and creates an edge for the sun
to fall over, leaving only darkness for seven whole minutes.
Over this section of the Mississippi there is a break between
the sun and the night lights of the moon and stars, a gulf that
blocks the two from replacing one another as they do in most
skies. For seven minutes there is no light but the artificial ones
created by the host. So, in line with nature, the gas-powered
lights also go out.

As the lights abruptly extinguish all over the house, both
inside and out, Palmer drops everything he is carrying and
reaches into the back of his suit, wrapping his hand around a
pistol tucked into his waistband. Xhosa follows and reaches

for his knife. Their eyes dart back and forth across the room, attempting to fixate on something, anything, while they wait for their pupils to adjust. Only whispers can be heard as people stand in reverence. Palmer and Xhosa stumble to gain their balance in an unfamiliar room. Everyone else sits quietly, waiting for the night lights to return.

Then, precipitously rounding the corner on the Mississippi River, a riverboat emerges with the moonlight following close behind. Two drummers on the riverboat establish a central rhythm. The bass drummer plays on the one and the three. The snare drummer improvises march-style beats that depart from the standard accents on the two and the four. A Second Line has ironically arrived first, with West African influences from Congo Square. The partygoers on land add layers of rhythm with hand percussion, bottles, sticks, and other improvised instruments. The rhythms of the Second Line spectacle coming off the Mississippi River, with the moon on its tail, roll in on waves of Caribbean rhythms and West African cadences. The spirit of the party is both rhythmically structured and wildly unleashed as everyone in the garden is up on their feet, moving to the beat of the drummers as if they were being marched off to a war. And while they are still moving to that beat, another pageant rounds the corner.

One strike of a big drum! Another strike! Another! And another! Then rapid repeated strikes on three different instruments explode from the riverboat. Pop! . . . Pop! Pop! . . . Pop! Pop! Pop! The drummers strike their instruments, horns blast in between the drumbeats, and then the loud click of heels is amplified by the cavern of the boat's shape and the cul-de-sac of the river. The crowd stops their own dancing to listen to the clicks as the moonlight, fully risen now, shines down on the dancer like a spotlight. She is dressed in only two small pieces of gold cloth. One covers parts of her breasts, and the other is strung loosely around her bottom, with only a flap to cover the lush gathering of plush between her legs. Her body vibrates with light and shimmers with the sound of the drums. She has a large heavy crest of gold-and-white feathers that sits atop a gold metal crown on her head. The crowd gasps when they realize she is the infamous Samba Queen from Brazil. The crowd goes wild with dancing, trying to mimic her moves. Everyone in the Great Red Room runs outside toward the sounds coming off the river, leaving Palmer and Xhosa to follow slowly, perplexed and puzzled.

The party has begun.

Once outside and immersed in the crowd of Second Line music and samba dancers, Palmer looks for the woman he had spotted in the corner before day abruptly transitioned to night.

"There she is," he says to Xhosa.

"Who?"

"The woman I told you I met while in Virginia."

"What is her name?"

"Amanda, I was told. But I never got a chance to ask her."

"The shape-shifter?"

"Yeah. That's her."

"Where? Where is she?" Xhosa asks with excitement, as he has not seen a shape-shifter since he was captured in the hills of Angola.

"There." Palmer points toward the blue roses.

Amanda stands with her arms rested on her hips and her hands clasped in front her. She's wearing a white dress made of Egyptian cotton, with strips of East Indian silk sewn into every other pleat. In between those pleats are strips of pearls strung from the waist to the ground. The string of pearls leaves swaths of her body exposed. The top part of the dress has a high collar with buttons made of pearls running from the neck to the top of the waist. Behind the pearl buttons is a white corset. It gives an air of both high art and moral turpitude.

Palmer is walking toward Amanda when a woman steps over to greet her, kissing Amanda on both cheeks. Still damp from the Temple Room, she is wrapping a red dress around her wet body. It is covered in sparkling stones delivered in a complex pattern of vertical and horizontal lines and abstract shapes. Her skin is the color of eggshells, a pale, warm, neutral off-white, she has hazel eyes, and her hair is long, straight, and dark black. It drops to the bottom of her back.

"You are still here," the woman exclaims in surprise.

Amanda gives her a polite and suspicious smile. "I am still here."

"I half expected you to be gone by now," the woman says. "Amanda?"

She looks in Palmer's direction, her smile warm and welcoming. "Palmer," she says with a relief that betrays her feelings for him. They embrace with passion and some hesitancy.

"What are you doing here?" he asks her.

She looks at him with the same question in her eyes, and without answering she introduces him to the wet woman. "This is Ismay, our hostess and lady of this town house manor."

Some say Ismay assassinated a French lord in line for the throne. Others say her grandfather, a general for the French army who established French colonial rule in New Orleans in 1682, built the city with his slave-trading empire. Another story says her father filled the new colony with expats from the Ivory Coast, forced to the Western shores as enslaved peoples. Still another story is that she is the reincarnation of one of the famed African Kandakes, empresses of Ethiopia, regarded as one of the most dreaded war generals of her time. Known to be a fierce, tactical, and uniting military leader, she had reembodied to help her people. These rumors are the byproduct of an astonishing and sensual woman with an exquisite frame who's never been married and only speaks of motherhood as if it would be a curse from the gods—she has a secret that has imbued her with a hatred for children so rich, it is unmatched by anything one can imagine. She guards her independence like her protected fourth floor, which is rumored to be a portal to other worlds, the presence Xhosa felt in that purple-tinted, pearl-lined hallway. The only thing people know for certain about Ismay and her fourth floor is that she goes there to pray.

Ismay greets the two men and excuses herself. She moves through the party in her iridescent translucent red dress, sweeping across the ground like a royal bridal trail. She greets one celebrity after another. As she does so, Amanda whispers to Palmer the identity and importance of each one. Xhosa takes his place behind Palmer.

"They are from Europe. There is the entrepreneur Louis Vuitton, known for his brand of leather products. His fashion house will be one of the biggest in the world, for a generation. And he is Vincent van Gogh, a famous Dutch artist whose work is known for its emotional intensity and bold use of color. He cut off his ear in a peculiar moment of inexplicability at one of these parties."

"Van Gogh?" asks Palmer as his eyes seem to search the back of his mind for familiarity. "My family collects art from famous artists around the world. We don't have anything of his. I've never heard of him."

Amanda cocks her head and a wry smile tugs at the corners of her lips. "Right," she says with a mischievous glint in her eyes. *He's not been born yet.* Then she continues her rolling introductions for Palmer as if nothing strange had just happened.

"Wait." Palmer considers pushing his inquiry further but decides on a different question instead. "How do you know these people?"

"I've made puzzles for them."

Ismay's move around the room continues, and Amanda continues to whisper important information about each cluster of people who have niched themselves away into cliques.

"There are the Chasseurs, they're doctors, and they experiment on black-skinned peoples. And the Joneses, who are exceedingly wealthy and equally as stupid. And the Pacifists, Joan and Edward, who do not believe in violence, but he is a general in the Spanish army. Over there"—she points in the opposite corner—"are the Quakers, who *really* do not believe in violence. They refuse to practice it in any form. They taught me and the other children on the plantation in Virginia how to read—secretly, of course. One of them was hanged for it. The next day the others came back and continued our studies. I have great, great respect for them. So when I learned to make puzzles, I made one for the slave trader who killed that woman. He's there. That one in the corner, swatting at the air. He sees black streaks flying in front of his eyes. Always. He will go completely mad within the year."

Palmer looks at Amanda with a mix of fear and curiosity about what it would mean to be in love with this puzzle conjurer. Amanda is interrupted by another partygoer.

"Over there," she continues, "are the politicians and social scientists. That's James Polk; he is the youngest president this country has ever had."

Palmer asks, "Why is he here? Why would the president be *here?*"

"This is one of those rare rooms where power breeds and conspires against history. And when history is rescored, it is realized . . ." Amanda pauses for a moment to savor that last word. "I love that word," she says parenthetically. "*Real-ized*—made real—in a future that becomes present in a process of having been." Again she goes back to her presentation of this room, where time is constantly pushing the boundaries of physics and of society itself.

"There are Karl Marx and Friedrich Engels. They've written interesting things about labor and work. And there, that's the son of Immanuel Kant, Johann Kant, an anthropologist. His father's doctrine of transcendental idealism believes that space, time, and causation are mere sensibilities. In his view, the mind shapes and structures experience, with all human experience sharing certain structural features." Palmer doesn't want to interrupt Amanda again, but he knows Johann Kant. They have been traveling together for years. Kant is the one who scouted the party and relayed the information that Palmer could get in without an invitation. "And that's Abraham Lincoln," Amanda continues. "The rumor is, he's Black. And there, that's Susan B. Anthony, a prominent organizer of the women's movement. Standing next to her is Elizabeth Cady Stanton; they both fight for women's right to vote. But not *my* right to vote. Though, to be fair, Susan is very involved in the fight against slavery, for which we respect her. She's also involved in the temperance campaign to limit the use of alcohol, for which we forgive her. Standing with them is Frederick Douglass, born under an important number, the year 1818. He escaped slavery and now writes and speaks about his life during those years as an enslaved human being."

Amanda's thoughts seem to wander. "This new kind of slavery is a strange thing. It is not like other slave histories, where one could convert to a new religion or simply hide in a sea of free people. They picked something that will always stick out and that will sustain over hundreds of years and generations: the skin color. And they said that slavery was inherent in that color. It is actually quite a brilliant war strategy." She continues the introductions. "Standing next to Frederick is Dred Scott. He is suing the United States for racism. I've seen the outcome. He will not win. Next to him is Harriet Tubman. Some people call her Moses. She helped my family escape from Virginia, but then we were caught again by the Coultoure family."

Palmer, who has never known what it is like to be a slave himself, imagines the horror based on the stories he's heard from his father. But his imagination is obstructed by how well his father treats their enslaved people. Xhosa is an example. When Palmer was a boy and in town with his father, he saw little boy Xhosa being forced off a ship in chains. Palmer walked over and took him from the slave trader and told his father to pay the man. Palmer made Xhosa his best friend.

Amanda's tour of the room is interrupted by the group of writers spread out along one wall playing word games. A challenge is proposed by one of them to the others to quote the perfect poem to Ismay, fitting to the beauty that she is, as she has made her way to their corner and now stands before them. One man begins:

"And the sunlight clasps the earth,
And the moonbeams kiss the sea;
What are all these kissings worth,
If thou kiss not me?"

"He was a dear friend of Percy Shelley. My heart aches that the world has lost such a formidable poet," says Amanda.

"The others in the circle?" Palmer asks.

"Edgar Poe, known for his poetry and short stories, particularly his tales of mystery and the macabre. He married his thirteen-year-old cousin. When she was dying, he asked me for a puzzle, and in return paid me with a look at his poem 'The Raven.' Denise Ron, she's a whore. Likes to do it with young boys. Every aristocratic father who wants to give his son a woman for his twelfth birthday goes to her. She's very beautiful. Is she not?"

Palmer wonders if this is a trick question.

After greeting Ismay, a musician walks over to a cello sitting next to the piano. The jazz pianist who was playing earlier joins her in the corner. The two of them release an improvisation that is haunted with what looks like the rings of Saturn as the colors from the Blue Garden, the gold of the samba, and the shimmering pinks of the Second Line waft into the room. "And that's Yudi," Amanda continues. "She's a violinist and a fiction writer. She writes of the horror of being a woman in Colonial America." The horror is evident in her music and her face and her fingers. Her impromptu piano accompanist weeps as he plays.

It's 3:00 a.m. and the full orchestra has arrived and is ready to begin. The conductor interrupts the crowd to announce that Lady Ismay has requested Hector Berlioz's *Le Carnaval romain* ouverture. The introduction of the orchestra is the cue to partygoers that the party is winding down. Only those who are willing to take part in highly inventive discussions stay beyond this point.

Ismay's butler is suddenly standing next to Amanda, Palmer, and Xhosa, delivering an invitation to the forbidden fourth floor. They follow him to a stairway and ascend three sets of twenty steps. The butler unlocks the gate that sits at the entrance to the landing. The three walk onto a floor the width of the house. In one corner is a set of Yoruba drums that have been baptized in the Mississippi. They sit inside a cage to ensure they don't get up and walk away. In the center of the room is an altar with four white candles lining the top, and in front of the altar is a small channel that runs the length of the altar and holds water from the Mississippi. Behind each candle is a porcelain white cup, reserved for use in prayer and working with the spirits.

Palmer is hesitant because he's never seen anything like this before. Amanda is curious because she never imagined such a room in this town house. Xhosa is charmed because he is in his element. Each one of them, standing separately and contemplating what they might do next, is startled to see Ismay walking toward them from the opposite end, her glittering red dress sparkling against the wall. She has been watching them in a dark corner of the room. Sizing them up. Trying to determine if she can get what she wants from them.

"I think that one of you knows what to do with this," Ismay finally says as she points to the altar. "It was given to me on my last trip to Haiti, four years ago, by an old witch, who told me to set aside the fourth floor of my house. I, of course, was intrigued because she knew nothing about me or my house, and it is unusual for a house to have four floors. She said I could use it to bend time."

Xhosa steps forward toward the altar. He lights all four candles by simply touching their wicks. Then he dips each cup, one at a time, into the channel and fills them with water. He takes the first cup and candle. Ismay second. Palmer third.

Amanda fourth. Xhosa begins the ceremony and instructs the others to do as he does.

Xhosa pours out three drops of water from his cup: one to the right, one to the left, and one in the center, in a straight line in front of his candle. The others follow suit as he explains that this exercise gives the spirits water, inviting them to move through and hear their prayers. Xhosa continues: "In order for our prayers to be heard, in order for us to reach the other side of time, which is what this particular altar is used for, we must not pray in the way that your family prays, Palmer. We do not recite lines of formulaic script. We pray the words that sit in the heart, in the soul. Not the words that sit in the mind. Words that sit in the mind do not open the *Door* of the veil."

Then Xhosa invites each of the three altar bearers to release their own prayers.

"But what do I say?" Ismay asks, despite the prolonged explanation Xhosa has already delivered. And Palmer looks to Xhosa in anticipation of the answer because he wanted to ask the same question.

"Listen," Xhosa whispers, so as not to disturb the wind that has already begun to move through the room. "Listen to the sound of the wind. What do you hear?"

At first, Ismay and Palmer struggle to hear anything. Palmer squeezes his eyelids together as if to squeeze sound through them. Ismay stares at the lit candle and feels a breeze glide past her arm.

"Let go of your eyes, my friend," Xhosa says to Palmer. And as Palmer relaxes his grip on his eyelids, he hears an ocean. Ismay, the mumbling of words that sound oddly like her own voice. Amanda, who needs no instruction on how to pray, has already taken flight from her body.

Their separate and single prayers take them to separate places both backward and forward on diverging time lines. Palmer sees one of his ancestors on a boat. Vanilla coffee–colored skin. A short Afro. A brown suit. A vest, a white shirt with a frilly collar that drapes in front. Long white socks that go up to the knee to meet his knickers. Black shoes. He is a botanist explorer who has hired a ship and a captain and a crew to take him to the West World. As Amanda moves through time, she stumbles upon a Heaven Council when the Sons of God came to present themselves before the Lord, and Satan came also among them. When she hears Palmer's name being mentioned, Amanda shape-shifts into one of the Sons and listens in. Ismay whispers that she is hearing the Lord's Prayer on the other side of a time veil.

Our Father, who art in Heaven.

"Our Father, who art in Heaven," Ismay repeats.

Hallowed be thy name.

"Hallowed be thy name," Ismay repeats again.

On the other side of time, Blue was sitting in the chapel, on her first day at The Ranch, for the daily sunset meditation and reading of the Lord's Prayer, and she started to hear *voices*. Voices other than her own as she recited the prayer aloud, in the chapel alone. She was sitting on the next to the last pew in the far right corner, next to the stained glass window with golden, red, and blue images of Catholic saints painted on it. The sun streamed golden light onto the right side of her body. She noticed the golden light lying across her writing hand, the one in which she held a pen, and which rested on the pages of her journal. The golden light bounced off her hand, creating a golden streak on the page. Blue looked up from her prayer book. She was slightly confused by what she heard. She angled her head toward a vent below her feet as if thinking maybe the sound was coming from outside the chapel, through the vent. She leaned closer to the vent as she continued to recite the next line:

Thy kingdom come.

"Thy kingdom come," again Ismay repeats.

Standing next to Ismay, Xhosa is pulled into the chapel on the other side of time with Ismay. He listens to Blue recite the prayer and Ismay repeat it. They sound like echoes of one another. Xhosa joins the echo and invites Amanda and Palmer to join them. Amanda refuses to be pulled away from the Heaven Council. Palmer accepts the invitation and leaves his 1600s boat ride. Together the three of them bend time into 2008.

Thy will be done.

"Thy will be done," the three repeat.

Blue continued to recite the prayer as she slid out of her seat and to her knees between the pews. She placed her left ear against the vent to verify whether the *voices* she was hearing were coming from that location. *Maybe it's a radio,* she thought. But she quickly corrected: *This is a place of silence. No one would be playing a radio all out into the open like that.* Then she thought, *Maybe it's the wind coming through the vent. The voices aren't very clear and they're almost like a whisper.* Her backside shoved up into the air as she pushed her head to the floor vent. The *voices* grew louder.

On earth as it is in Heaven.

"On earth as it is in Heaven," the three repeat.

They are repeating what I say. For the next few lines, as Blue recited and listened to the *voices* repeat, she experienced what it was like to be completely free of fear.

Give us this day our daily bread, Blue says.

"Give us this day our daily bread." Again, the three repeat.

And forgive us our trespasses, Blue offers.

"And forgive us our trespasses," the three return.

As we consider those who trespass against us, Blue said. She altered the line, substituting "consider" for "forgive" that would normally come in that spot, because she was running an experiment. Were the *voices* following her lead, or were they just reciting the Lord's Prayer?

"As we consider those who trespass against us." The three follow Blue's lead.

And lead us not into temptation; but deliver us from evil.

"And lead us not into temptation; but deliver us from evil," the three whisper.

For thine is the kingdom, the power, and the glory, forever and ever. Amen.

"For thine is the kingdom, the power, and the glory, forever and ever. Amen."

Suddenly, Blue became aware of the absence of fear. It was a sensation she had never felt before, and it caused panic to rise along the line of her back: *Oh my God, what am I hearing? Am I schizophrenic?*

Footsteps echoed in the memory, down the passage they were yet to take. Toward the door they were still to open. Blue heard a whisper from a place so distant that it seemed to be hundreds of years away.

Can you see that the other side of knowing is memory?

Can you see that the loss of memory is insanity?

Can you see, the voice continues, *that the blue is where God lives?*

4

"'You were a bad mother! We didn't do any of the things that my friends' parents had them doing. Like sports. Or camps.' That's what Zion said to me the day before I left for The Ranch," Blue told Father Kelley.

"Do you agree with what your son said?" he asked.

Father Kelley was the ranking priest at The Ranch and a member of the Oblates Order. He looked so much like her daddy, it made her laugh. Short. Slender. Strong angular facial features. The hot Texas sun made his skin a golden brown, so even though he was White, he and Blue's daddy were about the same color. When Father Kelley was a young priest, he had translated several volumes of religious work from Latin to English, Spanish, French, and Italian. After he arrived at The Ranch, he built the premier library that now lived on the first floor of the Big House.

"Are these occurrences real or am I having a psychological breakdown?" Blue asked Father Kelley.

"I would say you're not having a mental break. I would say the experiences are real. When the resurrected commune with us, it is actually God."

"But it seems so strange. How can it be?"

"The resurrected ones are so far beyond the type of communication that we are accustomed to that it can feel more like communion than communication. They were repeating after you, like echoes."

"Echoes?"

"The resurrected ones." That's what Father Kelley called the *voices*. "Whisper in echoes. This plot of land is a place where time is separated only by a veil. Though I have known only two other people who crossed over."

Cross over? Where did I cross over to? Blue wanted to pose that question to Father Kelley, but another more pressing question replaced it. "How could I have these extraordinary experiences and not have known about what was about to happen to my daughter? I could have gotten her out of there."

"Maybe it was too tragic, and the memory of the time veil was trying to protect you."

"The memory? Of the time veil? The time veil has a memory?" Blue asked.

"The veil is informed by our current circumstances, and its memory by our history. Some losses can be so tragic that they fortify the barrier between present circumstances and knowings of the future. If we know them, we might not encounter them. And if we do not encounter them, we cannot make our way to memory."

"And why is memory so important?" asked Blue.

"Well . . . memory is the container that holds the essence of who we are."

"Not who we are," Blue asked, "but a container that holds that information?"

"Yes," Father Kelley simply said, with a smile so reassuring that it pushed Blue back into another vulnerable place of remembering. She thought back on her conversation with Zion before she came to The Ranch.

"Tsitra was really messed up," Zion had said with such anger that Blue thought he might combust. "She had serious issues! We had to raise ourselves. You were never around. You were always working." She could see him holding his body together with all the energy he could muster. His eyes watered and his brows crumpled into a mess of abstract meanings. A longing to be comforted and at the same time repulsed by the same person created a continuum of emotions on his face.

Blue stared at her son, holding her eyes as wide-open as she could so that they wouldn't close. If her eyelids had come together for too long, they might allow tears to form in the darkness, behind the lids. She decided he needed to say these things and he needed her to hear them. To hear him without the interruption of her speaking or crying. He needed that. And she needed to give it to him. She strained to keep her eyelids from colliding against one another. She must have looked a little crazy. But Zion was so passionate about his need that he didn't notice. He only noticed that she was really listening.

"What is your relationship with your parents?" Father Kelley asked.

"My most vivid memory is waiting for my dad on our front porch at five. He never came. And my mother? MaryMadeline. My most vivid memory of her is when she moved out of the home I grew up in and left me there with a man I hated, the man she had convinced me to marry."

"Tell me about your dad," Father Kelley pressed. "Who is he? And how did he meet your mother?"

"For the longest time we thought my dad's name was Jack. Curly Jack Rose. It wasn't until he died that we learned his name was really Christopher Columbus Washington Rose."

At twelve, Christopher leaves his East Texas home, traveling along the Gulf coast to New Orleans, then up the Mississippi River.

"Keep the river to your left," Christopher says quietly to himself.

He is running. Hard. Breathing harder. Running low to the ground, sprinting like a fox. There is someone else with him. A four-foot-tall bobcat. Breathing hard and so close that Christopher can feel the cat's breath on his neck. That's good. Christopher knows he isn't alone if he can feel the breath so close. Their footsteps echo through time.

"Hounds!" Christopher whispers to nobody in particular. The dogs are barking, and by the tenor of their moving sound, he can feel them closing in.

Christopher is picked up by an unseen force and pushed from behind like a wind blowing a ship with sails. His speed triples and he is moving like spirits being blown through the gale. He is moving so fast, it all becomes a blur. Christopher is shifting.

The sound of the dogs disappears. And it is sudden, as if he took off like a flying bird and abruptly left one place and landed in another—the first home on the trail now known as the Underground Railroad.

It is a lavish home with West African designs on the walls. Relief woodwork on the ceilings. Wide-plank hardwood floors. A porch so big it wraps around the entire house, which covers two of the ten acres it sits on. Christopher peers at the house from the woods that surround it, deciding whether to approach it. *It is on the map that Momma and Daddy gave me.* But there are White people there. Christopher is still breathing hard. His breath seems to be breathed by someone else, making him feel as though he had to catch it.

An old Black man walks out of the house, toward the trees where Christopher hides. The man is carrying a porcelain pot as if he were going to empty it. *Slave,* Christopher thinks, *emptying Master's chamber pot.*

"You can come out of the bushes," he says. "We all know you're there. You're safe here. Amanda sent word that you were coming."

Christopher stays at that house for two days. On the third night he continues moving north along the Mississippi River, where boats are paddled by tall, slender Black men in ragged shirts and knee-length pants standing in canoes with long sticks, long enough to touch the riverbed. There is a whole clan of them, peppering the long black river. They are Black men in a black night on a black Mississippi River. They are picking up Black people coming from all parts of the South and carrying them north. They look like gondola taxis on the Venice sea.

They are wearing straw hats that are lit up by the blue moon; without that moon, most people would not be able to see them in all that blackness. One of them beckons to Christopher, as if to say: *C'mon. We've been waiting for you. Tomorrow's moon will be a white one. We can't travel under a white moon. We can't hide in it. The blue moon gives light only to our hats.* In the distance they look like oversized blue lightning bugs. The magic of it all frightens anyone who isn't supposed to be there. Without the blue moon, their trick would be seen through like a has-been magician.

The next house is like the last. Lavish in design. A welcome from an old Black man carrying a porcelain pot. He greets Christopher in the woods that surrounds the house. Then Christopher is off to the next house.

By the fifth house, and the fifth old Black man with a porcelain pot, Christopher asks his host: "Why does every man who greets me carry a porcelain pot?"

"To let you know that we are owners of this house. We, unlike too many dark-skinned folks, do have a pot to piss in.

"The next eight houses along the route will be Ismay's houses," the old man continues. "You will not be greeted by a Black man carrying a pot, as they will not own the house. But they are part of the underground railroad. They will take you in. You have your map, right?"

"I have it here." Christopher pulls it from a pocket on the inside of his pants.

"You know how to read it?"

"My mother—she taught me how to read it."

"Good! Then you'll be fine."

Christopher grows up moving from one underground rail-road stop to the next along the Mississippi. It takes him eight months to get to his intended destination, Canada, as far north as the underground rail line would take him. But at twelve he finds Canada to be a difficult place to maintain his freedom. The Canadian Quaker families insist on adoption. Back in East Texas, Christopher spent most of his days alone in the woods that surrounded their house or watching his mother's patrons suspiciously. He had been raising himself since he was five. Unable to take all the mothering of the Quakers, Christopher leaves Canada and goes back down the Mississippi then across the New River, known by Indigenous peoples and creatures as New Waters, through the Appalachian hills of western Virginia, where kids raise themselves. He promised his Quaker hosts that he would return in a few years. He liked Canada. But he craves his freedom more.

His first night in western Virginia, Christopher steps off the underground railroad water taxi into a thick brush of jungle. A few of the others on the blue moonlight gondolas also disembark. Christopher peels away from them, so quietly the others don't even notice him leaving. He's learned that it's harder to maintain his freedom from slave trackers when he's in a pack. Human hunters and hunting dogs can pick up on human scents much easier when humans are gathered in a crowd. Besides, even though he is only thirteen, Christopher likes traveling alone.

He makes his way through the brush in a night whose moon and stars are hidden by clouds. The drizzle of the fog makes the forest wet and sticky. The humidity is so thick, Christopher can see it. He keeps moving, slow and low to the ground, stepping lightly and being mindful of the water creatures that slither from the river into the forest at night when it's cool, in search of food. He loses track of time because he can't see the stars. The clouds and fog hide them. Suddenly he stops dead in his tracks when he feels a wet, cold body slither around his legs. At the same time, he hears faint sounds of music coming from the other side of a small rocky mountain.

Christopher stands motionless. He knows how to communicate with bobcats, but his parents had not taught him how to communicate with snakes. He approaches the situation the same way he approached Amanda's patrons. He listens with his body. He moves all of his speech into the nerves that run throughout it.

"What exactly do you want from me?" Christopher asks the snake.

"Knowledge," the snake says.

"I'm listening," Christopher says.

"There's a tree over that hill. Inside the fruit is the knowledge of how my ancestors used to walk upright. I want to know how to do that. I need to ingest a piece of the fruit. The knowledge will inform my DNA. And it will know what to do."

"Why do you need me?"

"The tree is guarded by large birds, wild boars, mongooses, raccoons, foxes, and, worst of all, bobcats. I've watched you since you left the small boat on the New Waters. You move like a cat. You can get to the tree and get me a piece of the fruit."

"And in return?"

"I will grant you one life that would have otherwise been taken by a snakebite."

Christopher agrees. Quietly and quickly, he runs to the tree. Then jumps, swinging his body up and onto a large branch. He walks across the branch on his hands and knees, snaps one of the fruits from the tree limb, and then goes back down the tree and the hill to drop the fruit beside the snake. The snake curls its body around the fruit and slithers back into the forest.

Christopher listens again to the music. He can tell by the tenor of it that Black people are making it. He approaches the building and inside are Black women dressed in bright, colorful dresses with matching colored flowers in their thick woolly hair. Black men are dressed in suits that make them look like they are entertainers. The crowd is dancing, laughing, and cutting deals for something called liquor.

Christopher has a knowing—*I can stay here for a while*—in the bluegrass mountains of Appalachia.

Ten years later, Christopher, now a master bootlegger, decides to leave the hills of Appalachia—and his First Peoples wife who had just caught him cheating—and go back south to run bootleg liquor from Appalachia to the southern region. He believes it's safe for him to go home, since the folks who chased him out of town are now dead. Unfortunately, so are his parents. Having birthed and sent Christopher away, Amanda felt her mission complete. One night she and Palmer went to sleep and walked off together into another realm.

After traveling around the south for years, Christopher makes liquor so good that when he moves to Dallas he supplies every speakeasy and dance hall in the southern region of the

United States. He takes on a job as a cook as a cover. At that time, the only Dallas cooks who work a midnight shift worked downtown on Elm Street, known by the African Americans and Eastern European–American Jews that frequented it as Deep Ellum, the only place in segregated Dallas where White and Black people converge for pleasure, knife fights, gun brawls, sexual adventures, good food, and the best music prodigies in the South.

When Christopher arrives in 1948 in search of a place to produce and disburse his liquor, when the owner of a South Dallas café asks him his name, he thinks about it for a second, then says: "Jack." Jack is a name that is typically given to cooks at that time. Looking at him out of the corner of her eyes is a young smart MaryMadeline who gets lost in the thick, black, silky curls of his hair and the light color of his skin. MaryMadeline, whose skin is dark brown, loved, absolutely loved, light-skin Black men. As a waitress in the café, she is washing down a table when he walks in. She must have washed that table for thirty minutes. When she hears him say his name is "Jack," she is stretched out over the table, her body peeking through her uniform and winking at this Jack, whom she decides she will name "Curly," since he isn't using his real name anyway. Three months later, when Jack considers his first marriage annulled—since it had been done under the name Christopher—he marries MaryMadeline, and Jack begins signing his name as Curly Jack Rose.

Father Kelley said, "Stories like that remind me that history is not only the property of nations and wars but can literally be embedded in our names. Tell me about MaryMadeline."

"There's a story she told me. My sisters don't remember the story, so honestly I'm not sure if I remember it or I made it up."

When MaryMadeline is just ten, her mother goes completely crazy, as crazy as a batsy bug—batsy bug crazy is the kind that they lock people up for in the hospital in Waco, Texas, the worst kind of crazy that Black people can go, and the only hospital in the South for Black people who go that crazy. Their father got a new wife and refused to keep his own kids, so MaryMadeline and her two siblings are sent off to live with their maternal grandmother, on the other side of town in Shreveport, Louisiana. While she is there, MaryMadeline's uncle rapes her. She is tall for her age. Long, thick black hair. Kinky curls that drop down to the middle of her back. It takes a hundred stitches and one month of a hospital stay for her to recover. On the way to the hospital, Grandmother tells MaryMadeline to tell the police she fell on a smoothing iron or they would take them away and put them in an orphanage. Further, if she thought the pain of having her anus ripped apart by the dick of a grown man with no mercy was painful, she would be in for a big surprise—it could absolutely get worse, her grandmother informs her. MaryMadeline lies there in the back of that car with her head in her grandmother's lap, bleeding like a hog from her rectum, unable to really make sense of what her grandmother is saying. She couldn't possibly be understanding correctly. *There is a place that is worse than my grandmother's house, where the young can be ravaged by the grown men and then be made to feel obliged to protect them? Hell itself couldn't be worse than that.*

MaryMadeline cringes from a pain banging in her head during that ride to the hospital. Her ears grow tired of hearing her own groanings. She takes leave of her body. She remembers a woman she worked for when she was nine. She opened the door for this woman when people came calling. She brought coffee. She smiled pleasantly and made the people feel at peace while they waited to see the old woman. MaryMadeline also knew how to make people uncomfortable. She could look deep into their eyes and expose their secrets to them. The old woman, who loved MaryMadeline, saw that the child had talent and she kept her close by to teach her how to use it. The old woman sometimes levitated people from the floor. MaryMadeline learned how to do that too. She remembers that old woman. And MaryMadeline decides that she will take care of her uncle herself.

When she recovers and returns to her grandmother's house, MaryMadeline does a practice run on what she had learned from that old woman who was from Hammond, Louisiana. She wants to see how much she remembers—and how much she will have to re-*member*. Her uncle is sitting at the kitchen table, his expression a mixture of meanness and oblivion. It confuses MaryMadeline for a second, and before she can finish her thought, a quiet commotion suddenly springs up outside. Two White people have come from down the road, from the other side of the tracks, in a twenty-year-old beige Model T Ford with orange wheels. They are rolling into the south side, right outside of Shreveport, in Arcadia, Louisiana. MaryMadeline's grandmother's neighbors are seduced by the unexpected and peculiar occurrence and slowly come out of their two-story houses to see who the pale visitors are.

Grandmother is standing at her clothesline, with clothespins pinned to her bosom. The two White folks drive up into Grandmother's yard. They are skinny, hungry-looking, and dirty. They look like they are hiding in plain sight. One of the visitors, the man, reaches back into the car for his shotgun. The men of the neighborhood look at their wives, who quickly start bringing out their own guns and handing them to the men.

The White woman says to her man: "Put that back. We don't need that. These are good colored folks." Grandmother motions to the neighbors that everything is all right. Grandmother is like the mayor of their neighborhood, settling disputes like Solomon. Everyone thinks she is the wisest person they know. And if they need help, she never turns anyone away.

What kind of wisdom chooses her son over her helpless granddaughter? Grandmother is flawed like Solomon too.

"Whatcha'll need?" Grandmother says to the White couple.

"Food," says the woman. "If you can spare some food and a night's rest, we'd sure appreciate it."

"Come on in. We don't turn nobody away who's in need."

The neighbors sit down on their front porches, where they would normally gather to talk about nothing. Leaning on their guns, the men start pontificating about the White strangers. A couple of the women go over to help Grandmother.

"What's your name?" Grandmother asks the couple.

"I'm Bonnie. And this is Clyde." Still alive, notwithstanding all the reports over a decade ago. And, despite Bonnie and Clyde's cozy relationship with Henry Ford—doing those impromptu ads for the power and speed of the Model T engine—the government needs them dead. Otherwise, how will they control people who live on the margins of society? How do they control the narrative of good versus evil? If "evil" can outsmart the "law," then what kind of society would they have? These small-minded ideas have been trying to "outlaw" me for centuries.

The couple stay the night. Later that night, two other White men arrive to meet the couple. One of them has family in the town next door; that's why they've come there. But the police tracked them there, so Bonnie and Clyde split off from the other two. They all reconnect at Grandmother's home.

Even though they were riding in that classic car, MaryMadeline can tell that Bonnie and Clyde had grown up poor. Well-off White people don't like poor White people. So poor White and Black people found they have an affinity for one another.

MaryMadeline asks Bonnie, because Bonnie is real approachable, "Why are y'all so hungry and driving that nice car? Why don't you just sell it?"

" 'Cause, we stole it, darling." Bonnie responds with such a welcoming smile that it makes MaryMadeline almost feel . . . pretty, like she was something to behold. Strange coming from a grown woman, and a White one at that.

"I think I know who y'all are," MaryMadeline says.

"And I think I know who you are," Bonnie replies. "You're one of them Geechee women. Well, you will be. When you're grown up. Now you're a Geechee girl. How old are you?"

"Ten. And what's a Geechee girl?"

Clyde sits on the porch with his feet propped up on the banister. MaryMadeline loves her grandmother's large front porch. It is so big it feels like she could get lost in another world from that porch. Clyde is smiling, but MaryMadeline feels safe. It is unusual; she has never felt safe like that with White people before. These two are different. Bonnie walks toward MaryMadeline, dragging her left leg. It sounds like shoes scuffling the floorboards.

"Geechee women can levitate people," Bonnie finally says.

"Can you levitate people?" Clyde asks with a cigar hanging from his lips and moving up and down as he talks. "Go on. Do it. I ain't never seen it. Bonnie here. She's seen it. Do it!"

MaryMadeline should be startled by a White man yelling at her to do something/anything, but instead she grows aggressively calm. The energy that should have been shaped into fear shifts into possibility as she re-*members* a memory from that old woman in Hammond. She looks at Bonnie with a question in her eyes. "Which one of you?"

"Him," Bonnie says, and MaryMadeline blushes as if Bonnie were flirting with her.

With her gaze, MaryMadeline begins lifting Clyde from his chair, her eyes fixed on his face as though she were looking through him into another world. She sees his whole history and his whole future. She sees the many banks they have robbed and all the ones they will rob. She sees how Clyde and Bonnie will die in a shoot-out with the police. She uses what she sees to cause a panic inside Clyde's mind. His chair starts to stir a bit, or that's what it feels like to him. Clyde fidgets. And suddenly, so quickly that it is almost unnoticeable, he floats into the air. Parallel to the ceiling of the porch. His nose touches the ceiling.

While amazed, Clyde is also terrified. He fixes his eyes on Bonnie, who is still smiling and entertained. "I knew you could do it!" Bonnie exclaims to MaryMadeline. "What do you see?"

MaryMadeline looks over at Bonnie. "I see Ivy. On the road. I think y'all better be on your way now. Don't stop and change no tires." Because MaryMadeline has turned away from Clyde to talk to Bonnie, he drops to the floor. Clump! He hits the floor with a thud, like a large axe swinging into a five-hundred-year-old tree. The whole thing takes no more than ninety seconds. And because it is so quick, once it's over, a few people who have been watching aren't really sure it had happened. But at the end of it, MaryMadeline says to herself: *I do remember what I learned from Hammond.*

MaryMadeline packs some personal things: a comb, a dress, a teddy bear, fourteen knives she stole from the Jewish merchant in town. Before the arrival of Bonnie and Clyde, she waited to see what her grandmother might do to the man who raped her, her own son. When nothing was done, a week before Bonnie and Clyde's arrival, MaryMadeline went into town to find the right kind of knife. She saw it lying in the display case behind the counter. The case was open on both sides of the counter. No glass to cover the sides, only the top where people leaned to look down at the objects. She walked into that store and started a conversation with the owner and he was so mesmerized that he didn't notice that she had stolen fourteen knives, slipping each one into her bag and rearranging the others so he wouldn't know any were missing.

The day Bonnie and Clyde leave, MaryMadeline leaves too. She goes to the other side of town, where throwaway kids live on the street. She uses her wit to identify and recruit thirteen boys into her newly formed gang, who become her new family. For their first act of rebellion, she instructs them to abduct her uncle and bring him to a stable, where she keeps him suspended in the air for three days before she finally leaves and allows him to fall to the ground, snapping his spine. His screams are so piercing they rouse all the nearby neighbors, who come running to find him impaled on the infamous smoothing iron that MaryMadeline had supposedly fallen onto.

She and her new family of boys live together on the streets of Shreveport, Louisiana. They take in strays of all kinds—animals, people, and unholy ghosts. She rules their house the way that old woman taught her to run a house: with love, kindness, strategic violence, and a complete detachment that she eventually passes on to her daughter, Blue.

MaryMadeline leaves the streets and joins the Catholic Church at sixteen. She is as tall as she will get by then, five-ten, still with the long black hair braided down to the top of her back. She is just about to take the vow to commit herself to Christ when she gets into a disagreement with the reverend mother about purgatory. She is kicked out, and old wounds of being kicked out of her daddy's house by the new wife resurface. She wanders around the South, looking for whatever she is looking for. She takes in people's laundry, cooks for them.

Odd jobs here and there. Until one day she comes upon what she had been looking for—a missionary trip to Uganda. It is an opportunity to do the things she loves most: travel, speak, and write.

She packs the night before and lies down to sleep with incredible visions dancing in her head. When she wakes up, all of her hair is lying on her pillow. She has rheumatic fever. She is rushed to the hospital for a six-month stay. When she reapplies, they won't take her.

Despondent but not defeated, MaryMadeline gets a job as a housekeeper for a liberal-minded White couple in 1947. Her hair grows back. Thicker. Longer. Black kinky. Curly. Strands that braid down to the center of her back. The couple travels a lot and they have a daughter. They want someone to travel with them to watch over their daughter. *It's not ideal but I still get to travel around the world.* She packs her bags the night before. When she wakes up in the morning, she looks back at her pillow. Again all of her hair is lying there. The same fever repeats itself, taking her hair along with it. It never grows back in its rightful thickness ever again. It comes in thin and weak and will only grow about two inches long.

So she gives in to whatever it was that had chosen her for its plan. Something she learned from the old woman who levitated people: sometimes when a thing refuses to come to you, it's because it ain't part of the plan. Each one of us has one. Peoples and things and places and ways of being are birthed through us, and if we deviate from that plan, they won't get created. By the time she sees Jack in that South Dallas café, she has resolved to just find someone who will not run off and travel the world without her or put her out of his house. At thirty-eight, he's twenty years older than her. But he loves her, and he makes her queen of their world.

She gives in, but this plan starts to eat at her, little by little. She notices pieces of her right wrist starting to peel away. Soon enough, she has a big wound on her wrist that oozes pus whenever it gets irritated. One day, while building her and Jack's first house—the one that the City of Dallas later condemned—a snake bites her on that same spot on her wrist. The wound starts to spread up her arm as they rush her to the hospital. Neighbors call Jack to tell him what happened. MaryMadeline is dying.

Jack is in a meeting with one of his customers. He excuses himself and goes into the back of the club and out the back door into the alley. He crosses over the alley and goes into the surrounding woods. He stands motionless and transfers all of his speech into his body. He calls out to the snake from the bluegrass of Appalachia. Jack-who-was-Christopher calls in the snake's debt.

At the same time, MaryMadeline looks at her wound and sees it for what it really is: a festering sore of disappointment. She is compelled by a spirit to pray in tongues and suck out the venom with her mouth and spit it out of the window. Yoruba gods are present. When MaryMadeline arrives at the hospital, the doctors want to cut off her arm to stop the poison from spreading.

"Nope. I need this arm. Pump out the poison. Wrap it up. And send me home," she says.

That's exactly what they do. The arm recovers, all except that one spot on her wrist. She knows what it is, so she leaves it alone. She gives in but secretly doesn't give up. She holds on to the concept of hope, mostly in dreams that end with sleep.

MaryMadeline lives a very fulfilling life; it is too bad that most of the filling is made of disappointment. She has to live inside her dreams to find what she knows exists . . . *Somewhere, just not here.*

"I see a common theme," Father Kelley interjected. "What do you see?"

"That my momma was searching for the thing that got away from her while she slept and the Devil cut off all her hair?"

Father Kelley smiled a soft smile.

Blue sighed. "And that my parents loved me. Dearly. I'm certain of it. I felt it every day of their lives. And despite their inability to accomplish even the simplest of things that they wanted for themselves, they made me believe I could breathe water, that there was nothing I couldn't do. But they were not there for me. Both of them were wanderers and felt cheated by life into parenthood."

Blue's thoughts went back to her conversation with Zion.

Three years before Tsitra was killed, Blue had called her and told her how sorry she was that she hadn't been there for her. Two years before Tsitra was killed, Tsitra had called Blue to tell her how much she loved her. One year before Tsitra was killed, Tsitra had told Blue: "I believe if I don't get out of Detroit, I will die." Blue had said: "Then come here. I'll send you a ticket." But every time Blue tried to send a plane ticket, Tsitra wouldn't answer her phone. Or she had a new phone. Blue couldn't get in touch with her. Blue has thought many times since Tsitra's murder that maybe she should have flown to Detroit and forced Tsitra back to Houston. Blue never stopped thinking that. She wondered, *If I was better at being a mother, would I have forced her to Houston? Isn't that what "mothers" do? Like going with their children to help them get settled into college, rather than writing their letters and completing their applications and filling out their financial aid forms?*

Questions like these created a halo of silence that hovered over Blue like the spirit of a god hovering over the dark waters at the creation of a world. She stepped into the fog of her daughter's murder and wandered around for nearly two years. She looked for answers to painful questions asked by her son, too painful for her to ask herself. She sometimes saw herself as the selfish baby child that her sisters described. She sometimes saw herself as the stuck-up Goody Two-shoes other people described. But she never saw herself as a mother. A mother would know how to take care of her children. Instinctively. She would know.

Blue assumed this knowledge about being a mother to be true because she had an ability to know things. *So, how could I not know that I should travel with my children to college and make sure they get settled in? If I didn't know this, I must not have wanted to know.*

The seer gift allowed Blue, like her mother, to look into someone's soul and tell them information about things they needed or wanted to know. But Blue refused to allow that gift free rein to roam into her own soul. Or the souls of her children. She looked nonchalant to other people, but she was a mess on the inside. She was a ball of emotions wrapped in fire burning itself off in the atmosphere of her life. She found herself constantly drained of energy, and at the same time ablaze with ideas.

It had been a strange mix of freedom and captivity when she suddenly found herself without her kids and believing that she should have been devastated about being without her kids.

She found release in the mercy her children offered her when they reveled in the apologies she had given them. She found solace in the light that emerged from their eyes as they realized that their mother not only loved them, and not only did she believe that she should take complete responsibility for their childhood nightmares, but also liked them and actually enjoyed being with them. She found peace in knowing that her life and theirs were watched over by angels disguising themselves as cussing homeless men on New York City subway cars. She found grace in her own wide-shut eyes clearly being looked through by God. She found a mercy.

"What do I do now?" Blue asked Father Kelley the same question she had considered almost two years earlier, on the day her daughter was hacked to death, the day the breach began peering into time.

Like the stillness of a South Texas summer day, Blue was starting to slow down inside herself. The natural rounding of the sun was starting to collapse into an enclave. Blue felt pieces of herself sliding into the opening that started with a crack at the beginning of the two-hour wait for an update from Detroit but had quickly, too quickly, become a small planetary black hole in the shape of a giant *Door* that looked as if it were the entrance to the inside of her mind or the other side of time. Gravity pulled away from her, but instead of falling she floated on the surface of short memories and long histories over the peaks of motherhood and satiable ornaments of grandeur leaping through ornate forests of flowing houses where porcelain pots sat in the windows of Black men alongside mud-caked riverbanks bathed in blue light, and little Black girls made mud cakes inside of meticulously carved cave doors that could only be seen in blue moonlight.

Blue caught herself and forced her gaze away from that *Door*—from a time more than a hundred years ago, in a room bathed in red—and looked instead at Father Kelley as the most real thing in the room to anchor her.

And morning passed.
Evening came.
Marking the second day.

5

DOWNSTAIRS IN THE GREAT RED Room of Lady Ismay's New Orleans town house, the discussion that always follows the orchestra has emerged. The recent annexation of Texas from Mexico is on the verge of making and breaking political careers. The expansion of the Atlantic slave trade in the former British colonies lingers in the air of salon parties in colonial conscious French- and West African–influenced New Orleans.

"The Mexicans will never let it go," says one man.

"Who says we need their approval?" retorts another.

"What do you think, Mr. Lincoln?" asks one woman. "You have written about this subject, no?"

As Lincoln launches into what will become a famous stump speech that will take him all the way to the White House, another woman whispers to the one who asked the question, "Of course he's for protecting the slaves. You know he's Black."

"No! I can't believe it. Look at him. He's as white as a sheet."

"You know some of the mulattoes can pass for White," she says. "I knew a woman in Hammond who absolutely could have passed for White. But she chose not to. I don't know why anyone would *choose* to be Black."

"More important than Mexico," another man chimes in, "is this business about the balance of power achieved in the Compromise of 1820."

"Well, if Secretary Calhoun had not so recklessly informed the British minister to the U.S. that he viewed Britain's meddling with the Texas question as a poorly disguised attempt to abolitionize the area, the two events would never have been linked," says a man wearing a white wig.

"That connection has surely complicated the matter," says Lincoln.

"Then you agree with it?" asks the white-wig-wearing man.

"I am a logical man," Lincoln says. "If it were up to me, if I could save the Union without abolishing slavery, I would."

"Why is it up to us to free slaves?" asks another man. "Why don't they free themselves?"

"And if they did, who would do your cleaning, cooking, planting, and so on?" asks another man sarcastically.

"Obviously that is not the point that I am making. I'm simply asking why is it our responsibility? When we decided to break away from the British, or the French, or Spanish, we did not make it the responsibility of our oppressors to set us free."

"Every time your enslaved peoples attempt to free themselves, you change the social contract," Amanda interjects as she, Ismay, Palmer, and Xhosa rejoin the Red Room conversation.

"Social contract?" the man asks.

"Yes, the unwritten, unspoken, but assumed practice that all members of a society agree to in order to get what they want from the collective society, usually through laws and political policies. The social contract you used to free yourselves from your oppressors was radically different than the one available to the enslaved African," Amanda says.

"How so?" the man pushes further.

"For one, you could buy your way out of slavery. Convert to a new religion. Learn the language! Change your name! And simply change your clothes and hide!

"You were not," Amanda continues, "kidnapped from your land, chained for weeks on a never-ending sea, raped repeatedly, and then dumped onto a shore where you did not speak the language, stripped naked, and handed over to laws that declared you not even human—laws that made it illegal for you to even learn to read. You were not stripped of your language *and* denied the language of your captors. And if you happened to earn your freedom, you were not suddenly subjected to new laws enacted that wrote your servitude into the color of your skin and all the children you would produce with the same skin."

Amanda isn't finished. "Were your history and libraries literally burned so that you would not know who you are, where you came from, or what you were capable of doing? Reducing you to a poverty so brutal that it ravaged even your mind of memory? Stripping your mind of re-*membering* its history?"

"I don't understand," Ismay chimes in, "how the two are related. I mean, why do poor people stay poor? Why not just rise up in rebellion, like they did in Haiti? There are surely more Blacks on any one plantation than there are Whites." She looks at Frederick Douglass and says, "You outnumber them by four to one at least. Why not just kill your captors?"

"Exactly my question," the earlier man says with a cocky smile, betraying his pleasure at the thought of being supported by the lady of the manor.

"For example," Ismay continues, "Spain took control of New Orleans in 1763, and after thirty-seven years of rule as a Spanish outpost and important trading and cultural partner to Cuba, Haiti, and Mexico my grandfather took it back. Then the U.S. took it. Why not Africans?"

"First of all, because Africa is not a country." Amanda's calm decisiveness makes everyone else nervous. "It is a continent made up of hundreds of countries. The people your father, Benoit Joseph André Rigaud, captured were taken from many countries. Some of whom were enemies, spoke different languages, couldn't understand one another."

Amanda looks in Palmer's direction when she drops Rigaud's name into the conversation. Palmer responds with a look of confusion because he saw Ismay and Rigaud in the bath in the Temple Room, involved in a sexual consummation ritual that he thought father and daughter should never do together.

"They were not one people. Why should they be expected to fight like one people, like the French? Because they have the same-color skin?"

Amanda stops and waits for an answer. No one has one. She looks to Frederick Douglass, who raises his glass to her and nods his approval. He is exhausted from speaking for all

Black peoples everywhere in this country, and he gladly hands the baton to the next runner.

Long pause, then Ismay responds. "Okay, but when placed onto a plantation, after years of serving together, can they not find common ground in their predicament?"

"But your family and friends work hard to ensure this allegiance is never achieved. They separate the fair-skin people from the dark-skin people and tell everyone that the fair-skin people are more like White people because their skin is whiter. As a consequence, fair-skinned Black peoples have better opportunities. The elite also tell everyone that the fair-skin people inherently have better morals and are closer to your god, who is forced on enslaved peoples. Despite the fact that their skin is fair because there has been an egregious act performed on their mothers, which most gods would call degradation and condemn the perpetrators to their hell."

Again silence . . .

Ismay finally breaks it with a question. "But in Haiti the slaves revolted. Why not here?"

"The enslaved in Haiti were of a privileged color class when they started their revolution, with access to weapons and soldiers," Amanda continues.

"Not Louverture," Ismay snaps back.

"You are correct: Louverture is no different from the Africans here. But the land is different."

"Always an excuse," Ismay retorts. *African slaves are weak people,* she thinks. *Like my father against my mother.* "Weak!"

Another man works up the courage to interject. "They are broken by their years of service. They are subservient. They are genetically inferior. And as you say, Ismay, weak. Even when exposed to the advantages of White society, they can't grapple with it and use it to their advantage. They will never revolt. Sambos, the lot of them!" He says this with a loud chuckle, and some of the other partygoers in the audience laugh harder than the occasion would call for because it is a much-needed relief from the tension with which Amanda has encircled the room.

"You both talk as if no group of enslaved people ever rebelled on this land," says Amanda. "To date there have been three hundred and thirteen such revolutions. I myself have fought in two."

Up until this point, everyone except Palmer, Xhosa, and Ismay had thought that Amanda was a White woman. When the crowd realizes she is Black, the women nervously shift in their seats. Their faces become hard. Their eyes reveal plots they would like to unleash on Amanda. The men subconsciously caress their weapons, whether holstered pistols or sheathed swords.

Amanda cannot tell what they might do next. She had learned a very important lesson from her owner, Dr. Coultoure: rich White people are fickle. They are easily persuaded to change allegiance when they are threatened. She considers toning down her argument to make them all feel better about themselves, *because they are much better than the Dutch slave-holders*, she thinks sarcastically. She considers just standing up and leaving the room, but if they should seize her from behind, she would be defenseless. Amanda looks at Palmer, but there is a look of dismay on his face that makes Amanda feel that she cannot depend on his assistance should she need it. He is too distracted.

Palmer is wrestling with what Amanda casually conveyed earlier: that Ismay is Rigaud's daughter. He, along with Amanda and Xhosa, just participated in a very intimate experience with Ismay, the daughter of the man who betrayed and enslaved his parents. He is wondering whether Ismay knew who he was and invited him to the fourth floor as a way to defuse his threat.

But Xhosa is standing ready in a dark corner. Like a warrior, one hand secretly cradles his knife, the other a pistol. Xhosa is wearing all black: a cultured expensive suit with an evening tailcoat, a black high-collared shirt, and a black silk necktie. A black top hat adorns his head, which is shaved bald on both sides, revealing ink drawings of Angola and hieroglyphic prayers; long black dreadlocks run down the center of his head and are neatly pulled together with silver and gold and ivory clamps. His black skin and black attire allow him to disappear into the corner. Amanda decides she is too far in and she will just have to continue delivering her argument. If she should need assistance, Xhosa will back her.

"I am not aware of any such rebellions, yet the Haiti rebellion is world-renowned," Ismay says, interrupting Amanda's thoughts, "and has placed fear in the hearts of every slaveholder. Mine included." She chuckles. Once more the crowd finds welcomed relief in laughter.

"Again," Amanda adds, this time with a smile that frightens Ismay, "because Haiti is such a small island, word would travel quickly and the revolutionaries could isolate their enemies. This land is vast. As you yourself have just proclaimed, you've never even heard of these rebellions, but they do rival the Haiti revolt, except they occurred on a stretch of land so vast that it kept the people from reaching others and expanding the revolution."

"Three hundred and thirteen? I cannot believe that. I have not heard of even one. Name one," Ismay demands.

"I myself fought alongside Nathaniel Turner in the revolution he led. I was just a girl . . . you might say I was about ten."

"You couldn't have," exclaims Ismay. "Nat Turner would have been dead by then."

"Not the son; the father, Nathaniel," Amanda says.

"What father? No one has ever mentioned his father."

"But you have to know he has one, Ismay," Amanda says with as much sarcasm as she can muster. "And his name is Nathaniel," she says, with eyes that almost seem like they're flirting.

"Please continue, Amanda," Frederick Douglass says.

"My parents had been fighting for decades in previous rebellions. Each one rivaled the revolution in Haiti, except getting word to those with 'common ground' was obstructed by hundreds of miles of desolate land, peppered only with unsympathetic White enslavers.

"Have you not noticed when you travel throughout the South how far each plantation is spaced from the other? One practical reason, of course, is the amount of land each plantation holder owns naturally separates them. Another unintended advantage is it also separates dark-skin people with a common predicament from one another. The plantation also sits inside towns that are filled with common-predicament White people."

Frederick Douglass is finally having a conversation that does not require him to be the *everyman slave* and it invigorates him. He is curious to know about these rebellions that even he hadn't heard of. "You say your parents fought in countless revolts? Tell us about one."

Amanda inclines her head. "In 1811, about forty miles north of New Orleans, Charles Deslondes, a mulatto slave driver on the Andry sugar plantation in the German Coast area of Louisiana, got fed up and took inspiration from the victory in Haiti.

"He led the largest and most sophisticated slave revolt in U.S. history. He recruited other enslaved peoples from nearby areas, and on a rainy evening at the beginning of the year Deslondes and about twenty-five purchased peoples rose up and attacked the plantation's owner and family. They hacked to death one of the owner's sons. Unfortunately, the father escaped.

"That was a tactical mistake that they would come to regret, but in the interim Deslondes and his army seized and ransacked the Andry plantation, which happened to be a warehouse for the local militia. They confiscated guns and ammunition and, some thought, oddly, uniforms. But it was a strategic decision—uniforms provided legitimacy for their cause, which proved to be pivotal as they moved toward New Orleans, intending to capture the city. Dozens more men and women joined the cause, singing Creole protest songs while raiding plantations and exacting revenge from the ones who had murdered and tortured the enslaved. The force ultimately swelled to three hundred.

"The father who had escaped turned out to be the Louisiana congressman, slave master, and genocidal butcher of First Land Peoples, Hampton Wade. And even with the U.S. Army and the militia, Wade overcame the protestors only when they ran out of ammunition. The protestors were only twenty miles away from toppling New Orleans.

"You see, Ismay, the subtle advantages that the revolutionaries had in Haiti are missing here and the difference is drastically vast.

"Once ammunition was depleted, most of the protestors surrendered. The enslavers ignored the rules of war—despite the soldiers' uniforms and irrespective of their surrender—and slaughtered all of them. Those who ran into the swamps were caught within the month. The heads of all revolutionaries were spiked onto tall poles along the road to New Orleans. They looked like man-made trees that invaded the sky, with rotting fruit sprouting from the top."

Amanda stops there for a moment of silence.

The white-wig man tries to say something in the gap of silence. He opens his mouth but is suddenly swallowing his words. Amanda stares at him as he starts coughing violently. Then he starts choking. He's gasping for air with his hands around his throat, trying to clear his esophagus.

Ismay looks at Amanda with eyes that say, *Enough!*

Amanda releases the man's throat. He can breathe again, but he cannot remember what he had intended to say. The rest of the audience is too frightened to say anything.

When the silence ends, Amanda's face softens and she looks toward Frederick Douglass, who says, "And there will be another revolution so great it will be called a war, where all the black-skin and white-skin people of 'common predicament' will join forces. These insurrections are just a prelude to the noble performance that is to come in the inevitable *civil war*, the war that will finally put an end to the evil institution that has chained more than nine million human beings to perpetual bondage."

"I don't mean to be disrespectful," Ismay reinserts herself, "but I still cannot imagine a situation where I would not choose death over bondage."

"Perhaps you might consider a social experiment," says Johann Kant, the anthropologist. "Perhaps you might try living as one of them for twelve to eighteen months?"

"Living as a slave?" Ismay asks with indignation.

"I think the beautiful lady has made valid points for you to consider," Kant says. "But you either cannot or will not see it from her perspective. Perhaps if you experience it from her perspective, then you might have more credibility to continue this line of argument that you are so committed to."

Ismay contemplates the wretched slave shacks with no running water or heat in the winter. Mud floors. Pig slop and leftover rotten vegetables for eating. The production of fair-skin babies through rape and power games. Then her face changes, as if she is considering it.

"But how could I do such a thing?" she asks. "I mean practically. How could it be arranged?"

"I can introduce you to Eugène de Mazenod. He's a Catholic priest who started an order of the Catholic Church known as the Oblates. They go to places that are so degenerate, no other order will go."

Ismay finds the idea of a social experiment intriguing and agrees to what she deems "research."

"I know Eugène," says Amanda. "He will take you along on his travels throughout the county. You can either dress as a slave—which, judging from your earlier response, I suppose you will not—or you can dress as yourself, and the lords and ladies of the plantations will introduce you to the best of the lot, like myself. Indeed, that is exactly how you and I met."

"Touché," says Ismay as she raises her glass to Amanda.

Amanda and Ismay had met in Virginia at the Coultoure plantation. Dr. Coultoure had become extremely fond of Amanda, the green-eyed mulatto girl who had designed a new game she called a *puzzle*. He took her to elite parties and introduced her as his ward. He never told anyone that he had raped her mother and produced her. She was always a peculiar child. Her eyes had a hypnotizing affect. With wisdom like a hundred-year-old enchantress, she could use her eyes to make rich, important people feel calm in her presence.

Some people said she was the reincarnated witch Ursula Southeil, better known as Mother Shipton, a sixteenth-century witch who could see the future with such accuracy that she was thought to have the power to *create* the future. A glint in one eye, which was oval, reflected flashes of light when she was *seeing* something. The other eye was round. Like Amanda's eyes. Once, when she was seeing the execution of Mary Queen of Scots, she made the foolish mistake of telling the queen herself, who threw a pot of boiling water into Ursula's face, garnering her the famous nickname "Hag Face." No one dared to use that name in her presence though; instead they called her "General" for her fierce and accurate battle plans. She could move through the camp of the enemy unseen and listen to their plans and then devise a counterplan that made her appear brilliant. Amanda, who also thinks like a shrewd war general, cultivates this belief about herself. Ismay has heard these stories and believes every one of them.

"But if you really want to experience life as a slave, I have a different proposal," Amanda says.

"And what is this proposal?" asks Ismay.

"Upstairs, on the fourth floor, we moved across time, both back and forward. I went to a council in your Heaven. You went to a ranch and pierced into the space of my future granddaughter. You heard her reciting your Lord's Prayer and she heard you."

Amanda moves slowly toward the dark corner where Xhosa stands, stirring a quiet panic among the docile audience members, as they are unsure of what Amanda is planning. Her speech is slow and drawn out, because she is concocting an idea as she walks. Her speech and her walk move at the same pace.

"You invited me to join you and listen in," Amanda continues. "But I refused your invitation because I was listening to something more important."

Amanda has now reached Xhosa. The audience is surprised to see him in the corner. He disappeared in the blackness. He slips something into Amanda's hand from behind his back. Moving from the corner to the center of the room with one step, Amanda holds Xhosa's knife to Ismay's belly, poised upward to cut through Ismay's heart. "Take her place," Amanda says. The knife is her counteroffer to the proposed social experiment. "Live half your life in this century and the other half as my granddaughter. She will be born into a gripping poverty. You will be able to live it and then, finally, as you say, *understand* it."

Four bodyguards emerge out of nowhere to protect Ismay. A series of sharp, almost convulsing inhales from the partygoers shudder the room. Palmer pulls one pistol from the back of his waistband and another from underneath his pant leg. Xhosa stands beside him with a pistol in one hand and his other knife in the other hand.

Ismay is surprisingly calm. "Amanda has presented her proposal as a question. I have not answered yet. She will not take my life against my will. She cannot. I know enough from my own witch mother that, if she did, it would not work to her best advantage."

Amanda steps back from Ismay. Although she is aware of Ismay's heritage, Amanda is surprised to realize that Ismay knows the ways of the occult. Ismay is correct. She would have to give her permission in order for it to have the effect that Amanda desires. The other guests are shocked to know that Ismay's mother was a witch. They assume, then, that Ismay is also Black. The Black-rumor-spreading woman from earlier whispers to her companion, "See! I told you. You cannot tell them apart from us!"

This granddaughter would not be born for more than a hundred years. To be exact, Amanda proposes the day and year of return to be April 5, 1968. The number five brings a message from the angels that important life changes are imminent.

Ismay had seen a glimpse of the girl's life during the time-bending experience. It had been brutal. Ismay tries to curve her mind around the idea that the two people who stand before her, Amanda and Palmer, would birth descendants who would end up so wretchedly lost and crushed under uncertainty and fear. So destitute of resources. Networks. Possibilities! *Perhaps I should take this challenge,* she thinks. *I cannot imagine that even if I were born in whatever hell that girl had been through that I wouldn't know how to get out of it.*

"If I say yes," Ismay says, breaking through the fear and possibilities running loose and chaotically around the room, "it cannot be now. I need more time here. There is something I have to do."

6

At 7:05 p.m. on April 4, 1968, MaryMadeline goes into an unexpected and ferocious labor. Blue, MaryMadeline's fifth child, is on her way into this world. Triggered by violent riots that broke out across the country in response to the assassination of the Reverend Dr. Martin Luther King Jr., MaryMadeline, a woman strong enough to build her own first house, is brought to her knees by an overwhelming pain in her belly that eradicates the idea of hope.

Memphis sanitation workers were striking, and King had gone to support them, bringing with him the national attention that had begun following him around the South. Before heading to dinner at the home of his local host, Minister Samuel "Billy" Kyles, King was hanging lazily over the hotel banister of room 306 (3 + 0 + 6 = 9) as sun affected-folks tend to do—right?—when a single shot released from a slender high-powered barrel slammed into King's face. Ripped flesh and shattered bone flew into the wind, leaving half of his skull exposed to the world. When the images made their way to the television, radio, and grapevine news networks, the nation imploded inside a blaze of fire and riots.

MaryMadeline lies on her side in the hospital bed, watching the news on the television above her head. Jack stands next to her, holding her hand.

"I'm not surprised," Jack says. "What made him think he would be safe enough to be out in the open like that?"

"I don't believe you," MaryMadeline says.

"Don't believe what?"

"I think you *are* surprised. I can see it in your eyes."

"What you see is not *surprise*; it's *disappointment*."

"Disappointment? With whom?"

"With Martin Luther."

"Why?"

"He's a fool if he thought White folks would let him live."

The pains that come periodically when a baby is moving toward the birth canal are so intense that they render MaryMadeline temporarily in and out of consciousness. Several attending doctors remember her from six months earlier, when they gave her only a few weeks to live. She had terminal cancer. At that time, they offered to more than double her life span and give her eighteen more months to live if she let them abort the baby she was carrying. MaryMadeline declined their offer, *generous as it was*. They sent her home to die. So, six months later, they were genuinely pleasantly surprised to see her.

"We heard that you were back, Mrs. Rose," says the lead attending doctor. "I've brought a few colleagues who want to meet you. Some residents and medical students are also here."

MaryMadeline looks at the group, which is so large it could very well have been intimidating, but instead she says, "So now do you believe in God?" Then she chuckles.

Another attending doctor turns to the medical students and says, "Six months into her pregnancy, Mrs. Rose was diagnosed with terminal uterine cancer."

"And she *and* the baby survived?" the cockiest of the medical students asks.

"We're not sure why," the lead attending interjects. "That's why we are all here now." The attending doctors study MaryMadeline's patient files while a maternity resident lifts the sheets to examine the dilation of the cervix. Whispers about the idea of *remission* are thrown about and bounced around the circle of medical professionals like a turn-taking talking ball.

MaryMadeline finally says, "If you sent me home to die, then can it really be called *remission*? Wouldn't 'miracle' be more appropriate?"

The student doctors secretly marvel at the idea but are afraid to admit to the attending doctors that they *could* believe it.

The maternity resident interrupts the chatter. "Though Mother is moving in and out of consciousness, the baby has remained fully conscious."

In fact, the girl baby is so conscious that she had a dream.

She dreamt that as a child—well, actually, even before she was a child—she was that Frenchwoman. Creole actually. With thick, long, black hair, an elegant top hat, and an overcoat made of a fine silk. A lacy dress, too feminine for the top hat and boots, but the boots, made of alligator skin, were fashionable and sexy. She carried a riding stick horizontally and in line with the straps of a beige leather purse with zippers and strings. She loved riding her horse to events instead of traveling by a carriage. It was the independence, the freedom that comes with being easily mobile. When she was that woman, before she was this girl baby, she had a dream. A dream is what she called it because, although she had made a deal with her friend, she didn't know how to say to anyone that the dream was really happening.

She dreamt that she was about two hours old. She had just been dropped into a very uncomfortable containment of too much skin. She was tired. The birth canal had been an exhausting trip. There were rolls and rolls and rolls of extra skin, still bluish from the blue it was. She was on her back with her head turned toward her shoulder in the baby hospital bed. She was connected to a bunch of tubes and there were lots of people in the room. She could see her momma lying in the bed across the room. Her momma was also exhausted from the experience of bringing her into this new world, this baby girl who didn't have a name yet because her momma had intended her to be a boy.

Everything was slightly disorienting. Her eyes—things looked funny, sort of washed-out and blurry. The people seemed surprised to see her looking at them. Before she was in the baby bed, she spent a couple of minutes on her momma's breasts. She recognized her mother, her mother's skin felt like the water she'd been floating in for the past nine months. (9 = completion.) She could hear people saying, "The baby won't make it."

"We're losing the baby!" the maternity resident says.

"Plug her into the respirator," the attending says as the too-large group of medical professionals hovers nearby. Then he inserts a tiny tube into each nostril.

"The next tube," he says to the nurse.

"Her pressure is dropping," the nurse responds.

"Adrenaline!" he shouts.

"Yes, Doctor."

"We have to get the heart going." He pushes a needle into her heart, followed by very, very light chest compressions interspersed with gulps of oxygen from the machine.

Twenty minutes later . . . the sound of a tiny heart flatlining pours into the room. MaryMadeline, who has been watching from across the room, says, "Well. Whatever God wills."

And then . . . out of the blue . . . the baby starts crying.

On April 5, 1968, a Friday, at 4:44 a.m., Blue arrived.

Two days later, the doctors detected an umbilical hernia.

"Can I be present when you inform the mother?" asked the cocky medical student. He had grown fond of MaryMadeline's poignant humor regarding medicine's limitations.

The attending doctor examined the baby without responding for what felt like seven whole minutes and then finally said, "No. I don't think we will inform the parents."

"How can you not?" the student asked before thinking about how to pose the question with less disgust. The attending responded with a look that terrified him.

"We are curious to know whether this hernia is simply her intestine bulging through the opening in her abdominal muscles or whether it has something more to do with her and her mother's survival." He spoke with logic and rationality while holding the baby with a look of empathy and benevolence.

The girl baby had a *knowing* that she would make her appearance onto this scene. *Wherever the hell "here" is. I gotta tell you, it's not looking familiar,* she thought. *Apparently there's a problem with the fact that I'm blue all over.* That's the reason for all the tubes. *Apparently, that's not normal. To be born blue means you were born dead. But where I come from, the color is blue.* And this is who she is: She is *roseofsharon Blue—Blue Washington Rose.* Inquisitive about simple things like her fingers. Content with herself and the world that she knows and doesn't know. Possessing a deep wisdom, a confidence in that wisdom, and a peace in the confidence. Affectionate. Playful. A *blue rose,* not made in *nature,* but made in *unattended-by-God agreements.* Agreements made of the intensity of a deep, deep beauty, like the night lights of New Orleans bathed in blue moonlight. Like a languid moment of rest and ecstasy in the presence of the unknown. But this calm confidence would not last.

In the unknown, the strange is knowable through stories. Blue's story is one of: *Blue kisses. Raindrops. Teardrops of sweet things. Love things. Violins stringing words like lollipops on a clothesline in the country yard where she grew up. And it feels soooo good, remembering where she grew up. Warm, hot Texas summer rain-soaked dirt. Momma lying on the couch, reading a book. Looking at her playing in the dirt. Eating it. Throwing it above her head into the air to be caught by the angels circling her. Dirt particles flying by their faces, being caught in their mouths. Blinking off their eyelids. Rolling off their lips. Dropping back down all around her as she twists in a circle with her hands up to catch it like her angels are doing. And Momma seeing all of them.*

Blue kisses . . . raindrops . . . teardrops of sweet things. Smiling like pickles and chimera bells whispering words into her mouth; lickable words running shyly down her face like her own tears. Sweet smells of blue apples. Blue turkeys clapping blue wings. Bluegrass in Appalachian Mountains making music in the dew. Blue blessings in a desert place. Blue offerings of sweet fruit glittering from the ground, squeezing lines of water from its mouth. Soft feathers from cotton trees blowing stifling air. Blue spiders spinning blue webs catching sweet blue babies that nobody wants.

Babies aren't born knowing how to put themselves to sleep when they're tired or how to wake up when they're well rested. This is all learned behavior. The blue baby girl slept all day and came alive at night. After spending nine months in a dark and watery womb, she had established her own sleep cycles, based on voyages in a sea so black it reflected its blackness in the sky. A sea so black, sound seemed to have been swallowed up by the vastness of the blackness, as a fleet of ships glided over the top of the black water. Attacking. Advancing.

When the sun rose, the ships would rest, as God did on the seventh day.

At night, Blue found it impossible to sleep. Even as a baby, she could find creativity living in the nighttime lights. Before her father left for work, for his midnight to sunrise shift, he would rub her belly until she fell asleep.

Blue, like everyone else in their house, called her father Honey. It was a name they picked up from MaryMadeline.

"Honey. Honey. My navel hurts," Blue lamented. Her family was unaware of the hernia still, as the doctors had never revealed it to her parents. To be fair, they worked at a teaching hospital that, like all teaching hospitals everywhere in the world, does harmful research on only the marginalized. (It would be some years, when Blue was twelve, and swelling and discoloration of her abdomen led to violent vomiting, before a trip to the emergency room would finally reveal the cause of the plum-sized navel.) Every time she called for her daddy, curled up in the fetal position, she was suffering from a thrust from inside her belly.

"Honey. Stop spoiling that girl," MaryMadeline would say.

"She can't fall asleep unless I do this. You know that."

"She can too," MaryMadeline said.

"She's been up all night," Jack retorted.

"Bring her to me," MaryMadeline would sometimes say. Other times Jack would say: "Having another baby was your idea! I told you not to go having another baby." But it was real clear to everybody who knew him that what he meant was *God dammit to hell! I'm doing this my fuckin' way! I wanna rub my baby's belly 'cause it hurts too much for her to go to sleep, and she wants me to do it, and that's that!*

When Jack wasn't home, MaryMadeline would hold Blue in her lap and play Tchaikovsky on the piano. The music would soothe Blue, who was troubled by things she didn't understand. Like if life had a reason for itself or if it *just was*. Feelings of wanting to be alone and yet wanting to be in her momma's belly and daddy's arms and the *place* she came from. MaryMadeline would hold Blue and play the piano. Jack would sit on the edge of Blue's bed and rub her belly. These were the ways she went to sleep each night.

Today was like all other Tuesdays. Blue waited on the front porch for her father to come home from his job. When he arrived, the two of them walked MaryMadeline to the bus stop four blocks away. Jack and Blue then kissed MaryMadeline goodbye as she got onto the bus and went to work as a cook in an elementary school. MaryMadeline was a terrible cook. Blue could never understand how she made a living at it. But back then nobody really questioned whether a Black woman could cook. If it didn't taste right, they figured it was something wrong with them. "I think I'm coming down with something. My taste buds are all screwed up."

All Black women could cook—and clean.

After putting MaryMadeline onto the bus, Blue and Jack walked the four blocks back home.

When Blue and Jack got home, Blue started pulling off her clothes, as she had always done. She was dressed in a pink T-shirt with white lace around the waist, and her hair was combed and neatly constrained with ribbons and barrettes— Blue had lots of long, thick hair that her sister Delilah reveled in as her fingers locked inside the strands and pulled through hair grease and water to moisturize the thick locks of black curls. Blue started with the barrettes and ribbons in her hair. She got down to her underpants and pulled them off. She felt utterly and satisfactorily free. Of clothing, underpants, and barrettes—it was just *her* in the pure essence of herself. It felt wonderful. No constraints of decency or acceptableness or cuteness. It was a revolutionary act. A refusal to abide by the rules. A wildness uncontained.

Feeling as though she had grown in size without the constraints of social etiquette, Blue walked around the big house
as naked as a jaybird, as her momma would say. And as happy
as one. Her uncle Roscoe, whom she never liked (and felt
guilty for it), came out of his room earlier than he normally
did. "Blue. Put on some clothes!"

Being only five, Blue's response was to throw one leg to
the side and vigorously scratch the inside of her thigh while
spitting bubbles out of her mouth.

"This is *her* house," said Jack. "She can do whatever she
wants." Jack's response to Uncle Roscoe not only silenced him
but, most importantly, planted a kernel in Blue about the power
of her station in life.

Vindicated by her father, who sent Uncle Roscoe back to
his hideaway without another word, Blue went to play in
their backyard while Jack took care of the chickens. After all
the chores were done, father and daughter sat on their large
front porch. Blue sat on Jack's knee while he stared into the
silence of space. He didn't talk much. Blue talked incessantly.
Blue accepted this behavior as *normal*. At nap time, Blue would
lie back on Honey's chest and he'd rub her belly, because
that hernia was always making its presence known, until she
fell asleep.

In the afternoon the house came alive again. Blue's siblings
came home from school. MaryMadeline soon followed. And
on this Tuesday, when MaryMadeline walked up onto the
porch toward Blue and Jack to wake them from their nap,
Jack was dead.

A year later, almost six years old, Blue sat on the front porch
waiting for Jack as she had done all of her life. She woke up

and out of habit, not out of hope, went to wait for Jack so it would be like the other times when he came home and they would walk MaryMadeline to the bus stop.

"I told you he's not coming. He's in Heaven now with God," said MaryMadeline, who had come onto the front porch and stood next to Blue, looking down at her.

Blue thought she knew this "god" that her mother spoke of—this god who Blue imagined must be female. But it can't possibly be the same god that was responsible for her miracle birth. *That god wouldn't take my daddy. This must be some other god. Who is this other god that takes little five-year-old girls' daddies and for no apparent reason doesn't let them come home again?* This god is male—and he is known by the Rose family as *God the Lord*.

Every day MaryMadeline walked onto the front porch and told Blue, "He's not coming." Blue didn't care. She decided that she would wait anyway. She developed a habit of waiting for something, not knowing what it was, but suspecting that she would recognize it when it came.

"It's been nearly a year, Blue. In a few days you will be six," said MaryMadeline.

Blue wasn't sure what she was expected to do with that information. "Does a year mean something special?" she asked her mother.

"It means he's not coming back."

Blue felt she was drowning in *time*. As she grew up, *time* haunted her with an inability to know where she was going, an inability to look back and understand where she'd been. Everything seemed as though it might not be real.

So, at five, she began to follow a path mapped out by loss. That was the day she decided God didn't exist. That was also the day she became afraid of *hope*.

MaryMadeline, on the other hand, felt free for a while. The most respectable way for a woman to be freed from the constraints of a man is through death. She had loved Jack, but she had never really wanted to be married. Of her options at the time, marriage was the best one. Ironically, it was this same hope-*less* thinking that she unwittingly passed on to her girls. But on the surface of her consciousness, she thought, if you have a marriage, then you might as well go all the way and have children too. Maybe one of them would come upon your dream and you could live it through their eyes, if they allowed you to see it. But if, in the meantime, you were relieved of the responsibility of marriage, then that was a freedom you just couldn't ignore. MaryMadeline went all in with what she felt was her calling: taking care of everyone except her own family.

At eleven, Blue had developed a habit of going to sleep when she faced a problem she didn't know how to solve. Once again, there was no food in the house. Not even a jar of mayonnaise to make a mayonnaise sandwich. No bread to make a sugar sandwich. Nothing. The chickens they had had when Blue's father was alive had been sacrificed years ago. MaryMadeline, who never learned money—the nature of it, or how to leverage its power—couldn't keep it, and when she had it, she had no idea how to spend it. She spent her monthly Social Security check in two days, mostly on her poor neighbors who had even less than her family did, which is actually hard to imagine.

So, in lieu of eating, Blue went to bed.

Blue would go for days without eating anything. Although no one would call it that, she had developed an eating disorder. It was easy to do. Her body had adapted to her family's relationship with anything that required money to purchase. When she did eat, she would often overeat, not knowing when she might get food again. Her sisters, who were all fifteen or more years older than Blue, had left home to start their own families after Jack died. So it was only Blue and her mother still living in the big house, and the occasional sister who would run into financial problems and go back home temporarily to re-*gather* herself.

Blue's sisters never forgave their mother for falling into a financial tailspin after Jack's death. Blue, however, even at eleven, had come to understand that her mother had never left the streets of gutter children where her grandmother had abandoned her. Blue watched her mother with eyes that were ready to look deep inside, if she could ever get past the wall her mother had placed neatly and firmly in front of them.

On her way to her bedroom, Blue passed by the black-and-white television screen. As an adult, she would appreciate the value of documentaries, but at eleven they bored the hell out of her. But this one had her glued. It was about two English-speaking missionaries, a husband and wife from Europe living in Africa, *or was it the Brazilian rain forest?* Her mother came into the room and wondered what had captured Blue's attention so resolutely, so she joined her daughter standing in front of the television set. The missionaries' goal was to take the knowledge of Christ to the Indigenous peoples of that place. However, the missionaries didn't speak the language of the people, and the people didn't speak English. So the missionaries spent ten years living with the people in order to learn their language. Ten years later, the missionaries discovered that there were no symbols in the language for "Christianity"—nothing for "Christ," "salvation," "Trinity," "heaven," "hell," "resurrection," etc. So the missionaries spent an additional ten years *creating* a new language by way of writing a dictionary.

Blue looked at her mother. "You can just create a new language?

"What exactly is creation?" Blue asked her mother, who always had an intelligent answer for everything.

"I don't think I know," MaryMadeline said. Blue couldn't remember a time when MaryMadeline responded to one of her questions with "I don't know." The idea of creation became the most mysterious of actions either of them had ever encountered.

"Do you think it's something that *I* could use?"

"I don't see why not. If they can use it," she said, referring to the missionaries, "then why not you?"

"How do you think it works?"

MaryMadeline tried to tease through this idea. "Since we are made in God's image—"

"What?" Blue asked.

"—and God created all things, then it must work like it did in Genesis."

"Which is how?" Blue asked, impatient with MaryMadeline's pace as she noodled through a logic.

" 'Let there be . . .' He spoke things into existence."

Could it really be that simple? Because if you can just create a new language, you can create anything.

A week earlier, MaryMadeline had been sitting in the living room reading a book. Something she often did, now that she had retired from her school cook's job. It was nearly sunset. Blue came into the living room. "Will you pray with me?"

MaryMadeline looked at Blue with wonder and confusion. Wonder because, despite never really wanting to have children in the first place, MaryMadeline had asked God for one more child in her and Jack's old age, because she wanted a preacher—so she wanted a boy. Actually, MaryMadeline wanted to *be* a preacher, but she grew up in a time and place where only boys could grow up to be preachers. So she wanted a boy. Nevertheless, she was not too disappointed with the blue girl baby because Blue was so peculiar that MaryMadeline had recognized Blue as a prophet.

"Yes. Of course, I'll pray with you," MaryMadeline finally said as she stood up and extended her hands to Blue.

"Can we kneel?" Blue asked, instead of taking MaryMadeline's hands.

"Sure," her mother said, with some hesitation.

"Over there," Blue said, pointing to the couch next to the front door, whose main door was open leaving only the screen door between them and the outdoors.

"Okay," her mother said slowly, thinking, *This is really specific.*

Blue and her mother knelt next to the sofa. MaryMadeline didn't say anything at first, because Blue had been so precise that her mother assumed she also knew which prayer they should pray. But Blue just knelt with her head down. Finally, after several seconds of quiet, MaryMadeline decided to pray aloud. Within sixty seconds of her starting that prayer, Blue and MaryMadeline heard a rustling on the front porch, less than two feet away from them. The two of them looked up to see who was at the front door. The visitor, a stranger, a Black woman, hadn't knocked but stood at the screen door.

"Hello. Can I help you?" MaryMadeline asked.

"Oh no! Don't let me interrupt your prayer," the woman said. "In fact, may I join you?"

Blue went back down on her knees, her mother next to her, and the woman next to MaryMadeline. Blue looked at her mother with questions in her eyes, and MaryMadeline responded with a look that said, *I don't know.* This event was not as strange as it may sound. Friends, neighbors, church members, salesmen, and strangers often came to Blue's childhood house. It was almost like it was a stop on the underground railroad. So Blue's mother led the three of them in prayer. Blue knelt in silence. The stranger prayed with MaryMadeline as if they were regular prayer partners—spiritual groaning and utterances in tongues that none of them could understand, but all of them could feel the blessings of those words that were spoken through MaryMadeline and the stranger. They spoke expressions of praise, with gratitudes of life, and lilies of the field dressed in grandeur that even Solomon could never match, or something like that.

Twenty minutes later, MaryMadeline ended the prayer with a simple "Amen." MaryMadeline stood with her hands on her hips, looking at the stranger. Blue stood with one foot snaking around the back of her other leg as though she were going into a yoga pose. Both mother and daughter were anxiously waiting for the woman to announce her reason for being at their front door precisely seconds after they had knelt to pray at the urging of some mysterious guide.

Finally the woman said, "I came here to give you this eviction notice. The bank is planning to take your house. But I'm not going to give it to you. I'm going back to the bank and I'm going to figure out a way for you to keep your house."

Then, without the normal pleasantries of polite conversation, the woman simply left. MaryMadeline looked at Blue and said, "You. Are. A. Prophet."

Blue stopped telling her story. Took a long pause. And cried for the little girl who too often went to bed without food.

Blue felt a wounded pounding in her chest. It felt like someone was stuck in there and was trying to get out. The feeling reminded her of those random images of a staircase that used to flash into her vision. Images of standing at the bottom of the staircase. Looking up. An ornate staircase that felt like it was from a historical time but suspended in a time that looked like the future. There was a feeling around it that Blue couldn't quite language—she couldn't articulate. She had hoped that the language of anthropology would have helped her figure it out by now. Anthropology helps to put words to those things that get lost in between the lines of thoughts and imaginations. But the image kept getting stuck inside her. And the whole thing made her feel like her life was too big for the historical poverty she was living, and it just wanted to get out!

She abruptly shifted her eyes from her future/history and looked at Father Kelley, who simply said, with the sweetest smile, "Go on."

Blue fidgeted in her chair for several long seconds; then, as her eyes moved back and forth into the room and out of it through memories, she haltingly asked, "Have you ever felt like . . . the life you were living . . . was too small for the life . . . that was really yours?"

"You already have acceptance letters to college," a high school senior asked Blue. "Aren't you just a junior?"

"Yeah," Blue simply said. She felt proud to be the only one with an opportunity no one else at her school had and embarrassed by what felt like ridicule from the older student, who had intended for her to feel mocked.

"But why would you have acceptance letters in the eleventh grade?" the boy asked, unaware that in the rest of the world, outside of their neglected neighborhood, eleventh grade is actually when such agreements are made.

Blue turned up her lips as if to say, *The hell if I know.*

"Which schools?" He suspected that it would be some community college in the middle of nowhere, because he was a senior, a popular football player with what he thought should have been limitless possibilities at his fingertips. But he had no acceptance letters yet.

"University of Texas at Austin and Southern Methodist University."

"*What?*" the boy said with the strongest surprise he could muster. "You must be a genius."

Both colleges were looking for smart Black students to whom they could extend an opportunity and were offering a full scholarship. But Blue couldn't imagine the idea of representing her entire race in all-White colleges that only wanted her skin color for their own gains. She also couldn't imagine living with only White people. The ratio would have been Blue to several thousand White students on either of those campuses. Blue also couldn't imagine school being an imaginable place at all. She hated school. She only went two or three days per week. She didn't need to go five days to learn what they were teaching her. If her mother had not been an incessant reader who read to Blue every day, Blue would have been as unlucky as her classmates.

What Blue didn't know about the world is that prestigious American institutions only want anyone for their skin color. Usually that color is White. But because Blue would graduate high school after the accomplishments of the civil rights and the Black power movements, some universities were looking at themselves and saying, *Damn we're too fucking white!* So Blue was catching a break, because she wasn't only a Black girl; she also happened to have a genius mind. But Blue grew up in a sea of limits. Her experience was shaped by her mother's understandings, and MaryMadeline didn't know how to help Blue dream big. So Blue couldn't see these school acceptances for what they were: her big break.

Blue was abruptly pulled out of her recollections of her childhood with a question from Father Kelley: "Are these *memory sessions* useful to you?"

A long silent pause, then an exasperated "Yep. The most devastating event that happened to the descendants of my ancestors is that we forgot. We forgot everything that started in 1604 because it was too painful to remember. On top of that, our oppressors wiped out our history before 1604 with disease, insanity, war, death, and the burning of our texts. We grew up with a *collective forgetting*. So it's been good. These sessions. Remembering is like re-appending a leg to your body. It's painful as hell, but once it's back on, you can walk straight again."

And morning passed.
Evening came.
Marking the third day.

Now there was a day when the *Sons of God* came to present themselves before the Lord, and being the firstborn and, although disappointing, favorite son of God, Satan also came among them, as he typically did to give a report of his roamings. You see, he had been kicked out of Heaven and condemned to roam the earth when he launched a coup against his father and lost.

God the Lord says to Satan, "Where have you come from?"

Satan answers the Lord, "From roaming throughout the earth, going back and forth on it."

Then the Lord says to Satan, "Have you considered my servant George Washington Rose? There is no one on earth like him." God would typically offer up his best servants as a challenge to his wayward son. He would dare his son, in a war of loyalties, to persuade a faithful servant to curse God.

"Does George worship God the Lord for nothing?" Satan replies. "Have you not put a hedge around him and his household and everything he has? You have blessed the work of his hands, so that his lands have multiplied, and his slaves are spread throughout the land. He has won unwinnable battles against the British Empire and the French Empire. He has been sold into slavery and within a few short months became owner of the wealth of his former owner. But if you allow me to strike everything he has, as you did with Job, he will surely curse you."

God shrugs. "You may choose one branch of his family line."

After a contemplative pause, Satan considers the most ironic of numbers. "Then I choose the tenth member of the family," says Satan.

"The tenth?" God the Lord turns to an old man to his right—an old man with a long white beard that extends from his chin, drops down to the floor, and drapes between his sandal-clad feet. He wears a pointed hat with magical writings scrawled around it in a looping, sloping line; he holds a golden book with off-white pages and uses a pen that writes in golden ink; he writes in straight, vertical lines rather than horizontal lines. He is writing Amanda's granddaughter's story.

From the crowd of Sons of God, Amanda rolls her eyes over the vertical lines of golden ink and sees an image of the goddess of chaos, and, startled, nearly stumbles into view. "Who is the tenth member of the family line?" God the Lord asks the old man.

"That is Palmer. He will have a granddaughter with a shape-shifter, and the granddaughter—a blue baby girl—will be the seed of their last son. If Satan is successful, the family's history will end with the blue baby girl. The irony is ten is the number of new beginnings."

Satisfied with his win, Satan goes out from the presence of the Lord, and the Heaven Council comes to an end.

When Amanda hears their plans, she gasps so intensely that it nearly pulls Ismay, Palmer, and Xhosa back to the fourth floor into 1848. When Amanda returns, Xhosa again invites her to join them in listening to Blue reciting the Lord's Prayer. Not only does Amanda listen and repeat, as her cohorts do, but she travels through the veil and sees Blue, her future granddaughter that the Heaven Council is currently discussing.

The shock of this knowledge ripples through the historical line, up to the moment in the chapel in 2008, and past it. Amanda collapses into a convulsion that disturbs the wind, which blows through the fourth-floor room, extinguishing the candles and licking up the water, leaving the gutter, filled from the Mississippi, dry.

In the chapel, Blue has heard the whispers of the same Heaven Council. While Amanda hears them as the future, Blue has heard them as the past.

"Has she cursed God yet?" one member of the Council asks.

"She hasn't cursed God. But she has acknowledged that she's not sure of His existence," another says.

"Why has she come to The Ranch?" another member of the Council asks.

"She's looking for answers to her life."

Another member delicately poses a question to God. "Her trials have been severe. And this latest one, perhaps, was too brutal?"

"I want to hear from her," another member says. "Can we not bring her before us?"

"I think we have already heard from her. Her tears have been clear," another says.

"I want to know what she has learned," yet another says. "And what was done to prepare her for this moment?"

"Has she been too injured by the experience?" someone asks. The Sons of God don't recognize this one and turn as one to face him. He looks as if he belongs there, so they ignore him and turn back to God, who finally speaks: "I had hoped she would learn how to travel to the other side of life without losing herself, without losing her mind."

"Why?" asks the mysterious Son of God.

"On the other side of life is a dimension that is invisible and unnoticeable to most. Some can touch it when certain conditions happen. Some brush past it and know they've brushed past something but can't explain what. Some know about it but have never been able to travel there. They think too hard about it. It goes further away from them, rather than drawing closer. Some can travel there at will. Like you," God says to the stranger.

"I have a vested interest here. She's my granddaughter. And she can see through the veil. But what good does it do her?"

God responds, "This knowledge will allow her to understand that manifesting something is just a matter of time and space coalescing into an intention. It's all she needs to rewrite her story. And *Time* has come due."

Amanda's shape-shifting is born of an old-world tradition of reshaping the story of a person. When Amanda is four years old, her father (and owner), Dr. Coultoure, notices her making a toy that his acknowledged children adore. She shows him how to play with it, and he finds that he too falls in love with the game.

Amanda draws elaborate images on pieces of stiff white paper and colors them in with paint she makes from plants she cuts, grinds into powder, and pours into a mixture she concocts from the kitchen and the forest. She paints the image with a delicate brush she fashions from the hairs she cut from her siblings' heads while they sleep. Then she cuts the image into hundreds of pieces in strange shapes. She carves and shaves the edges perfectly, mixes them up, and then challenges her audience to put them back together again.

She calls her game a *puzzle*.

The year Amanda turns seventeen she has made her father—an already rich man—an even wealthier man, creating thousands of these puzzles that he taught her how to sell to the upper caste of Europe and North Africa. She has traveled extensively with him and learned to speak French, Portuguese, Spanish, Italian, Russian, and Arabic.

Seventeen is also the year that Amanda begins reordering her own story.

It's Monday and, as has become customary for the past twelve months, Amanda is on her typical weekly stroll through the town behind her father's wife, Mrs. Coultoure, who is so fond of Amanda that she ignores the fact that Amanda is the product of the careless rape of Mrs. Coultoure's personal "slave." Mrs. Coultoure has not always felt this way.

Amanda, who has cream-colored skin, wears a wide-brim white hat and a long white dress with blue lace trim that hugs the contours of her body. She carries a lacy blue umbrella to match, an outfit that she picked up in France on a trip with Dr. Coultoure.

The day starts out like all the other Mondays, but as the two women parade through the town, something new occurs. Amanda sees a man she's never seen before. His spirit blows past her like a roaring wind, and in the wind Amanda sees all the pieces that this man is. She, the Seer, has a way with seeing. She sees all the names he's adopted for his own description, and the ones he adapted from other people's descriptions of him. Beneath that, she sees who he really is. She sees the history of this broken creature and how that history can put him back together again. She sees the beauty of the dirt he grew up on that has expressed itself in his skin—reddish–light brown, cream. She sees the explosiveness of the ocean that his father crossed settling in the man's eyes. Amanda sees a girl grand-baby that will come that will be Amanda's chance to put the broken pieces back together again for a whole generation of two enslaved families—hers and his.

The man, who is so despondent, feels his spirit slacken and sees himself as though he were in a slow-motion picture show. Initially he assumes Amanda is a White woman. He recently developed a habit of not looking at White women. He has learned that such a simple act is legally justifiable cause for hanging a Black man. But the woman's eyes pierce his soul and compel him to look back, and he looks right into the eyes of the most beautiful woman he's ever seen.

"Good morning," Amanda says to him. And immediately he knows she's a Black woman. He recognizes the subtle accent that is commonly used among people passing for White. To Amanda's own surprise, Mrs. Coultoure hisses at him. Amanda looks at her with a piercing gaze and Mrs. Coultoure calms again.

"Good day to you, sir," Amanda says to the man. "Perhaps you will join me for tea in the square in five minutes?"

The man cautiously accepts, his eyes darting back and forth between Amanda and Mrs. Coultoure. He's trying to understand what is happening, but it's too strange for him to comprehend.

"Shall we continue our walk?" Amanda asks Mrs. Coultoure. She has learned that way of talking from White people. They always pose threats in the form of a question. So Mrs. Coultoure and Amanda continue their walk through town. A few feet down the road, they run into Mrs. Coultoure's three friends having tea in the outdoor café.

"Oh, there you are, Evie. Why are you late?"

"I had a situation to handle with a strange Black man attempting to approach Amanda," Mrs. Coultoure says as she joins her friends and sends Amanda to wait for her in the square.

"Why do you let that nigger bastard child behave like she's one of your children?" asks one friend.

"I don't know," Mrs. Coultoure says in exasperation.

"Maybe you've been hexed," suggests one friend.

"You don't believe in that nonsense, do you?" says Mrs. Coultoure.

"No, I don't. But as I understand it, it doesn't matter if you believe it to have it done to you."

"What other reason is there, Evie, for you to act like you've plum lost your mind? Walking around town with that whore baby like she is a china doll you are displaying for the town," says another friend.

"That's just it: I find it terribly pleasurable to display her. She's an object. I own her. And she is so exquisite. You should see how she charms the royalty in France. People who would never invite me onto their estates. She has opened a lot of doors for us. Speaking French like she's spoken it all of her life."

"How'd she learn to speak French?" asks one of the women.

"I don't know. She sat there. Listened for a few hours. And then just started talking to the duke and duchess."

"Well, I would never admit that!" says another woman.

"Well, I'm not admitting it, honey. I'm telling my closest friends. I don't know what the hell is wrong with me. But I can't seem to help myself."

"Like I said: hexed!"

"What exactly is being hexed?" asks one of the women.

"It's real popular where I come from. Down in Louisiana. Well, my mother knew a woman who could levitate people from the floor. Down back off deep inside of Hammond. Nobody can remember when she came there or a time when she wasn't there."

"Oh! Stop that foolishness! Ain't no such thang." When Mrs. Coultoure is upset, the accent of her no-count daddy—that's how her dance-hall-dancer-turned-socialite mother describes him—peeks out from behind the polished New England accent that Mrs. Coultoure worked so hard on to snag the dashing lieutenant who became her husband, the father of her ten children, and the father of a whole bunch more slave children. The man loves Black pussy.

"Then what other reason is there for you to parade that whore around town?"

"Everyone wants one like her," Mrs. Coultoure said defensively. "I am the envy of the town. And y'all know I'm not lying or delusional—if there's one thing I know, it is uppity-ass White folks pretending to be descendants of royalty. And they all want them an *Amanda.*" All the women shake their heads in agreement and turn their lips up in a frustration they can't explain.

Amanda was twelve before she realized that her puzzles could be used to affect the characters they were based on. She discovered quite by accident, when she decided to put the oldest, and cruelest, Coultoure boy into a puzzle in chains at the bottom of the ocean. Two months later, after she sold the puzzle to a Portuguese trader, Coultoure Junior went missing and was later found at the bottom of the Atlantic, wrapped in chains from a Portuguese slave trader.

For her sixteenth birthday, Amanda made herself a *Monday* puzzle in which she paraded through town in her finest French fashions with Mrs. Coultoure.

After changing and testing the *Monday* puzzle for months, crafting the perfect experience, Amanda created a *Tuesday* puzzle.

The *Tuesday* puzzle took even longer to complete. It was intricate in detail, because it would be her time away from the

Coultoure family, something she'd never had since her family was caught and returned to the Coultoure plantation. Amanda didn't even have the ability to imagine what a *day off* could be. She heard Mrs. Coultoure and her friends talking about *a day off*, but *from what*? They didn't do anything. Amanda decided she needed *a day off* to find out who she was.

She has been testing the *Tuesday* puzzle for three months.

When Mrs. Coultoure sends Amanda to the square, the strange man is there.

She sits next to him. "Thank you for waiting for me."

"Why is it okay for us to sit here this way? Do people not know that you're Black?" he asks her.

"They know. But I've taken care of any potential hostilities."

The more she talks, the more confusion she causes. The man wonders whether he should try to get clarification or whether he should just enjoy sitting next to a pretty girl, something he hasn't done since he left home five years ago.

"Will you meet me in the morning?" she asks him.

"For what purpose?"

"Just come with me into the forest."

"What time?"

"Before dawn. Sleep outside my Big House and wait for me."

The next morning her new admirer follows her into the woods.

Amanda moves through the woods like an indigenous cat, sleek, quiet, effortlessly. But also like a ghost. She is constantly shifting, merging with nature around her and the spirits running with her. Her admirer can barely keep up. It is only his keen sense of being stalked by slave trackers that makes it possible to continue to find her trace. She frequently loses him. Then allows him to find her again.

She comes to a clearing so clean of brush it looks like it's been cleared by otherworldly forces. She attunes to the sounds of the woods. And listens—she can speak several of its languages. Her head is perched, her hands positioned as if she were about to conduct an orchestra or lead a choir. She stands there frozen in a moment while her soul takes flight to somewhere else. Her admirer watches from the bushes. Finally, she says: "When will you come out from hiding? What is your name?"

"Palmer." He steps from the shadows, holding his gut like he's been hurt. He can feel movement in his cells, as if they've been separated into thousands of pieces and are waiting to be put back together again.

Amanda holds out her right hand, cupped to receive his naked heart—to hold it, beating, in her hand. She has decided his heart needs mending and that it should belong to her. She massages it and the whole future encapsulated within it.

There is a *cloud of witnesses* circling Amanda. Palmer can hear them. He can't make out what they are saying, but somehow he knows it's about him.

"Welcome back," the *cloud of witnesses* say. "You have brought a friend."

"Who is he?" Amanda asks. "I mean, to me? Why am I drawn to him?"

"He's your way off this slave plantation—and your way to rewrite the future and carry out your *order*."

Amanda and her kind believe that before they are planted into their mother's womb, they have a conversation with their god. Each week Amanda is made to remember that conversation. She appreciates that it was a *conversation*. She was a participant, not simply made to do or to be something. She offers possibilities as well as listens to options. Ultimately she chooses. As we all do. The *conversation* is made up of what the person will do and who they will be on this side of life. Once there is an agreement, the order is made and *sealed* into their history to come. The *seal* ensures that the person lands in the right space in time, location, family, and circumstances, to carry out the order. The *seal* is the person's anchor—and the beacon that their *cloud of witnesses* look for when it's time to reveal themselves.

Palmer's family, the Roses, have a similar tradition with their god. But with their god there is no *conversation*. Decisions are made between gods and the impulses of the spirit world.

When Amanda calls Palmer from hiding in the brush, she has been told that a great council will strike a deal that will condemn the future of Palmer's family to a poverty so abhorrent that it will breed insanities deep in their minds. Amanda will be needed to break them free. She looks at him and sees the incredible beauty in his eyes, the color of sand. She sees the brilliance of a blue baby that will change this afflicted world with the words she will write. And since she sees nothing of the sort in her own line, Amanda decides to leave the Big House and follow the winding path that she can see in her immediate future: south to New Orleans, up the East Coast to Canada, then back down the Mississippi, then west to Texas.

This Friday is special. The Coultoures are entertaining the Rigaud family from northern France. Upon her return from the forest, Amanda is instructed to prepare to *puzzle* the guests.

The Rigaud family arrives at the Virginia plantation with all the pomp and circumstance of French royalty. A ceremony of grandeur, a very formal celebration welcomes the Duke and Duchess Rigaud and their twenty-year-old daughter, Ismay. It is common knowledge that they are all mulatto, but their skin is white and they are French royalty, so everyone disregards it. It is not even a problem in most of Europe. It is only a problem on this side of the world. So the neighbors and invited guests experience a cognitive dissonance between their honor to associate with *real* European royalty and their repulsion to honoring Black people.

But they are so regal are the thoughts of the crowd that line each side of the red carpet leading from the drive to the grand front door—a door so big and round it should be written *Door* and so black it looks like a small black hole in the sky.

Ismay walks with her father while her mother trails conspicuously behind. Her mother has given Ismay to her father to produce additional Rigaud children with increasingly milky white skin. Their goal has been to whiten the family. It was her mother's idea. Ismay, both disgusted and flattered, agreed to it, though her agreement meant little, since the practice had already commenced without it and would continue until the *puzzling* of her parents. Ismay has already borne five sons as her brothers. The daughters are killed. Her mother has no need for another girl.

The practice began when Ismay first began to bleed at fourteen. When Louverture expelled Rigaud from Haiti, he took his wife and child to the French northern countryside, where they hid in isolation from the rest of the world. Only their immediate family and servants lived in the castle. Lady Lola Rigaud, Ismay's mother, felt the urgent need to produce sons to secure her family's status and fortune. She quickly became pregnant when they moved to the castle, but three months in she lost the baby. Six months later the same process repeated. And again a year later. Lady Lola could no longer produce babies. So when her fourteen-year-old daughter came to her bed one night to tell her mother that she had started bleeding, Lady Lola waited a week for the bleeding to complete; then she sent the girl into their master bedroom to bed her father.

Ismay and her father had a uniquely close relationship. When nobles asked Ismay, as a child, whether she would marry this or that prince, she had always answered, "I will marry my father." Everyone laughed.

The first time it occurs, Lady Lola tells Rigaud that she will send someone to comfort him. She will sleep in her own chambers. This is not unusual. Rigaud allows Lola to choose his women to play with.

It's late. Lady Lola rises out of bed and quietly leaves the room. She goes to Ismay's quarters, where servants have been preparing Ismay in a bath of vanilla milk, cinnamon, oils, and incense. Lady Lola takes Ismay back to the master bedroom and tells her to quietly slip into the bed, which she does with pleasure because she loves her father and her mother has never treated her with affection.

Her father, thinking Ismay is the woman Lola promised him, rolls over and starts caressing Ismay's face. He buries his face in her hair, breathing in the vanilla and cinnamon. He runs his feet up her legs and his hands over her breasts.

Ismay's body stiffens as she struggles with two separate and simultaneous feelings. She welcomes her father's warm strong touch as she had always done, but she's aroused between her legs and she doesn't think she should be.

Her father continues to explore her body with his hands. He shifts to get on top of her and looks in her face and discovers it is his daughter.

Startled, he pulls away.

She looks at him and, with wisdom beyond her years in her eyes, pulls him back to her.

Nine months later, their first son is born.

Ismay refuses to look at him. "I don't want him. I only want my father."

"He's not yours. He's mine," her mother says.

Ismay's relieved that she doesn't have to be responsible for a child, but she carried it for nine months in her own body. This unbreakable bond that she cannot and will not be allowed to express causes her great emotional distress. Ismay sleeps with her father for comfort every night for three months, taking her mother's place in their private chamber. Nine months later the second son is born.

This practice continues for five more sons. Then the next child is a girl. Ismay watches her mother from the castle window carry the baby to the edge of the cliff and cradle it in her arms. Then, without notice or hesitation, Lola tosses it over the cliff. The little body bounces against the rocks for a hundred stories until it hits the water below.

Ismay confronts her mother. "Why would you do that?"
"I don't need girls," Lola says.

"What does that even mean? What kind of person are you?"

"You've always been overdramatic, Ismay. Calm down. You are not so naïve that you haven't realized that women are nothing in this world without a fair-skin, titled, or landed gentry man."

"So you're creating your own personal army with my body?"

"We all make sacrifices for the family."

"So you need at least one girl?" Ismay snaps back.

"You've proven useful," Lola says with detachment. "Girls are only useful for one thing, Ismay. We have five sons. Our status is secured. I have no need for any more girls attempting to displace me as the matriarch in this family."

For her sacrifice, whenever she gets the opportunity, Ismay subtly humiliates her mother, like making her mother walk behind her in public. She despises her father for being weak toward her mother. She is looking forward to meeting the famed puzzle maker. She needs three puzzles made immediately.

In a display of absurd pretentiousness, the Coultoures' Victorian home was ironically built to mimic an Italian castle. Inside there are wings and bays in every direction. In the Party Room, Frédéric François Chopin is the leading pianist with an orchestra. The lords and ladies of Europe are dancing a waltz. The women's dresses are soft pastel colors. The men are dressed in formal wear. Grinning faces move in triple time as they turn together in circles. Dancers move their shoulders smoothly, parallel with the floor, as they strive to lengthen each step. The colony settlers are generally people who were exiled from their European homelands. They circumvented their caste and circumstances with stolen riches from their new West World. Whenever they can reconnect with Europe, they are both elated and overcome by melancholy, and so they celebrate with drunken dance.

The Puzzle Room has been reserved for the duke and duchess from northern France. Amanda has set up her materials in elaborate rows that take over the entire room. The guests are instructed to walk up and down each row so that Amanda can see where their spirits land. Ismay's excitement is almost out of her control. Her mother notices it and becomes frightened as she begins to realize that Ismay plans to use this magic to reclaim her body. As a witch herself, Ismay's mother knows that losing her hold on Ismay will also mean losing her hold on her own power.

Amanda watches them move through the aisles. She follows a few paces behind them, gathering materials as she is directed and lays their choices ceremoniously on three separate tables. She requires one last thing: a piece of their hair for the paintbrushes. Then she sends them off to the party while she spends the next two hours crafting puzzles.

Two hours later, Amanda sits in a high-back chair that mimics a throne. In front of her are all three tables, one for each of her guests. She calls them in one at a time.

Lady Lola first: "Your sons are everything to you. So your puzzle depicts long life, over a hundred years for each son. And each one has a crown on his head. One son has a king's

crown. Another son has a warrior's crown. Another son has a
cardinal's crown. Another son, a bishop's crown. Another the
crown of the wealthiest man in France."

"And my daughter?" asks Lola.

"Yes. You want her dead. But I have need of her. And she
is your payment to me for your puzzle."

Rigaud next: "You love your daughter. You want her to
be at your side as you run your people-purchasing empire.
Your puzzle depicts your daughter at the head of your fleet
of ships."

"Wonderful," he says. "Thank you."

Ismay last: "You want both your parents dead. Your puzzle
portrays your mother lying on the floor of a great room, holding her throat and dying. From your mother's body a ghost is
floating toward a perfectly painted illustration of you."

"But the ghost looks like a snake," Ismay says.

"It is. It's your mother's magic. Did you know that your
mother is a witch?" Amanda asks Ismay.

"Is that how she made me produce six children for them?"

"Yes, you've been under a spell. But I've broken it and given
her power to you. And this is your father. He is floating in his
own blood in a Roman bath."

There is also a small image of something that Ismay can't
quite make out. Amanda skips over it.

"And in return," Amanda asks Ismay, "what will you
give me?"

"I didn't realize," Ismay says with disbelief, "that a return
favor was required. Are you not a slave? Who requires this
return? Your masters made no mention of it."

Holding Ismay's life literally in her hands on the puzzle pieces, Amanda says, "You would do well to simply ask me what I want."

"Then: What do you want?"

"Only to be free. I've heard that you have a party every week in New Orleans. Send for me to come. Pay the Coultoures for my services. And when I arrive, set me free."

"Do you really think it will be so easy?" Ismay asks. "You are very valuable to your masters, and the doctor loves you. He will not allow it."

"Together, both of our magic will be strong enough to achieve it."

Ismay contemplates what she can do with this magic. She even considers using it against Amanda. "I wouldn't if I were you," Amanda says. "I have taken precautions for that as well. Should you ever try to use your magic against me or my family . . . well, see this here?" Amanda points to the mystery image on Ismay's puzzle. "It is a boomerang."

In the Party Room, the dancing has become so furious that people are stumbling in a haze of dizziness as they are whirled around one another at an increasingly dangerously faster pace. Several men and women stumble to the floor. Ismay's mother drops. The standing guests run over to check on her. Ismay's father falls to his knees and lays his ear to her mouth. She is no longer breathing. Rigaud looks up at Coultoure with a menacing look. "What was in the wine?!"

Coultoure looks around at the guests, all of whom are affected by something. They weave and stumble against one another, trying to hold themselves up. "I swear! Nothing. I've done nothing!"

One of the guests interjects, "It's not the wine; I didn't have wine. It's the music. It's blue music. We have to get out of here. We'll all go mad or die."

The crowd of people moves slowly and wobbly toward the door, to their carriages.

"How can I fix this?" Coultoure asks Rigaud and his daughter, who are both cradling Lady Lola's head.

"The puzzle maker," Ismay says. "I want the puzzle maker."

Coultoure thinks about it. He loves Amanda, and his mind wanders aimlessly across their relationship. He wonders why he hadn't already gone into her bedroom. He doesn't know that Amanda had used her magic to forbid it. He had planned to move Amanda into the big house, into his bedroom, displacing his wife. So he hesitated when Ismay asked for the puzzle maker. But he kept seeing his head on a chopping block or worse. To be responsible for the death of a French noble could mean war. So, reluctantly, he finally says, "Of course. Of course," feeling that it is the best of no good choices.

That night Ismay leaves the Coultoure mansion with her father, with her dead mother's body, and with Amanda, who packs her bag of magic, a flower, some seeds, and the knob to her bedroom door.

8

A DREAM NEVER GOES AWAY. It's always there. Even if the dreamer doesn't get to it until they're thirty-five, forty-eight, or sixty years old, it's still there for them to live it. No matter how wonderful, impossible, or nightmarish the dream may be. It lingers, waiting to see if someone will embody it. After high school graduation, in 1986, instead of going to university, Blue embodied her mother's nightmare dream for her and got married.

The wedding was held at the house of one of Blue's sisters. It seemed like the most logical option to Blue, because neither she nor her husband-to-be had the money to pay for the kind of wedding Blue wanted. Although Blue never planned to be married, she had often imagined a wedding. But when she imagined it, it looked more like a coronation than a wedding.

It would be held in a museum; she would wear a long red dress made of different shades of red silk petals stitched together. Each petal would have a pearl in the center to match

a crown of pearls on her head. A long veil would trail behind
her as she descended a flight of winding stairs into a grand
hall with walls covered in masterpieces. The exchange of vows
would take place underneath an ornate chandelier dripping
with rubies.

Her sister's house had brown shag carpet, gold furniture,
and a decent-sized living room for guests. Blue wore a beige
wedding dress that looked more like an Easter dress. Some
said she wore beige because she felt guilty for not being a virgin on her wedding day. They were wrong. At eighteen, Blue
was still a virgin. She chose beige because, despite her limited
possibilities, she was looking for a way to be different. They
cut the cake and shoved a piece into each other's mouth. Then
they went home to an apartment that they would not be able
to afford three months after they were married. Guitar's job
as a maintenance man at the bank couldn't support them on
its own, and Blue lost her job because she called in sick every
other day. Blue was pregnant.

A year earlier, when Guitar moved from Detroit to Dallas,
he was following a dream of his own. He could just go for it,
despite all odds against him ever catching up to it and wrapping his hands around it. But that's what dreams do to you.
They make you do illogical things. He was six foot four and a
hundred and sixty-five pounds. And he wanted to be a football
player. He ignored the facts that he was too thin for football,
too old for the Dallas Cowboys at thirty-one, and that he was
not a bad basketball player. That's what dreams will make you
do. They will make you ignore facts.

When they first met, Guitar had been standing outside her house, smoking a cigarette. Blue had been startled to see a shadow off to the side when she came home at night. Guitar hid the glow of his cigarette from her, so all she saw was a tall, thin, dark-skin shadow engulfed by a haze.

Her nerves jumped but she quickly composed herself when he smiled. She responded with a nervous polite smile. She made her way to the front door and into the brightly lit kitchen where her mother sat at the kitchen table.

"Who is that outside?"

"That's Guitar," MaryMadeline answered.

"Why is he there?" *And what an odd name,* Blue thought. Guitar is actually his brother's name, so named for the prodigious legacy of their hometown, Detroit City. His parents thought they saw a musician when they first looked into his eyes. They thought they saw a scientist when they looked into the eyes of this man and called him Garrett Morgan Co'nartist, named for the famed inventor of the traffic light. But he assumed his brother's name after he was released from prison, where he had spent five years for killing his mother's boyfriend, who moved into their family home after their father's random murder and rendered all sorts of humiliations on his mother. Since Guitar was now a felon, he couldn't do anything normal citizens do. Get a job. Get a loan to buy a house or start a business. Take advantage of redevelopment opportunities. Vote. But, to be fair to the law that rendered him formally invisible, his most recent act of murderous lawlessness was only one in a long line of others that started when he was fifteen. The co-opting of his brother's name—and while his brother was still using it on the other side of the world as a grunt on an oil rig drilling off the coast of Helsinki—was the latest.

"He was just thrown out of the YMCA where he was staying. He came down here to try out for the Dallas Cowboys and didn't make it. Now he's lost. So he came to church, hoping he can find something that gives him direction. He needs a place to stay. He's staying here."

"Fool scared me half to death," Blue said.

Blue was a senior in high school when Guitar moved in with them, and Guitar found himself lost inside her eyes. He wanted to just stare into them, hoping he would somehow be pulled into the space that existed inside of them. He was sure there was one. A place where things happened, people lived, beauty created itself out of purple images of Heaven. Where people were quiet. Still. Peaceful. Always knew who they were, where they were going, and why. Of course, Guitar couldn't articulate any of that. All he knew was that when he wasn't staring into Blue's eyes, he felt lost.

Blue, on the other hand, had little use for Guitar. He was the ugliest man she'd ever met. He had deep crevices on his face, scars left over from his teenage pimple years that followed him into his early thirties. His hair was thin. His teeth were small and pointy. And his skin was too dark for Blue. Guitar was so ugly, she once got mad at him because of it. Blue looked like her father, Jack. Both of them had skin the color of sand, hazel eyes, and loose dark black curls, though hers were woollier than his.

Blue and Guitar worked at the same bank. Guitar had finally found a job downstairs in the maintenance department, and he heard that the bank was also hiring upstairs, someone to count money and checks. He told Blue about it. To her dismay, she got the job easily. At the end of each workday, they took the bus together to go home. One day, on the bus ride home, three boys got onto the bus, none of whom Blue knew or who knew her, but they were good-looking and about her age. They were loud and jovial among themselves. Blue, with the window to her left and Guitar to her right, watched the boys as subtly as she could.

Their bodies were carefree as they laughed and talked. Each took up a whole row of seats for himself. They were athletes and boasted incessantly about their performance in one sport after another. Basketball. Track. Football. They looked so free and happy—and sexy. One had a crooked smile that revealed the straightest, whitest teeth that Blue had ever seen and a charm that she couldn't explain. Another one had green eyes and made Blue feel like she was watching an exotic actor in a play. The other one had muscles bulging from his T-shirt that Blue imagined would be wonderful to touch.

The more she looked at them, the more uncomfortable she became with Guitar. She found herself hoping the boys would not look toward the back of the bus, where she and Guitar sat. She didn't want to be seen with a man who didn't possess any of the traits that made these boys so cocky.

The longer the ride, the more unreasonable she became about the possibility of these boys seeing her with Guitar. He shifted slightly next to her in his seat, pulling her out of her thoughts. She looked at him, and before she knew it, she was full-on mad at him.

As the bus approached their stop, Blue stood up and, instead of waiting for Guitar to exit their row, crossed over him, pushing her body against his to move him out of the way, stepping on his feet. She wanted to leave first because she wanted to ensure they exited through the back door, so they didn't have to walk past the three boys. When the bus came to a stop, Blue pushed the doors open so quickly and with such force that they nearly slammed in Guitar's face.

Off the bus, she walked ahead of him as if they were not together. "What's wrong with you? Did I do something to you?"

Blue gave him a look that ripped a piece of him away. "Leave me alone!"

Guitar was thoroughly confused. And, frankly, so was Blue.

It was not in her nature to be ashamed of people. She always befriended people who nobody wanted to befriend. She never made fun of anyone, and if other people did, she would go over and sit next to the person they were making fun of. She wouldn't say anything. She would just sit next to them so they wouldn't feel so alone. Nevertheless, with Guitar, she became the bully from whom she had protected others.

But when Guitar asked Blue to marry him, she said yes.

MaryMadeline fell hard onto the floor. She was a big woman. Not fat. Big. Six foot one and a hundred and eighty pounds.

"Sister Rose!" Guitar screamed, and knelt by her side. Blue came running into the hallway and leaned over her mother. Guitar remembered a story MaryMadeline had told him about her god healing her when she was six months pregnant with

Blue, and another story about her god raising some woman from the dead when MaryMadeline prayed for the woman. So he thought he'd try it. He had never thought much about her god before meeting MaryMadeline, but she had taken him in and didn't ask for anything in return, and if that hadn't been enough, she had given her daughter to him.

When MaryMadeline first brought up the idea—a move of mercy for Blue, like them old slaves who would kill their own babies rather than see them become slaves—Blue sat on the side of MaryMadeline's bed with her head hanging down.

"He has money," MaryMadeline had said. "I saw his bank account records when I was cleaning his room. He has a thousand dollars in the bank!"

"Is that a lot of money?" Blue asked.

"It is. And he's still saving. And he has lots of creative ideas for starting a business. He's smart in that way." MaryMadeline ignored the fact that it took Guitar over a year to save that thousand dollars.

Blue just sat there. MaryMadeline was both her mother and her best friend. She would do anything her mother told her to do, but she always needed time to come around to the idea from the place of desire. She had never been able to make herself do anything that she didn't *want* to do. So she was left with this conundrum: *How do I want to do something so repulsive to me?*

The dilemma made her head hurt and made her very, very sleepy. Even at eighteen, Blue found solace in sleep when she encountered a problem she couldn't solve. The habit that she developed as a child had turned into an addiction. She was sleeping a lot.

As her mom tried to show her how good a catch Guitar was, Blue found herself overwhelmingly sleepy. Blue lay on her mother's bed, on her left side, curled up like a baby. She said to herself: *I don't know,* then drifted off into a deep sleep.

Now she was kneeling next to her mother on the floor. Not breathing. And Blue was so panicked that her tears were even betraying her. They were crying in reverse—crying inside, not out.

Guitar started praying and decided he should pray loudly because he wasn't sure how it worked. He might need to get God's attention. Loud, real loud, was the way they did it at the church where he had met MaryMadeline. He yelled to God, "Heal Sister Rose! Please, God! Don't take her! We need her here! If you've raised people from the dead before, then please do it at least one more time! Do it again! Do it now!" He prayed like that for fifteen or so minutes, and then MaryMadeline started coughing.

Blue, who had drawn herself up in a ball in the corner as she watched Guitar pray, slumped over her momma in relief. Guitar got them both up. He and Blue helped MaryMadeline to her bed. Blue lay next to her mom in the bed and waited all night.

Just before dawn, MaryMadeline's body was cold. Her breath was sporadic and faint. Blue didn't know why, but she knew that if she just placed her hands on her mother's body, she could heal her. But she was afraid to try. *What if it doesn't work?* Blue couldn't stand any more disappointment from God. But MaryMadeline was dying. So she ventured a try.

She crawled up onto her knees and stretched both arms out to *lay hands* on her mother's body, and she felt power moving through her own body. It was like an ocean of nothing, like the nothing of Genesis that the Spirit of God hovered above at the creation of the world. The power was without form but full-bodied and pronounced. Blue imagined that it must be the creation power that she and her mother discovered when she was eleven. So, like God, Blue simply let the power flow through her. She closed her eyes and looked at the power. A calm force barreling through her from someplace that was ancient and boundless and sounded like loud methodical breathing of her own breath. In. Out. In. Out. In. Out. Then. She saw it.

Blue. Red. Purple. Haze. Engulfing a staircase: a recurring image that she only started seeing a little while ago and that had always been shrouded until now; an image of an antique staircase from somewhere in *the* future—*her* future—that was pulling her onto its fourth floor. An altar. Made of time. Dark waters floating in a gutter and sitting in four cups. And a woman who looked like the Messiah passing a cup to her.

"Ah!!!" Blue shrieked and teetered backward, tumbling off the bed and plopping onto the floor. MaryMadeline stirred and groaned a quiet groan. Blue jumped up from the floor to check on her mother. Her body had warmed, and life had come back into her face, and the sleep looked like rest.

MaryMadeline rested like that for a week. When she regained consciousness and came back to herself, she looked over to see Blue lying next to her and erroneously thought, *I've sheltered her all of her life. She would never survive on her own. God, what will happen to my daughter?* MaryMadeline knew that

Blue didn't want to be with Guitar. But in MaryMadeline's limited experience with the world, she couldn't think of a better option for Blue. In the best way she knew how, she wrapped Blue inside a cocoon and handed her over to a move of mercy, saying to her: "When I die, where will you live?"

Blue released a thick, flowing trickle of tears.

"You can't stay with Eve"—Blue's oldest sister—"because you're not safe around her husband. I don't trust him. You can't stay with Delilah"—Blue's favorite sister—"because her husband's too selfish. You can't stay with Jo"—Blue's third sister—"because she's too selfish. You can't stay with Janelle"— Blue's fourth sister—"because her husband I trust least of all. He might kill you and her. Where will you stay?"

Blue thought about the college acceptance letters. But she'd had a dream once that she was jumping up and down on a bed in the dorm in her slip in front of her new friends. They were all laughing as if they were drunk. The dream scared Blue. She told MaryMadeline about it. MaryMadeline had told Blue it was a warning from God. Blue assumed "college" was not an answer to MaryMadeline's question.

So when Guitar asked Blue to marry him, she said yes in a whisper that was so soft, she wasn't sure she had actually spoken out loud. She was trying to be quiet enough for her own spirit not to hear.

Blue waited for her belly to grow, but she was always quite thin and quite tall, so she didn't see any sign until four months into it, and it was not until she was nearly seven months pregnant before other people could see it. Then they asked the usual

questions they ask pregnant women: "What do you want?
Boy or girl?"

She would say: "Nothing."

She secretly hoped the little one inside would not make it.
She couldn't bear to say that to herself, but she could tell other
people that she wanted "nothing." Saying it to other people
was her way of saying: *Help me.* Her favorite sister would step
in and *clarify* her answer for her. She would say: "Blue's just a
little depressed right now. She'll get over it."

She didn't. It got over her. She sank so deep into depression that she got lost in it. She couldn't find her way out. But
she had to survive, because that is what poor people do. Poor
people are taught how to survive horrible conditions and
that survival is the most important thing to do as a human
being—because if you stop trying to survive, you have actually lost your humanity. So Blue resigned herself to living in
the depression, in order to remain human.

Zion was born inside the veil of Blue's depression. But his
father, Guitar, was there and so proud of his son. Blue's mother
and sisters were there. There were so many people hovering
around her while she was in labor that she sent some of them
home. She told the nurses not to let anyone back in but her
mother and the baby's father. The pain of labor was so intense,
she really, actually, literally felt she was dying. Blue wondered
why God had chosen this as a punishment for disobedience in
the Garden of Eden. *Maybe we were supposed to understand how
immensely difficult it was to produce "life."*

Blue pushed Zion out of her body and into the hands of *a*
doctor, not *her* doctor. Poor people don't have their own doctor.

They have *a* doctor. One who passed the baby on to be cleaned up and then placed into Blue's arms. Blue felt so strange. She wanted to love this little baby boy. He was so precious. So beautiful. So small. So sweet. She wanted to love him with everything in her. But she had nothing in her.

At only nineteen, Blue had accepted a life she had sworn never to live, and it had become as unbearable as the summer Texas heat with cotton trees for air.

"Why don't we move back to my mother's?" Blue suggested one day when money got tight.

"We can figure this out," Guitar said, although he was torn between wanting to build something of his own for his family and the prospect of not having to pay rent.

"We can save money," she said, because she knew that the best way to convince Guitar to do something was to show him how he could either save or make money. He was consumed with the idea of money, yet he made so little of it.

"But don't you want to be on your own?" he countered. "In control of your own life?"

The idea appealed to her, but that would mean that she neither went back to her mother nor stayed with Guitar. "How will we afford a decent place?" she said.

"You could get a job," he said.

She also couldn't imagine a job that she could get. She had hated the work at the bank. She hated mornings. She hated everything about her life. Guitar. Marriage. Motherhood. All of it.

"I'm going home!" she said finally, with a resolution that left no more room for discussion.

Guitar's job couldn't pay all the bills and feed them. She felt unprotected and steeped in the kind of confusion that only comes from poverty. None of her life seemed real. It felt like it was happening in a dream space, but not in a dream. Like when those random visions of standing at the bottom of a staircase would just pop in front of her, like a parabolic jack popping up out of its box, making her literally stumble as she tried to avoid walking right into it. When she was a child, she had more control over her body's interaction with the vision. As she got older, she became less commanding. Like that one time, only one time, she reached all the way up the staircase onto the fourth floor before she could pull herself back into her own reality. It frightened her so intensely that she *decided* that it would never get that far gone again. To her surprise, deciding was all she needed to do in order to retake control. Trying to make her life work with Guitar felt as disorienting as that fourth floor. She needed something to make the world under her feet stop spinning and the jack-in-the-boxes stop popping into her way. So, she made another decision. *Home,* she thought. *I'll go home.*

The old house had a cottonwood tree in the backyard. In the summer it bloomed and cotton flew around the house like snow. It caked over the window screens and blocked the wind from coming into the big house. There were no air conditioners, only fans framed in the windows. At night they slept with the fan right on their faces, pushing their beds as close to the wall with the window fan as possible. Some of their neighbors had water cooler fans, the kind you have to put water into and then the fan would blow out cool wet air. It made the whole house feel like a swamp and made everyone in the house feel like they were trying to breathe underwater. Blue hated those fans. She was grateful they couldn't afford one.

The big house didn't seem to be what Blue had remembered it to be. The toilet looked like it might fall through the floor. MaryMadeline had nailed a piece of plywood on top of the splitting wood floor and that did help, but not enough. The wall around the tub was soft and putrefying. The water in the bathroom sink ran at a trickle, so everybody brushed their teeth in the kitchen sink, but the countertop that surrounded it was rotting through. Blue and her mother would clean that counter until the rotten wood crumbled, but it was still not clean.

There was an antique china cabinet built into the south wall of the kitchen. Although Blue had never known it to be used for china, she could imagine the stateliness of its design accommodating and properly showcasing the exquisiteness of china. It was used for the everyday dishes they had. Blue had always tried to stack the dishes in a way that would honor the beauty of the cabinet and the display of the glass doors. The house had been built in 1898 as a two-story Victorian in South Dallas. MaryMadeline and Jack had moved it to West Dallas when they bought it, because Black people couldn't live in South Dallas with White people. In the move, the city of Dallas made them cut off the top half of the house, where all the bedrooms were. The foyer that held the staircase that used to lead to the upstairs with all the bedrooms was closed in and converted to a small bedroom. The front sitting room was turned into a bedroom, as was the dining room, and its French doors connecting it to the living room were covered with curtains to provide privacy. A beautiful historic home turned into a picture of poverty. When MaryMadeline first saw that house, she fell in love with it. Even after it had been distorted, she still loved it. It was hers.

But now MaryMadeline didn't love it anymore. It was run-down. And at night, most of the house was dark. The electrical wiring needed repairing, but MaryMadeline had no money to attend to it. In the winter, the air came in under the doorways and overwhelmed the gas heaters. There were only two rooms that were warm, so that was where everybody spent their days and nights. It was not at all what Blue had remembered it to be. She didn't understand how her memory could have been so faulty. She had only moved out a few months earlier. *What could have happened in just a few months?*

Blue sat most of the time in her bedroom, the old dining room and the biggest bedroom in the house. Her mother had given it to her and her new husband. When Blue wasn't sleeping, which she did a lot, she cried. She had no plan for a future. She just was. Her tears crusted into crystals on her eyelids and made them very heavy. She removed the fan from the window and opened the screen so the cotton could fly onto her face. She loved the color of it. The beauty wrapped inside the softness of it. It attached itself to the crystals on her eyelids, transforming her into a magical creature from a hidden world. She sat and let the sun bathe her body before the night came and the house went dark. Her body craved the sunlight. Her spirit craved the work of the *lightworkers*.

When Zion was only six months old, while Blue and Guitar were still living with MaryMadeline, Blue was pregnant again.

Guitar wanted Blue to abort the baby.

"We can't afford the one we have," he said to her. "And·you look so miserable when you're pregnant. I don't want you to go through that again."

"What if I die while having the abortion?" Blue asked Guitar.

"Why would that happen?" he asked instead of answering her question.

"Where would I go?"

Guitar looked at her with halting eyes.

"I could go to Hell if I died in the process," Blue said. And she really believed that, even though she wasn't really sure *Hell* existed—because she wasn't really sure *God* existed.

Guitar was in the bathtub when they started this conversation. He leaned back into the bath. His eyes wandered off as he tried to picture this "Hell" that he had never heard of before he met Blue and her mother.

"I'm having the baby," she said, fiercely defending the right to have a baby she didn't want. Each time they launched into this discussion, she lost a part of herself. By the time the baby was born, Blue was somebody almost completely different.

This different someone questioned Blue's logic for arguing for a baby she never anticipated for her life. If she wasn't sure *God* was real, why would she be so sure *Hell* was? But if *Hell* was real, could it really be any worse than having two unplanned babies in an unimagined marriage? *I mean, really, how bad could it be, this unknown place engulfed in fire that no one has actually seen? When Jesus went there, there was no fire. Only a gulf that divided two groups of people who couldn't cross over from one side to the other—where one side was separated from the god that made the place. And this "God"—who is he really? Do you really give a fuck whether you're separated from him? Look what he's done to your life.*

Blue, startled by the language of her thoughts, abruptly turned her attention to the baby girl she had just pushed into the world. This time no one went to the hospital with her. Guitar was afraid the hospital might try to force another bill on him that he couldn't afford. He was still dodging the bill from Zion's delivery. So he dropped Blue off at the entrance to the emergency room and let her walk into the hospital alone. MaryMadeline was at school. She thought she had time to get to the hospital. Blue's sisters were at work; they also thought there would be time to get to the hospital. But unlike with Zion, who took twenty-six hours to deliver, Blue didn't have much time before this baby pushed her way through the birth canal.

Alone and feeling as she had felt when she was five years old, waiting on the porch for her daddy who would never come home again, Blue regretted her decision. *But how can you regret a human being?* Blue held the baby girl and looked into her eyes and saw a painting of a woman who was literally larger than life, taking up most of the space on the canvas. Cool hues of blue, red, and purple fractured the woman's face into a prism of planes and geometric shapes that resolved into the parallel lines in the background. All parts of this picture seem to be in motion, chaotic and asymmetrical.

The image felt too familiar, given Blue had never seen anything like it before. She was mesmerized by it. Couldn't stop staring into it. Then it splintered off into branches of other images. She could see artists in a red room. One cutting off his ear. Another one painting the woman who oddly made Blue feel like she was looking into Snow White's mirror and being reminded of her youth—specifically, of the college acceptance letters in high school.

Her sadness congealed within her and forced itself through her eyelids. The tears dried and the salt flaked on her cheeks as Blue turned those letters over in her mind. She wondered why her mother hadn't pushed her to go to school and expand Blue's opportunities beyond her own limited possibilities. Blue had always appreciated the trust and independence her mother afforded her, but at this point she hated it. She wished she had had a mother with bigger dreams for her daughter and who had been willing to push her into them. And that wish made Blue wonder what dreams she would have for her children. She searched the back of her mind, but she couldn't find her children in her wonderings, only another somebody who seemed to be trying desperately to get out of this life.

Several nurses walked into her room, which she shared with five other women, and announced that they had the papers for the mothers to sign.

"What papers?" Blue asked.

"For a tubal ligation," one nurse said cheerfully. "If you consent to having it done before you leave the hospital, they'll do it for you for free."

Blue felt that the chaotic fracturing of the image was not only a commentary on her life but also a prediction of her daughter's life.

So Blue decided to name the baby Tsitra—"artist" spelled backward. Then she signed the papers.

MaryMadeline didn't want to take care of people anymore.

When she unexpectedly survived the last attack on her body, and her last daughter moved out with a husband, MaryMadeline thought that she was free.

"What's your plan for moving into your own place?"

Blue wanted to say, *I don't have a plan, and I wouldn't need one if you hadn't forced me to marry this loser,* but what she said was, "I mean . . . I don't . . . uh . . . I don't know."

MaryMadeline had taken her daughter and son-in-law back into the house begrudgingly. She had been taking care of herself and other people since she had to go live on the streets at age ten. She deserved to do what was right for her at this stage in her life. All of her children were grown. Her husband was dead. *If not now, when?*

MaryMadeline had done this once before, when Blue was barely a toddler—put herself before her children—when Eve had gotten pregnant by a man who was twenty years older than her and already married to someone else. But neither the man nor Eve wanted the baby, so Jack kept the baby girl. It was his first grandchild. He adored her. MaryMadeline acquiesced, but she didn't want to raise her own children, let alone anybody else's. So she got fed up one day and took the baby girl and all of her things to Eve and told her: "You raise your own baby." Six months later the family found out that Eve had put the baby girl up for adoption. Her sister Delilah was devastated. She tried to go and get the baby girl back. But she had already been adopted. Delilah never forgave MaryMadeline for that. Delilah also said the shock of losing that baby was what killed Jack. (In actuality, it was poverty that killed Jack: he never went to the doctor and died of a curable disease, something that never would have happened if he hadn't been separated from the Rose family history and wealth.)

MaryMadeline was looking for a way out of motherhood once again. So, two years after Blue and her husband moved back in with MaryMadeline, she sold her house for five thousand dollars to the pastor who had put her out of his church when Blue was thirteen, a devastating experience for Blue and one that MaryMadeline buried alone with the other events of abandonment. Blue was horrified at the thought of the pastor taking advantage of her mother, but in MaryMadeline's eyes it was her way of getting back at the pastor. The house was nearly irreparable. It had liens of more than fifty thousand dollars that had been placed by credit card companies. MaryMadeline got her freedom back, she escaped prosecution by the credit card companies, and she got five thousand dollars from the deal to boot.

Blue and Guitar had thirty days to vacate the property. MaryMadeline immediately moved into a small apartment only big enough for herself. She left Blue in that old house. Alone. Crumbling and falling apart. With Guitar and two new babies. Blue never could have imagined that MaryMadeline would actually do something so sinister. Blue cried so hard that she couldn't feel anymore. She stopped feeling. Walking dead. Stillborn.

Still born. Still alive. Not moving, but still here. Moving through life without living. Blue decided that it was what she would have to do to get through this horror. She didn't have the capacity to hope that this was temporary, but somewhere inside of her a hope did exist. There was a knowing this phase would end. Somehow. It had to. Nothing ever lasted forever.

Two years later, living in a nightmarish miniature version of her childhood big house, with decaying floors and disintegrating plumbing, Blue had a dream that she had a job as a cashier at a supermarket. She had been looking for another bank job but had been unable to land one. So, when Blue went to her local supermarket, she decided to ask them if they were hiring. They were. Two months later, Blue and another cashier were talking about how inefficiently the bulletin board in the break room shared company news. Blue decided to start a newsletter and she was good at it. She took a few writing classes at the community college and the professor encouraged her. One day, after class, Blue looked across the street and for the first time noticed that one of the two major newspapers in the city sat on the corner. Blue called the main switchboard number.

"I'm a writing student in El Centro and I'd like to do an internship in the newsroom," Blue said to the older woman who answered the phone with a thick twang. Blue imagined she had big hair and she walked like a peacock in heels.

"We don't give internships," the woman said curtly.

"Oh . . . okay. Thank you." Blue hung up the phone.

Immediately, Blue called the same number. "I'm a writing student in El Centro and I'd like to do an internship in the newsroom," Blue said again.

This woman said, "Oh yes. You want the city desk. Hold on. I'll transfer you."

Blue imagined this woman's hair to be normal size—not big Texas hair—and her walk to be graceful. One of the city desk editors answered the transferred call. "Drew Marks," he said.

Blue repeated her line. "I'm a writing student in El Centro and I'd like to do an internship in the newsroom."

"I'm on deadline and I can't talk now," Drew told her. "Call me back tomorrow."

Blue called him back the next day and Drew said, "I'm busy now. I can't talk. Call me back tomorrow." Blue and Drew carried on with this dance every day for two months. Finally, Drew said, "You're never going to stop calling me. Just come on in."

Blue held the phone's receiver in her hand for a long time before she hung it up. She couldn't shake the feeling that she was experiencing something important. That this moment was pivotal to something on the other side of something. She just couldn't make out what the "somethings" were. But it felt . . . *good* . . . like in the first chapter of Genesis, when God created something and then saw that it was *good*.

Six months after starting work at the *Dallas Times Herald*, Blue told Guitar she was leaving him.

He stared at her for a long time without saying anything, as if he was trying to make her say something more, like why she was leaving, or if he did such and such, she wouldn't leave. But she said none of those things. She stared back at him until he finally broke the silence: "If you leave, you're taking the kids with you." It was an attempt to jar her into understanding the gravity of her decision.

She simply wrapped her arms around herself and, without missing a beat, said, "Okay."

Guitar stared again, as if he was waiting for something else profound to come to him, so he said, "How will you take care of them? Yourself? Where will you live?"

Blue turned her lips up as if to say, *Whatever.* But she didn't actually say any words. She had a habit of being completely silent with Guitar, sometimes for days. When he dismissed her feelings or thoughts, she would disappear into herself and become completely and utterly silent. It was maddening to him, something she hadn't expected. She hadn't intended the behavior to be a punishment, but she was pleased with its effect on Guitar. But Guitar wanted an answer, "Are you moving in with someone else?"

Fuck you! is what she thought. *I can fucking take care of myself!* But still she didn't say anything.

"Fine!" Guitar announced in a moment of desperation. "If you leave, then you're not taking the kids!"

Blue looked at him and simply said, "Okay."

At that point Guitar realized that Blue was leaving him no matter what. That there was nothing he could say that would change her mind. So he decided that he would let her have the kids for now, only to steal them and hide them from her so she would have to chase them. One way or another, he would use the only weapon left to him, since he had no money to threaten her with: he would use their kids.

She was in the process of filing for a divorce when MaryMadeline became sick again. She was dying. Blue wanted to give her something before she died. She understood her mother in ways her sisters could not fathom. Blue pitched a story to another one of her editors, Paco, an old-school editor who loved, loved, loved his job. She pitched it as a story about a woman who at ten was raped by her uncle and left her family to live on the streets and take in other street kids and who grew up to continue that benevolent practice and was now dying of cancer. Blue didn't think any reporter would want to write her mother's story, so she pitched it as something she would write. She pitched it so well, however, that Paco wanted to write it.

"He stole your story?" one colleague asked.

"No!" Blue said. "It's an honor that an editor would want to write my mother's story."

The paper sent over a photographer. The photographer snapped a photo of MaryMadeline playing the piano. The story made the front page of the city's largest newspaper.

Two months later, MaryMadeline fell into a coma. Three days after that, she stopped breathing. Blue stood next to her, shaking all over. They had taken MaryMadeline to the hospital the last time something like this happened. But MaryMadeline told her and her sisters not to do that again, so they just stood there in a panic.

MaryMadeline momentarily breathed again and said: "It's so beautiful there. There's no pain. It's so beautiful there. There's no pain. It's so beautiful there. There's no pain. I want to go back. I didn't want to leave. I didn't want to leave. I want to go back. I'm tired. I want to go home."

After several minutes, she fell back into a coma for four more days and then she died.

Blue, since she was five, had been highly suspicious of God's existence, but her mother had given her an important gift before she died: her mother described an actual place with the word "there." Blue reasoned that life on the other side of this one *must* be real, though she still wasn't sure if the other side was a *heaven* or just on the other side of time.

After Blue and her sisters buried their mother and before the divorce was finalized, Guitar put his plan into action: he stole the children, who were three and two years old, and ran away one night. Blue looked for them but she couldn't find them. For Blue, the ground was spinning beneath her. She took some time away from work. She stepped deeper into detachment to preserve her sanity. It was impossible for her to connect to anyone, and she couldn't even reach her kids. She gave up searching six months later. The terror of the decision to give up haunted her, but the freedom of having no children and no husband charmed her.

The cognitive disjuncture was profound, but loss overruled freedom. It moved in and set up camp in the flesh of her spirit. It took on her identity and masqueraded as her.

"Blue has always been selfish," Delilah told Janelle, who'd asked Delilah when the last time was that she'd heard from Blue.

"What do you mean?" Janelle asked.

"She hasn't seen those kids for months."

"*What?* Why? Where are they?"

"Apparently, Guitar stole them, and she can't find them."

"Why do you say 'apparently'?"

"Because if Blue really wanted to find those kids, she could. I mean, *I* would. *You* would."

Janelle didn't say anything. She wondered if she would.

Delilah broke the silence. "Well. Wouldn't you?"

"If Blue needed help, she should have asked me. She knows I would keep the kids for her. I've done it before."

"Blue has never wanted kids. We all know that."

"None of us have ever wanted kids," Janelle said.

"Yeah. But we took responsibility for our decisions and we raised our kids."

"But did we?"

"What do you mean?"

"What about Eve?"

"Eve and Blue are just alike. Except Blue has had more opportunities because she was born twenty years later. And that's why Eve hates Blue."

"Why?"

"Jealousy."

"And a bit of evilness," Janelle added.

"And Blue is just selfish," said Delilah. "That's the reason she can live so carefree without her kids. Like they never existed."

Contrary to what her sisters, what society—what her *guilt*—screamed so loudly into her ears that it made her head hurt constantly, the gaping hole in the center of her being, created by the absence of her kids, that slowly leaked vital fluids she needed for survival also emptied out space for her to be filled by something she hadn't felt since her father died when she was five years old: motivation, freedom, desire. Blue started moving up in the world. Her dreams got bigger. Her job got bigger. But the motivation was different than what it had been when she was five. Now it wasn't her essence that drove her—it wasn't her. It was loss. Loss had taken over her speech and her walk. It made people think she was all right. It prompted her when to show sorrow and disappointment so that she would look normal. But in truth Blue walked the path of the world with her eyes wide shut. Each day was so normal without her father, without her mother, without her kids, that it was anything but normal.

She blended in as best she could. But secretly she had been captured by the circumstances of her own life.

And morning passed.
Evening came.
Marking the fourth day.

9

HE'S TWO KLICKS AWAY FROM the oncoming sails on the blue water shimmering in the sunlight.

He's on a flat, open stretch of ground. To his left and right are sparse piney woods. That is where George would have sent a regiment of soldiers. One regiment for each side. Palmer hears his father's instructions in his head: *Move like a big cat through the woods. Light and quick and without sound. Pounce out of the shadows on your adversary. Let them think the land is easy to be captured. Let them walk into the open plain. Then surround them from all sides, coming out of the woods.*

Palmer has led more than fifty rebellions, but he is not leading this one. He came here looking for Rigaud.

Instead, two White men attack Palmer in the saloon for not giving them his seat. He kills them both, which initiates an unscheduled revolt, and so more White men, at least twenty, come into the saloon. Word is sent to the White militia. Within the hour, the town will be swarming with them. They will take

Palmer, and because they will blame all Black people, they also will attack and enslave every Black man, woman, and child within fifty miles.

When the group of twenty White men comes in with axes and pistols, another Black man in the saloon moves with a precision that betrays his military training. He nudges a third Black man and the two of them slip behind the group of axe-wielding White men and out the door. He motions for Palmer to leave through the door at the other end of the saloon, where he is greeted by a group of Black men. They bar the doors with large wooden posts that prevent the White men from escaping, and the leader of the Black revolutionaries scrambles up the side of the building to the thatched roof, cuts a hole in it with his axe, and throws a torch inside. More torches come in through the thatched roof, burning parts of the roof as they drop into the saloon. The twenty men burn alive, and their screams tear through the town square.

Some of the White townsfolk bolt their doors. Some run out of the town into the surrounding woods, fearing the same fiery death as the saloon-goers.

The Black men jump onto nearby horses and ride furiously through the town, dumping torches onto the thatched roof of every single building. Some of the men go after the townsfolk who ran into the woods. They slaughter them with swords and guns, capturing and killing women and children and old men and the young. The horsemen continue their ride out of town for twenty miles. Palmer jumps onto a horse and follows them.

When their leader stops, he looks at Palmer. "You have started a shitstorm, my friend. I sure hope you can fight. What is your name?"

"Palmer. And yours?"

"Jeremiah."

"Mr. Jeremiah, it was not my intention to begin an impromptu fight—"

"*Impromptu*," Jeremiah says, mimicking Palmer. "You're an educated nigger."

Palmer rolls his eyes. He hates when Black folks talk like savage White slaveholders.

"Where you from?" Jeremiah asks, with a thick accent that Palmer doesn't recognize. "You have a Southern twang underneath that King's English."

"Texas."

"You left a neutral state to come east to a slave state?"

"It's only a matter of time. That's why I'm here. I'm preparing for the inevitable." That's a lie. But Palmer thinks it's a good enough reason to give for that moment. He is still searching for why he felt compelled to leave the comforts of his East Texas home.

"You fight like a free man," Jeremiah says. "You don't give an inch."

"I didn't mean to drag you and your men into my fight, though I am grateful for—"

"Those motherfuckers had it coming," Jeremiah interrupts Palmer. "Why do you think we were able to act so quickly? That whole town had been picking on us for three days. Even the children! We had already devised the plan. You just ignited it."

Relieved that he hadn't started a war all on his own, Palmer asks, "Where are we?"

"The Whitley Plantation. In the Geechee Corridor." *That's the nature of that accent,* Palmer thinks. *It's a Gullah accent. They still speak the languages they spoke two hundred years ago.* "There are twenty fighting men on this plantation," Jeremiah continues. "Twelve of them are Black. We're taking it over. There are weapons and plenty of ammunition. It also backs up to the Atlantic Ocean. The others, the militia, will be coming by sea. We'll cut them off before they can get into town."

"And what about the townspeople who got away?"

"There's only one way into that town, and it's the sea."

"What about the mountains?" Palmer asks.

"Only Black folks would even consider traversing those."

"So what are you going to do with them?"

"Starve them out. Then kill 'em. If they survive the bobcats."

"What's your strategy for the seafarers?"

"There are seventy of us. We'll take them head-on."

"I would recommend a different strategy."

"I'm listening," Jeremiah says.

"The woods . . . In the same way that you hemmed them into the saloon, I would hem them into this plain."

"You're not only educated; you're a trained military man," Jeremiah says, making fun of Palmer. The other men laugh. "Then you will lead the wooded regiments. And I will lead the plains regiment."

Two days later, Jeremiah and Palmer's battle plan delivers a decisive victory. The ships are carrying purchased humans who join the Black men on land, growing their numbers to more than three hundred. And now they have four ships. They conquer the island known as St. Johns, Florida.

When Jeremiah allows Palmer to choose what he wants from the spoils of the ships, Palmer chooses Johann Kant.

Palmer will have been trekking across the country for two years when he meets Kant. Two years before, one day, out of the blue—*I always say the blue is where God lives*—Palmer decides to leave his home, the Texas Rose Plantation, and go discover the world. In 1843, that is a risky proposition for a Black man. Palmer doesn't know that world of risk. In his East Texas town, his family is feared and treated like royal warriors. They own fourteen hundred acres of land and seven hundred purchased people who care for the land, the family, and serve in their military. The purchased people on his parents' plantation negotiate their labor and there is an end to their contracts, though most never leave. It is a good place to live. Nevertheless, feeling restless, Palmer decides it's time to move. He feels like the waves of an ocean are moving through his lungs and suffocating him from the inside out while at the same time compelling him to ride on those waves. As Palmer comes of age, he is discovering a nomadic impulse seeded in his soul.

Initially Xhosa goes with him. But after they are captured and imprisoned for the third time, Palmer sends Xhosa back to the plantation. Palmer has learned his first lesson. It is too dangerous to travel with such a dark-skinned man.

Xhosa pleads with Palmer to return with him. But Palmer is compelled by something that he can't articulate.

"But why?" asks Xhosa.

After the tenth time, Palmer devises a reason that feels like it's real. "Rigaud."

"What about him?" asks Xhosa.

"He sold my parents into slavery."

"And now they run East Texas. So what?"

"But I think it broke me!" Palmer yells. "Something has broken me . . . " His voice trails off.

Palmer frequently hears a voice calling him out of East Texas. At first, it is calming and content, but then it is like the voice suddenly splits into two different directions—while speaking the same words in both directions.

"You are correct, my friend," Xhosa says. "You need to go find the voice that is calling you."

Palmer is captured so often by White marauders that it's too depressing to keep count. Each time, he escapes and leads a revolution made up of the surrounding purchased and free Black peoples, and moves on.

Now, as Palmer picks through the treasures on the ships he and Jeremiah have just confiscated, Palmer notices that most of their prisoners are attempting to hold on to muskets, rifles, pistols, swords, currency, or jewels. One man is holding on to a book. Holding it like it is gold.

"May I?" Palmer says with his hand extended to take the book.

The man is surprised to hear Palmer speak the King's English. He is also caught off guard by Palmer's mannerisms. He concedes to Palmer's request—not that he thought he had a choice, but he did so out of pure curiosity.

Palmer skims through the book and discovers all sorts of important information about everyone from the most heartbroken slaves to kings and wretched holy men around the world. "Who are you?" Palmer asks. "What is your occupation?"

"My name is Johann Kant. I am an anthropologist."

"And what is an anthropologist?" asks Palmer

"A type of scientist who studies how people interact with one another. A social scientist."

Palmer continues to thumb through the pages. Kant is surprised that Palmer can read it. Palmer remembers the story that his mother told him about his father's god in a garden that held the *Tree of Knowledge*, and it was forbidden to the first two humans. But it was so enticing that they had risked exile from their god to have it.

So, when Jeremiah permits Palmer to choose his spoils of the skirmish, Palmer knows he wants Kant and his book—and as a son of a massive slave-holding family in Southeast Texas, Palmer feels completely entitled to take what he wants. Kant thinks that Palmer is the best option out of nothing but bad options, so he feels "lucky," in a sense, to be essentially "purchased" by the man with whom he could at least have a decent conversation about a cause that they share—which, ironically, is freeing the enslaved Africans.

The first person Palmer wants to meet after reading Kant's journal is Father Mazenod, who is at the center of a massive and intricate spiderweb connecting abolitionists from the North, South, East, and West. By now, Kant and Palmer have been traveling together for the past three years, and Mazenod's order supports the cause to organize uprisings with the ultimate intention of leading to a great civil war.

10

Two days after the new Orleans salon, Eugène de Mazenod, the Catholic priest who started the Oblates, has reluctantly agreed to take Ismay on his visit to a plantation so she can experience what it's like to live as a slave. When Kant escorts Ismay to meet Father Mazenod, Palmer, who is there with Xhosa, greets them both. Before Ismay can respond, Father Mazenod's shadow darkens the doorway.

"Finally, I meet the great Lady Ismay," Mazenod says as he approaches Ismay with arms extended toward her. She steps into his arms like stepping into a doorway to an unknowable place—hesitant, a bit timid, but with the nonchalance of the rich. Then he approaches Kant and greets him with a double kiss on the cheeks. He greets Palmer with much more affection. Palmer introduces Xhosa as his best friend and Father Mazenod falls into Xhosa's arms. "Forgive us," Mazenod cries to Xhosa, who finds the small priest odd.

"Father," says Kant. "Ismay Lafayette Rigaud is interested in an ethnographic study of the slave life."

"To what end?" Mazenod asks Kant.

"Understanding," Ismay answers for herself.

"And what do we get in return?" Mazenod retorts.

"My father," Ismay answers.

Without hesitation, Mazenod, Palmer, and Xhosa say in unison, "Deal!"

Rigaud has been financing militias who capture runaway enslaved peoples and return them to their slaveholders. The militias have often captured free Black people and sold them to new holders. Rigaud sees it as an inevitable consequence of the greater good.

"Today, we start with a visit to St. James Parish. It's half a day's ride away. We can talk on the way," Mazenod says to Ismay.

"Why are we going so far from New Orleans?" asks Ismay.

"In order for you to see a true picture of what you say you wish to know, you will have to get away from the people who know who you are. So, we go fifty-four miles to the west. Fifty-four is a good number. Isaiah, chapter 54 verses 3 to 4, says, 'For you will spread out to the right and to the left; your descendants will dispossess nations and settle in their desolate cities. Do not be afraid; you will not suffer shame.'"

Six warriors on horseback ride alongside the wagon that carries Father Mazenod, Ismay, and Kant, who sit atop a mountain of food and other supplies. Palmer and Xhosa ride on horseback with the other warriors.

"Who is this food for?" asks Ismay.

"The people who need it," answers Mazenod.

"Why take them food? Doesn't that simply fortify their dependence on you?"

"Do you get your own food, Lady Ismay?"

She smirks. "But I pay for it. I don't simply lie around and wait for it to come."

"When we arrive, I will ask you if you think these people are simply lying around and waiting for food to come. You said you want to *understand*. What exactly do you want to understand?"

"Why do people continue to live in wretchedness? So many others have risen up and done away with, as you say, injustice—"

Mazenod interrupts Ismay. "You disagree? That what is happening is injustice?"

Raised as her father's daughter, Ismay retorts, "It's economics."

"The sale of people? Is economics?"

"Precisely. The *sale* . . . makes it economics. So many others have flipped the circumstances and found a way out. Why can't the dark-skinned people do the same?"

"So many? Who has 'flipped the circumstances,' as you call it?"

Ismay rattles off the names of dozens of people in her inner circle who have managed to change their circumstances with a precisely negotiated marriage or the granting of a title or lands.

"Your list has one thing in common," Palmer chimes in. "They're all the color of sand."

"Are you suggesting that no dark-skinned person has ever changed his situation?" asks Ismay.

"I am not," retorts Palmer. "I am pointing out that all of *your* examples look like you."

"Meaning?" she asks.

"Meaning: you don't know what you don't know."

Four hours later and the caravan arrives in St. James Parish. They left at six that same morning, so the noon sun is beaming and burning the skin of the fairer-skinned people. Xhosa goes into the woods lining the roadside and comes back with a bucket of nutrient-dense black mud, so dark due to the high amount of decomposing plant and animal material it contains.

"Put this on your skin. It will protect you from the sun." He gives it to the priest, Kant, and Ismay first. Then he passes some to Palmer.

"I don't need it," says Palmer.

"It doesn't make you less Black. Use it to protect your fair skin, brother. Put it on. We learned about this medicine from the Egyptians, a race of Africans that look just like you."

Palmer grudgingly takes the offering of mud.

"Look! I'm putting on some myself. And so are these warriors," Xhosa says as he passes the mud to the horseback riders who all have skin so black, it looks blue.

Palmer slathers the mud on his skin. The cool, rich nutrients seep into his membrane, bringing down his temperature and releasing a tingling sensation throughout his body. Ismay is so pleased by the feeling of the mud that she gets an idea. At her next party, she will offer this treatment in one of the unused rooms. *I'll call it the Mud Room.* Kant is feverishly making notes in his journal as mud plops from his face onto the pages.

When at last they arrive, Xhosa and Palmer notice something's off. Palmer looks around them into the forest and detects movement. Overseers are riding horses among women harvesting sugarcane in the opposite direction of the mysterious movement in the woods. The overseers are slapping leather whips across the backs of the women who stop for only a moment to straighten their spines. When Ismay sees this, she flinches.

"What are they doing?" she asks in distress.

Palmer looks at Mazenod to tell him, "We're surrounded by—"

Before Palmer can finish the sentence, a swarm of armed White men are riding toward them. Xhosa and Palmer take a fighting stance. "Wait!" says Father Mazenod. "If you fight now, you will lose. We're outnumbered."

Palmer and Xhosa have already realized this.

"Who are these men?" asks Ismay.

"I don't know," Mazenod replies.

"I know them," Palmer whispers. "They've been tracking me for three years."

"With that mud on your face, they may not recognize you," Mazenod says. "Listen carefully. There isn't much time. This is what they will do. We will be separated and imprisoned. Ismay, you will be put in a locked room in the house along with Kant and myself. Palmer, it's a toss-up. If they recognize you, they will want to make a spectacle of hanging you. If not, your skin is light enough for them to think you might have a connection to money. If so, they will lock you up in the house with us, but in a different wing, planning to ransom you for a reward. Xhosa, you and the horsemen will be put in chains in the shed. When the sun rises tomorrow morning, you will be hanged. So we have no choice. We must escape into the woods when the moon turns blue. They can't see in the blue moonlight. Neither can I or Kant or Ismay or Palmer. We will be running blind. We will have to follow Xhosa and the other horsemen. And we must do all this in silence. If we scream out, we will give away our location. These are expert trackers, and they will have dogs. Find water, Xhosa. Run through it. It will break our scent."

"Which way?" asks Xhosa.

"North-northeast."

"The water does break the scent, but it can be found again pretty easily. But if we run in circles, it will confuse the dogs and they will run themselves to death," says Xhosa. "Just stick close to me."

"I can also see in the blue moonlight," Palmer offers.

"Ah. So you are a Black man," Xhosa says sarcastically.

"How do we escape chains?" asks one of the horsemen.

"With this." Mazenod gives each one of them a small one-inch metal stick encased in a capsule. "Hide it well. They will check your mouth. Make you strip naked and check between the cheeks of your derriere and under your testicles. They will take your clothes and leave you naked and bound. We, in the house, will need ours to unlock the doors."

"Where can we hide this thing?" Ismay asks in exasperation.

"You will not be stripped. Hide yours in your underclothes."

"What about them?" she asks.

"Swallow it!" says Xhosa.

"Then what?!" asks Kant.

"They know what to do next," says Xhosa.

"*What do they do?* I need to record it!" Kant replies.

"Do it! Now! They are almost upon us," says Mazenod.

"Do you have the herb?" one horsemen asks the others.

"Here," another says, passing it to all of them.

"What is it?" Kant asks.

"Use your imagination," Palmer replies.

The swarm of White men approaches the convoy. "Who are you?" Mazenod stands up so that his priest's collar and cross are blatantly visible.

"There was a slave rebellion up north and we were chased to this plantation. Now we protect it."

"When did this transition of power occur?" Mazenod asks.

"Six months ago. And what is your purpose here?" the man asks.

"I bring food and other supplies. Are you in need of anything? Please take freely."

"Who are these horsemen?"

"They are my slaves. They protect me and the lady here."

"Lady of what?"

"Her father is Benoit Joseph André Rigaud."

"Lady," the man says, and bows his head, "you are most welcome here. And the other one, who is he?"

"He's my biographer," Ismay says.

"And that one on the horse? Even though he's covered in mud, I can see that he's White."

"He's my brother," Ismay says without even thinking.

"Why have you come with the priest to such a wretched place?" the man asks Ismay.

"To meet the lord of the manor. Is he here? I have word from my father," she says.

"He is not. He had a sudden heart attack and died."

Father Mazenod performs the sign of the cross over his heart and head. "Should I perform a Christian burial?"

"No need. It has been taken care of."

From their response, Mazenod knows that these men are not militia but marauders. They have illegally taken this plantation and killed the owner. They have some respect for Rigaud, but it will not keep his caravan alive.

"You will not need your guards here," the man says as he waves his arm and men with rifles swoop out of the brush and overtake the horsemen.

"When will they be returned?" asks Mazenod.

"No need to worry. We'll protect you now."

As Mazenod predicted, Xhosa and the horsemen are chained in the barn; the rest of the convoy are locked in separate rooms in the Big House. At dinnertime, Ismay is brought from her room to dine with the leader and his two lieutenants in the dining hall. The leader calls himself "General."

The dinner is an eight-course meal exquisitely prepared by the enslaved people of the house. The general and his two top lieutenants dine with Ismay. They want to know more about her father and her relationship with him. Ismay knows these men are trying to determine her worth. Should they hold her hostage for ransom, or should they join her father's war? Conversation is strategic and halting from both sides of the table. Ismay, a master of political play, dazzles the three men with wit and femininity that makes them rethink their options. They now wonder whether they should just rape her.

Sensing the change in mood, Ismay asks the general to dismiss his lieutenants so that he and she can be alone. But because they are not a real army, the lieutenants refuse to leave. Ismay is annoyed, and her annoyance titillates the general.

"Aren't you even the least bit afraid?" he says to her as he pushes back from the table and moves toward her. Ismay leaps onto the table and slithers over to the general, plunging her teeth into his throat. The two lieutenants push back from the table, pull their swords, and charge at her. Ismay turns to face them with blood dripping from her mouth, like the head of a twenty-two-foot python. They run out of the dining room. Ismay walks out the front door, nearly missing the others who have already emerged from their various prisons and are running toward the woods.

Ismay catches up to Kant and the two of them run harder than they ever imagined they could. They are trying to catch up to Xhosa. Palmer lets out a sound like the call of a bobcat. Xhosa recognizes it. They begin a conversation in a cat language that enslaved people running from White militia have used for years.

"Slow down," Palmer says. "The others can't keep up with us."

"Then we will have to use other evasive measures, or we will be caught."

"What other measures?" Palmer asks.

"Amanda."

"What? How?"

"That voice that's been calling you for years is her. She can hear you. Call her."

Amanda, who is still in New Orleans at Ismay's town house, abruptly sits straight up in her bed. She has been awakened by an excruciating, grinding, brassy sound, like rock dragging across metal. Palmer's soul is in distress. She leaps to the floor and positions herself as if encircled by her *cloud of witnesses* in the forest. She transfigures into a bobcat running beside him.

"I'm here," she says to Palmer.

Palmer can hear her. He can feel her presence. But he can't see her.

"We need help," Palmer says.

Amanda peels off from the group and goes off into the woods, calling all nearby bobcats, who have already been alerted by Palmer's first call to Xhosa. Amanda leads her army of bobcats toward the White marauders and dogs tracking the runaways. The growls of the bobcats can be heard for miles, and the vibration of their running shakes the ground. Ismay resists the urge to scream out as she hears their shrieks. Palmer reaches out for her hand. Ismay is surprised to see Palmer's hand coming toward her. It occurs to her she can also see in blue moonlight. She relaxes into his hand. He pulls her along, comforting her that she is not alone and that they will not lose her.

Amanda releases a roar and a cacophony of bobcat screeches tear through the woods and bounce off the trees, creating a tunnel of sound. The cats tear into the dogs and the men. Blood and bones and flesh are thrown into the air, catching in the treetops and sliding onto the ground, glittering in the blue moonlight.

Xhosa and the convoy burst through the woods and onto an unexpected patch of manicured green grass. At the center is a little white church. The music coming from inside is familiar to Xhosa and the riders. It is music that is played during a ritual offering of one's self to a divine mission that could take place at any time, at all times, across time. Xhosa is careful. The music itself is a powerful portal. And he's not sure if he's strong enough to go inside without getting lost in it. Father Mazenod has heard the music before but has never understood it. Ismay and Palmer feel as if they're being lulled into a trance. The convoy is cautious. Amanda, who is still in the woods decimating the trackers, senses a portal in the little white church. She stops pulling apart the lieutenant of the marauders long enough to tell Palmer, "Go inside."

Palmer walks toward the church and the rest of the group follows him. An older gentleman is standing there. Coal-colored skin. Full white beard. Partially bald. Brilliant white hair. He is wearing a tuxedo and carrying a Bible. But the Bible looks different than the one Palmer is accustomed to. The writing on the front is vertical and it's in motion. The old man enters the church stage right, through a door that leads from a circular time line. Following him are several young women, each one in a different-colored cotton dress with white flowers and a white lace collar. Dresses a five-year-old would wear. All of them have puffy, curly, cotton-like hair.

The puffy-hair girls have strung themselves across the front of the church like clothes on a clothesline. They dance to a mesmerizing and spell-casting music, like Cab Calloway stringing an incantation over his audience, compelling them to sing along to words that he just made up on the spot. The lead dancer is a *war leader*. She is performing the *Ghost Dance*, which reunites the living with the spirits of the dead. The New

Orleans convoy watches in amazement. Amanda's *cloud of witnesses* have arranged this event for Amanda's and Palmer's future. The dance is a prayer to free the family line from the Agreement between God the Lord and his favorite but disappointing son Lucifer, also known as Satan.

Licking blood from her lips, Amanda leads the bobcats into the clearing. Out of fear of the portal, she does not enter the church. She can either step into the abyss or step back from it. She cannot walk along its edge. She calls for Palmer to come out into the clearing. The rest of the group follows Palmer, who looks for Amanda but he doesn't recognize her in the pack of bobcats.

Xhosa says, "That one there. That's Amanda." Xhosa looks at things with different eyes. He can see spirits.

As Palmer approaches Amanda, she grows in size, becoming the largest bobcat any of them have ever seen. On all fours, she stands four feet high. The length of her sleek body matches her height. Palmer walks over to her, cups her face in his hands, and pushes his face into her fur. Amanda whispers into Palmer's ear. Mazenod and Kant are not sure what they're witnessing, but Ismay has seen a shape-shifter before. With her mother's magic she nearly shape-shifted herself into a serpent at the dinner table with the general and his two lieutenants. Ismay took on the spirit of the serpent, but not the body. She's still learning how to use the magic. Palmer thanks Amanda, who gestures for them to follow her and their escort of bobcats into the woods, over the hills, toward the sea.

"That's the wrong direction," Mazenod says.

"You go the way you want to go," says Palmer, "but Ismay is coming with me and I'm following Amanda."

In the moment that came before, Amanda whispered into Palmer's ear, telling him to follow her and bring Ismay with him—by force if necessary. Amanda knows that going in any other direction would be fatal. And Ismay will be needed when Amanda and Palmer move to Texas. Xhosa, of course, follows Palmer. The six horsemen as well. Kant decided some time ago never to be separated from Palmer in situations such as these and follows Palmer as well. The group proceeds to leave Mazenod standing in the clearing alone. Amanda stops so abruptly that Palmer stumbles over her.

"He is also needed," she says of Mazenod. "Wait for him."

Palmer stops and waits for Mazenod to reason with himself. Not wanting to go back through the forest alone, blinded by the blue moonlight, Mazenod finally acquiesces.

On the other side of the time portal, Blue was sitting in the chapel in South Texas for the fourth day of sunset meditation. She saw a vision and, startled, jumped up from where she was sitting and scrambled away. Her vision was a small window into another time into which she peered to see eleven people. Two White men, one of whom looked familiar. He's in clerical clothing—short, with a thin frame. One White, maybe a Black woman passing for White. One definitely Black man who could pass for White who also looked familiar. And seven black-skinned men. They were walking into a little white church that looked like a mirror image of the chapel Blue was sitting in. There, it was nighttime, with darkness so dense the trees were a darker black version of themselves. Amber light was emanating from inside the church, so bright that its light pierced all the way through Blue's little vision window, bathing Blue's face in its color. *Amber is a healing agent.*

Blue could hear music from inside the church. And the church had precipitously begun to dance. *It was a dancing church?* The steeple went up and down to the left and to the right to the rhythm of the music playing inside.

Father Mazenod reluctantly follows Palmer toward the rocky hills covered in green brush. As Mazenod walks past the *dancing church*, he looks to his right into the open field and sees Blue on the other side of time, sitting in a chapel—a mirror image of the *dancing church*. And for reasons Mazenod cannot explain, he proclaims: "I'm here to help you write your story."

Reciting the Lord's Prayer, Father Kelley pulled Blue away from the vision window.

Amanda guides the group through a treacherous piece of rocky and hilly forest terrain to the sea, where there is a ship sitting in port. The army of bobcats stops at the edge of the woods. Ismay recognizes the flag. It's one of her father's ships. The emblem on the flag is the same on her signet ring, which is designed to verify her identity in moments like these.

The ship's deck has been damaged. Faint moans can be heard as far away as the edge of the beach. No movement can be seen on the ship's deck. A visible storm has driven the ship off course, slamming it into this rocky beach.

Having assessed the damaged deck, Palmer and Xhosa move quickly to commandeer the ship. Most of the crew are dead. The others are badly injured. Palmer picks up a titanium steel sword from the floor of the ship and summarily proceeds to slaughter all those crew members who are still alive. Ismay is horrified by Palmer hacking, hacking, hacking, even hacking at those already dead. Palmer recognizes this ship. He's seen many of them in the past five years. He was captured and sailed in the bowels of two.

Belowdecks, there is moaning. Purchased people are chained together and floating in water filled with their own excrement, vomit, urine, and seawater. Surprisingly, more than half of them are still alive. The dead died months ago in the Middle Passage.

"My God," Father Mazenod gasps, and without hesitation leaps into the knee-deep water below deck, pulls out his holy oil, and proceeds to try to bless the chained passengers.

Ismay has never seen this part of one of her father's ships. She's never even heard of this practice. She is sickened by the stench. She vomits into the water on one of the dead bloated bodies floating so serenely in a stew of human fluids diluted with seawater.

There are so many of them, Ismay thinks. The only way to get all of them in that hole was to chain them together lying side by side like sardines in a can. Ismay cannot imagine how any of them survived. Palmer hacks at their chains with his newly acquired sword and Xhosa and the horsemen follow suit. They move quickly, for they know these people will not live long if they do not.

For many of the captured enslaved, their minds are broken. When they are set free, *all* the women immediately run up the stairs to the deck and throw themselves overboard against the rocks. One man talks in a clicking southern African language that only Xhosa, whose distant cousin is from that region, can understand. He translates: "The colorless snatchers raped them every day when the sun rose and when it set. Some of the women died. And the colorless men didn't even notice it. They kept on raping them. The ones who survived were too damaged. The leap into the rocks is their only way forward."

Ismay will never be free of the sound of the bodies hitting those rocks. Amanda stands quietly in the shadows of the rocks in reverence of the lost minds. She will help guide them to safety.

Ismay looks at Palmer with opposing thoughts flowing through her mind: one thought—*Now I understand that these must be the strongest people on the planet*—and also *But they must have done something to deserve this.*

Palmer orders all the crew, dead and alive, to be thrown overboard against the rocks. The bodies of fifty-seven men are bashed against rocks so sharp, they pierce right through. They lie next to the bodies of the women they raped for nine months.

Palmer inspects the ship and leads the team in repairing the small holes with clay they find on the beach. Miraculously, there is very little damage to the bottom of the ship, which is why the cargo below deck survived. Father Mazenod is in shock. He slumps in a corner, unable to move his limbs. He clutches his cross, held close to his chest. Xhosa too is overcome, but his body keeps moving out of habit. Plugging holes. Lifting and throwing bodies. Lifting pails of water from below deck.

Ismay walks to the head of the ship, climbs the mast, looks out over the sea. She wonders what it would be like to leap against the rocks. To so freely end one's own life. To exert control of your own body.

Palmer sees her and orders one of the horsemen to retrieve her. "Amanda and I will need her. She can't leap just yet."

11

ON THE FIFTH OF HER seven days, Blue walked into a secluded section of the basement in the Big House where Father Kelley was now hosting their *memory sessions*. The architecture was completely different from the rest of the House. It was avant-garde and looked like a floor in a lavish decadent New Orleans town house. But it was filled with mementos of spiritual awakenings and events waiting to happen when the stars aligned just so, or something like that. Father Kelley doddered around the room, moving things out of the way to clear space for them to sit. The fluorescent lights that had replaced the original bulbs in the ornamental light fixtures made Blue think of public school classrooms. The flowers on the couch made her think of someone's grandmother's living room. Not Blue's grandmother—she had gone crazy before Blue was born and spent all of Blue's life, and three-quarters of Blue's mother's life, in the crazy house. The crazy house was what Black folks in the South called *a hospital for the mentally ill.* The Catholic statues made her think of idolatry. The Yoruba peoples who were transported through the slave trade had taken on Catholicism in an effort to stay alive and masquerade their worship of the Orishas. They took on the Catholic idols but they named them after their own gods. The irony is that Christianity insists that you make no graven image of God and worship God in spirit. It was quite similar to Yoruba worship, but in order to practice the Yoruba religion, the peoples had to place their spirit gods into the graven images of Christianity. Mary, the Mother of Jesus, Saint Christopher, Saint Peter, and a few other saints sat on the knickknack shelf in the corner. One in particular caught Blue's attention.

"Who is this?" Blue asked Father Kelley as she picked up the figurine.

"Saint Eugène de Mazenod. He started our order and founded this House of Prayer. The precise location of the chapel was chosen from a vision he had before his arrival here. It sits between time."

"I've seen him before," Blue said. "But I don't remember where."

"There are no images of him here. He was insistent that there be no paintings of him. He wanted the attention to be focused on the work, not someone to worship. For Saint Mazenod, the work was paramount."

A real Christian, Blue thought. "But I have seen him somewhere before—"

"Sit here," Father Kelley interrupted to offer Blue a chair. "What's on your mind today?" he asked.

"Work."

"Why work?" Father Kelley was surprised. The people who came to The Ranch were upper-middle-class or rich people. They never wanted to talk about work. They might want to talk about finding themselves and how their jobs were stopping them from doing that. But never about *work* itself, as a concept.

There were hints of Karl Marx in Blue's thoughts about the buying and selling of one's labor, coupled with colonial obsessions with an economy of buying and selling the bodies of others. *How do I value my labor and decide on a wage for it when it's so wrapped up in the flesh of my spirit? How do we detach such an intricate part of ourselves in order to hire it out for money? And then use the money to pay for things we hate, like the raggedy-ass houses we live in. The only broken-down cars that we can afford. The horrible food, the only food we can access, that kills us one bite at a time.* This is what work means for poor people. And they will risk everything—their health, their children, their homes, their dignity, and especially their happiness—for it. They wager everything on work.

Blue was on the verge of foreclosure of her home, but she couldn't force herself back into the work she had been doing for the past fifteen years. She hated the education industry; nor did she like kids. That she had ended up there and that she was so good at it was a giant cosmic joke.

Blue had always been confused about what work should be. She persisted in her belief that work should not be something she simply did for money, and when she did find herself simply working for money, she did so in a state of fully conscious sleepwalk.

She was Stillborn.

So when Blue found herself unable to produce work for herself, she grieved it. Any work that she could imagine for herself, even in an industry that she hated, afforded her an opportunity to create something. And if she could create something, she didn't feel so crushed by the fact that she was forced to do work she hated in order to survive. So, without work, not only could she literally go hungry, but she would also starve to death creatively. And that death felt more gruesome than the death of her daughter, which made Blue feel ashamed. Blue wondered: *What kind of person grieves for work like they would for their own child? What kind of parent? Mother?* The guilt was caving her body inward, like a building that implodes, the debris of her emotions going up in blue smoke.

Before Blue came to The Ranch, she slept most of the day. When she was awake, she walked around her house slumped over with her arms wrapped around herself, trying to hold herself up. And when she was able to hold herself up, she worried about money.

"What do you think work *is*, exactly?" Blue asked Father Kelley.

"Well . . . " Father Kelley said slowly. "Father Mazenod was a friend of Karl Marx. They discussed questions of *labor* all the time." Father Kelley paused for effect but continued easefully, "When we talk about labor, we are usually talking about what a person gets paid—usually with money—to do. But in a system based on *capital*, money is used to buy a commodity only in order to sell it again for something else that you need or want."

"So capital is money used to obtain more money?" Blue pulled two journals from her bag and placed them on the desk. She went back and forth between the journals, writing on the same topic in each but from a different perspective.

"That is correct," Father Kelley answered.

"And slavery was a commodity?" Blue asked.

"Yes. Slavery was a commodity."

"So an enslaved person was a unit of capital?"

"That is correct."

"It is also hideous," Blue added.

"That is also correct," Father Kelley agreed. "Commodities are the fundamental units of capitalism. The basic criterion for assessing a commodity's value is its essential usefulness, or how well it satisfies needs and wants."

Blue pulled out two more journals. In one of them she wrote: "So money communicates value and capitalism is the ideology that shapes the language? Money, then, was a new *currency*." *It is not naturally occurring, unlike trading two chickens in your hand for a basket of apples at a market,* Blue thought. *It must be made up, like the new language the European missionaries created.*

In the other journal, she wrote: "And if you can just create a new language, you can also just create money?"

Blue then wrote: "What about labor?" She posed that question to Father Kelley.

"To increase their capital, capitalists rely on workers. Workers treat their labor as a commodity and sell it to factory owners. But in order for the owner, a capitalist, to make a profit, the working day must be extended to generate more value than the worker's labor earns for himself. Their work must generate surplus value, which goes to the capitalist himself. This is the essence of exploitation."

It's not money I need to create but capital, Blue thought. "So," Blue asked, "commodities emerge through exploitative systems of wage labor?"

"That is correct," said Father Kelley. "What was your first job?"

Blue got her first job at the age of fifteen through a program that placed high school sophomores in government jobs half of the day and in school the other half. It was a good job, but she barely went. It was mostly secretarial work, and Blue didn't actually mind doing it occasionally. But not every day, all day. The work itself wasn't a problem. It was the job that Blue hated.

She would call in sick at least once a week, sometimes as many as three times. Nothing about the job stimulated her curiosity. Once Blue randomly asked her mother, "How did we decide to call the color of the sky blue?" On another occasion she confidently announced, "I think I can breathe water." MaryMadeline had always engaged Blue's imagination with her own curiosity as they noodled through the possibilities. The monotony of this job dulled Blue's mind and she dreaded the idea of the dullness so much that it literally made her vomit, sick with stomach cramps.

Blue would not have been able to tell you why she found herself suddenly vomiting on the days she was scheduled to go into the office, but she did get a glimpse of the problem one day. On her birthday, her supervisor had gotten a cake for her, but Blue had been out sick for three days. When she finally returned, they surprised her with it. Blue felt terrible that they had been waiting for days to give her that beautiful cake, so she smiled and admired the white icing and pink and yellow flowers on top and her name written in blue letters. She knew she should have been happy, but she wasn't.

Her supervisor, a really nice young White woman, Becky, who really did care about Blue and who had a nervous laugh that followed all of her sentences, was helping her director, an old White man who was also really nice and who supervised everybody in the department, get ready for a trip. Becky passed on the responsibility to Blue so that Blue would have something to do. Blue was in the storeroom gathering papers, books, and such when Rita came in.

Rita was an older White woman who must have marched with civil rights advocates. She introduced herself as a field agent. She rarely came into the office and was excited to learn about the program that had hired Blue.

"How does it work?"

"We spend the first half of the day at school taking required classes, then work here in the afternoons."

"How do they recruit the students?"

"I learned about it from my high school counselor."

"Who pays the students?"

"My check comes from the high school."

Without warning, Rita's questions got personal. "So what do you want to be?"

Blue had taken a liking to the law, so she said: "Maybe a legal secretary."

"Well. Have you thought about being a paralegal? I mean, if it's the law you like, I'd like you to do something other than just being a secretary."

Blue had never had anyone expand her dreams for her like that before. (We will overlook how the White woman didn't offer the possibility of being a lawyer to the little Black girl.)

Blue didn't know exactly what she wanted, but the conversation with Rita tickled her curious brain until just moments later when she realized something profoundly broken about herself: she was doing the work of a secretary at that time and she hated it so much it literally made her sick, and yet, when asked what she wanted to do, she selected the very thing that was making her ill. But was it really a choice if she didn't know about her options?

"It's too bad you can't travel with us to the conference," Rita said.

"You're going?" Blue asked Rita, surprised.

"Yes. We're all going. Didn't Becky tell you?"

Blue carried the items from the storage room back to the table where she was packing up the other resources for the trip. She looked sadly at her birthday cake with its white icing. Blue had wanted to go on that trip and she had told Becky so.

Noticing the expression on Blue's face, Becky said: "Oh, Blue, I'm so sorry. You wanted to go on this trip. Listen. Don't worry about this stuff. I'll take care of it. I'll find something else for you to do."

Blue felt the need to relieve Becky of the guilt she was feeling, so she said with a genuine smile: "Oh no. I didn't really want to go. I was just talking. It's okay. It really is." It wasn't okay with Blue, but she liked Becky and she didn't want her to feel guilty about something she had no control over. Becky's guilt also embarrassed Blue. Blue felt responsible for inflicting such a weight on someone whom she genuinely liked and thought was a good person, who was doing her best inside an idea fraught with the failings of history. Blue wished that her school had higher expectations for the students and had taken more care to find opportunities more suited to the students. She blamed her school more than Becky. She wanted to live in a society where the smartest students in her school weren't groomed to be secretaries in jobs where curiosity is a handicap. Blue had watched her mother, the smartest person she had ever known, be tracked in a similar way into the expected profession for Black women: cleaning. It had crushed MaryMadeline. And this new secretarial track was crushing Blue.

Blue's first big break with a job that she actually liked was at the Dallas newspaper at twenty-two. After working there for two years, she realized that she needed to go to college, a real college, a university. Community college didn't count. In order to compete with her peers, she had to go to a college like the two whose acceptances she had ignored five years earlier, even though most of the White male editors on the city desk never went to college. They worked their way up, the way Blue had attempted to do.

Blue used her community college transcripts and applied to Columbia University—not for its prestigiousness, but because she wanted to get out of Dallas, now that her mother had died and she had no husband or children to hold her back. Now that she had spent two years with White people, learning to think and dream like them, she wanted to move to New York City.

Blue sat across the desk from the dean of the registrar. He had impeccable grooming habits. His hair was cut and neatly shaped around his face. His skin seemed attended to on a regular basis. The lines in his forehead and those that shot from the sides of his eyes were typical of White people, even the younger ones, so Blue didn't pay much attention to them as she tried to guess his age. *Late thirties?*

He leaned back in his chair with one leg thrown over the other. His clothes were fashionably all black: black turtleneck cashmere sweater, black light wool pants, black leather boots. His fingernails were cut close and clean. The thumb of his left hand was placed underneath his chin as if to hold it up, while his left-pointing finger lay perfectly against his left cheek. His right hand held Blue's transcripts.

"These are very good grades," he finally said as he glanced at Blue and then back at the 4.0 transcript.

An eager smiled pulled at the corners of Blue's lips.

"If they're real," the dean continued.

The smile sagged but refused to leave Blue's face. She didn't respond to the dean because she didn't have anything to defend.

"We'll have to get your official transcripts from the school. And we won't accept most of these classes. You'll have to take the basic core classes here. We have our own way of doing things," he said.

Blue, still silent, and a soft smile still on her face, just continued to look at him. He shifted slightly in his seat. His posture remained confident, unbothered by what he had just implied. "These are *very* good grades—if they're real," he said again.

He planted both of his feet firmly on the floor and pushed his chair away from his desk. He finally looked up at Blue, as if the chore of looking at her was the equivalent of doing that very last push-up before your body crashes to the floor. He stood up, reached to shake her hand. She reciprocated and walked out of his office.

Before Blue moved to New York City, she applied for four jobs in the city. Three newspapers and one book publisher. All four offered her a job. The three newspapers offered her the part-time job she applied for and the publishing company told her to come back when she had graduated from Columbia University for a full-time job.

Life in New York was mesmerizing, especially at night. The lights of the city inspired her writing, and one of her university professors, who was also the program director for the Film Society of Lincoln Center, offered to help her get into television writing after graduation.

But in Blue's second year at the university, she received a call from Detroit.

"Guitar's been arrested," his sister said on the other end. "You need to come pick up the kids."

Everything changed. That was the first time she had heard from them since Guitar stole them away four years earlier. Blue had given up looking for Guitar and their kids six months after they had disappeared in Dallas. But now they had come back.

The anticipation of reuniting with her kids produced a mix of apprehension, guilt, and grief.

Blue had to move into a larger space, big enough for the two elementary school–age children, which meant she also had to take on more work. She worked three part-time jobs, piecing together enough money to almost match one full-time job. A full-time job wouldn't have allowed her to finish her studies, so Blue worked her three jobs while also taking fifteen hours of college credits per semester. Her time was stretched so thin that she slept on her train commutes. In her final year she took eighteen credit hours per semester so she could finish early and get a full-time job to support herself and her kids, because even with three part-time jobs Blue still struggled to pay the rent and buy food.

"Make sure you eat lunch at school today," Blue told her kids as she dropped them off at school. She wasn't sure she'd have food for them when they got home.

At the end of three years at Columbia University, and twelve thousand dollars in debt, she applied to work at the New York newspaper where she had been working part-time while she was in school. She didn't get the job. Overwhelmingly disappointed, Blue couldn't figure out her next move. She couldn't imagine a job that she could go to every day without being sick in the morning before she left for work. The only job that had ever been that for her refused to hire her as anything more than a clerk.

Blue was exhausted. Her exhaustion produced an erratic thought pattern that betrayed Blue's memory. She forgot that the publishing house told her to return after graduation. She forgot that her professor promised to help her after graduation. She forgot that her perseverance had garnered her an internship when she was told it would never happen. She forgot about her ability to simply *decide* and actually change the course of her life. She was overcome by the violent spirit of poverty.

Blue was jolted out of her thoughts by Father Kelley's question, "Where did you eventually land in the job market?"

"An industry I hate. Education."

"How did you get into education?"

"After completing school, the only job I could find was a full-time job at the Brooklyn Museum for nine dollars per hour. I couldn't support my family on such a wage in New York City. So I took a summer job at a new school, one that was just starting out. And then that turned into year-round work. There were only six of us teaching there, and we worked from seven in the morning until ten at night. My kids, who were in middle school by then, took care of themselves until I got home. At first I loved it. But after two years it was easy, and I became bored. I lost interest. I found it impossible to go on. Do rich people feel this way about work?" Blue asked.

"No. They don't need *work* to provide their basic needs, like food and medicine. Work is different for them. It's a life's mission or an accumulation of accomplishments. A compilation of ideas, studies, or research."

"I think that poverty is the place where work becomes difficult," Blue said. "It renders the worker irrelevant."

"I think Marx would agree."

"For me," Blue said, "work is money. But I've spent my entire life trying to change that for myself. I want meaningful work, the way you describe it for rich people."

"Do you need the adrenaline of a challenge?" Father Kelley asked.

"Yes. I think so. I think that's why I wanted to be a journalist. When everybody is running away from a fire or a hurricane or a war, journalists are running toward it."

"Education and journalism have a lot in common," he said. "They both look for the truth and attempt to communicate that truth with as much accessibility as possible."

"Hmm," Blue said.

"Let me read you something that Marx says." Father Kelley pulled out *Das Kapital*. " 'The second essential condition to the owner of money finding labour-power in the market as a commodity is this: that the labourer, instead of being in the position to sell commodities in which his labour is incorporated, must be obliged to offer for sale as a commodity that very labour-power, which exists only in his living self.' "

"What does that mean?" Blue asked. "I mean for me. What does it mean?"

"Well. What Marx meant is that the only thing that the poor have to make money with is the time they spend working away from their lives. But I see it slightly differently: I see one's labor power as a unique *something* that only exists in *your* living self. Like an *essence*. *Something* that precedes existence."

"What does that mean?" Blue asked. "How can anything that exists precede *existence*?"

"There is a school of thought that believes that human existence comes before essence. For example, I am a man. You are a woman. Man or woman is the essence that we are born into. There is another school of thought that believes my essence existed before I was born into a man. Or that your essence existed before you were born into a woman."

"So man or woman, and even girl or boy, are social constructs of who we are but not our essences?" Blue asked.

"That is correct. What do you think is your essence?"

"I wish I knew," Blue said.

"Can't you see it?" Father Kelley gestured to Blue, where she sat with four different journals and multiple pens spread out in front of her. Each journal meticulously assigned to a different perspective on the same topic. Pen colors methodically chosen to help her follow her ideas across all four journals. Ideas written in pink, for example, were written in pink in all four journals.

"Can't you see it?" he asked. "Can't you see? You're a writer! And the words you will write can change your story!"

Blue then remembered where she'd seen Saint Mazenod before. "I'm here to help you write your story," he had said to her from yesterday's sunset meditation.

And morning passed.
Evening came.
Marking the fifth day.

12

"It's been three months," palmer says to Amanda. "And I need to do something."

Amanda just looks at him. They have just finished making love and Amanda is customarily sleepy afterward.

"Have you forgotten the beach of St. James Parish?" Palmer asks accusingly.

"I will not answer that, since it is clearly a rhetorical question," Amanda says. "After those women threw their bodies against the rocks, I had the responsibility of guiding their minds safely home, to a place where *Language* could overwrite their memory of worthlessness."

"What does that even mean?" Palmer asks. Then, without waiting for an answer, he continues in exasperation, "Never mind. You know why? Because I don't think I give a fuck. I. Need. To. Do. Something! Don't you want to do something!"

"Of course. But what I see in your eyes is restlessness. Not justice," Amanda finally says.

"Maybe you're right," Palmer says as he unsuccessfully tries to calm himself. "I've been on the move for the past five years. I get antsy when I'm stationary. But I'm also enraged, Amanda! The horror of that ship is not the exception. It is the rule!"

Sarcasm spills from Amanda's eyes as she rolls them. She's becoming impatient with Palmer's insinuation that the ship didn't have the same profound impact on her, that she doesn't know the ship is the rule or that she's not been devising a plan to respond.

"We have to do something! Something! Don't you agree?"

"I do," she says, and calm washes over Palmer. Amanda has a plan.

Two weeks later. "That's your plan?" Palmer says. "Steal ten Rigaud *war*ships? How exactly would we do that? They are armed to the teeth."

"With Ismay Lafayette Rigaud at the helm," Amanda replies with a clever smile.

"Why would she do that to her own father?"

"I constructed it in her father's puzzle in Virginia. It was what he wanted. For his daughter to run his people-trading empire alongside him. I gave him what he wanted, with a twist in our favor. Also," Amanda continues, "Ismay hates her father for what he and her mother did to her." Amanda shakes her head as if to wipe it from her mind's eye. "Let's just say, she wants revenge."

So, three months and two weeks after the St. James Parish slave ship incident, at Amanda's directive, Ismay and Palmer commandeer a fleet of ten warships from Rigaud, sitting off the coast of New Orleans. Palmer names the fleet Geechee Corridor.

The New Orleans Six, as Ismay, Amanda, Palmer, Xhosa, Mazenod, and Kant will become infamously named, launch a plan to travel from New Orleans, around the tip of Florida, then up the East Coast to Nova Scotia and over to Montreal. Then they'd go back down the Mississippi River from Winnipeg to New Orleans, setting up underground railroad sites and conducting strategic and repeated raids on Rigaud's fleet, effectively bankrupting his people-trade business.

Before they embark on their journey, Palmer, who received word from Cuba that help is needed, takes the New Orleans Six and the fleet south to aid the Conspiracy of La Escalera, a revolt that has been run by a ragtag group of *mutts*—free and enslaved peoples, some of African and European descent, rich and poor, royalty and common. Palmer is so intrigued by the inconsistencies that he ignores the inevitable dangers of approaching an island in clear tropical weather. The Geechee Corridor arrives as the conspiracy's leaders are being prepped for hanging on the beach. The ropes are already around the necks of three men and one woman, who is their general. Palmer instructs his archers to release arrows to slice through the ropes.

"You'll only get one opportunity. Once the first arrow pierces, the levers will be quickly released to complete the hangings," Palmer tells the archers.

"The weather," he complains. "I forgot to consider the weather. Once we round that bend, we will be completely exposed. It would be nice if we had some sort of cover," Palmer tells Amanda, who's standing next to him on deck.

Suddenly a wind begins to spin around Amanda, who shape-shifts into a fog that works like a two-way mirror: on one side the ship's crew can see through it like a glass window; on the other side, where the shore is, it is impenetrable fog. Neither Palmer nor the others notice Amanda's shift. Except Xhosa. He sees it.

Their ship creeps toward shore slowly and quietly. The archers stand ready.

As they enter range, Palmer commands, "Release!"

Arrows shoot through the air and land precisely, both slicing the ropes around the necks of the revolutionary leaders and piercing the hearts of their captors.

The Geechee Corridor anchors off the coast, and the New Orleans Six stay overnight in Havana at the invitation of one of the recently saved rebels, the poet Plácido. The Six celebrate their victory with Cuban rum and samba dancing all night. Amanda and Palmer stay in the home of Plácido, who in gratitude offers them the master bedroom of his town house.

Readying for bed, Amanda opens her luggage. The doorknob she swiped from her bedroom door at the Coultoure family mansion before she left with Ismay is sitting on top of her clothes. The jostling of the luggage dislodged it from the place where Amanda had tucked it away. She pulls it out and notices for the first time that the crystals in the knob are arranged into a map of five countries in Africa. After a long moment, an instinctive feeling—one that comes without the need for conscious reasoning—leads Amanda to replace the doorknob on Plácido's bedroom door with her knob. It fits the room perfectly: *It will glimmer in the sunlight that will flood the room at dawn,* she thinks. The next morning, as they prepare to leave Cuba, Amanda stares at the flickering knob. Although made of crystals, it looks like a giant blue diamond.

After Cuba, their first stop is Jamestown, North Carolina. The fleet anchors in the Atlantic, while the lead ship carrying the Six docks in port. They disembark and walk through the town. Amanda is carrying her signature umbrella above her head with white-gloved hands.

They have arrived in the middle of a slave auction. Dark-skinned people are standing on rudely crafted pedestals fashioned from tree stumps or wooden crates or the backs of wagons. They line the main street coming from the port from the Atlantic to the center of town. Slave traders, slave breeders, local merchants, and entire families, including young children, parade past the pedestals, inspecting the human product in the same way they inspect animals they're about to purchase. All of the buyers follow the same protocols. It's as if they have all attended a seminar on *how to purchase a person*. The National Center for the American Slave Trade recommends the following:

> *First, breed standards are important, but there is great varia-*
> *tion between different lineages of niggers within the same*
> *breed. Still, there are a few breeds you might consider first.*
> *Senegambia, the area comprising the Senegal and Gambia*
> *Rivers and the land between them—Senegal, Gambia, Guinea-*
> *Bissau, and Mali—and west-central Africa, including Angola,*
> *Congo, the Democratic Republic of Congo, and Gabon. These*

heritage breeds have long histories of selection for strong graz-
ing and breeding abilities.

Second, if you're interested in farm production over breed-
ing, look at crossbred niggers.

Third, go for the beefy build. Smaller-framed, stockier
niggers can turn forages into muscle.

Fourth, high-strung niggers are harder to control. A
calm temperament is a trait that you should look for in any
farm nigger.

And lastly, know what you're getting. You can find a few
young bucks for an inexpensive price, but you don't really
know the lineage. If you're serious, focus on the body type for
breeding purposes.

So the buyers tug at the mouth of the product, pulling the
lips apart to reveal the gums, which are poked with sticks.
They fondle the genitals, scrutinizing for healthy breeding
parts. Traders shove their fingers into women's genitalia and
squeeze their breasts like they're milking cows.

Each one of the Six has a different reaction to the proceed-
ings. Being from Texas, a free state, and a plantation that treats
its purchased people like humans, Xhosa has never seen one
of these horrifying events. And being from a protected class
of exploitative assholes, neither has Ismay. Traumatized by
seeing too many of these experiences, Amanda feels exposed.
Palmer, who has escaped from a similar wood stump in various
previous situations, works extremely hard to subdue the panic
that threatens to overtake him. Kant scribbles feverishly in his
journal what he sees. Father Mazenod, who has seen many of

these occurrences, knows exactly what to do. He calls Xhosa over to him and says, "Walk behind me." He positions Ismay, who looks every bit of White, next to him. He places Amanda and Palmer behind Ismay. They walk through the trading post unnoticed, until a small black-skinned boy steps up onto the auction block. Without moving his mouth or making sound, he warns Amanda.

Upon receiving the warning, Amanda shape-shifts into sound waves and moves around the Six to protect them from what is about to happen.

The boy looks around at the various people at the auction. There is an entire family, dressed as if they are going to a Sunday picnic; a lot of traders; a woman who looks as though she runs a saloon, with big hair and a big dress, calloused hands and hard eyes; and several other dark-skinned people up on blocks of wood, standing naked and shivering, muttering old languages and ancient prayers that haven't been spoken in more than a thousand years.

The *Languages* begin to create an invisible ring around the trading post. Amanda, now part of the sound, travels in the same wave pattern as the *Languages*. The vibrations bounce off each person at the auction, searching for those whose creation story is recognizable—searching for those who were created with words, with language. Amanda swarms around the other five of her group to make them recognizable. The *Languages* moving through the crowds of people hit a sound barrier when they encounter the New Orleans Six and move on. Palmer, Ismay, Mazenod, Xhosa, and Kant stand in the middle of this commotion, untouched and confused.

"Amanda!" Palmer calls out. "Where did she go?"

"She's all around us," Xhosa says. "She's shifted. She's in the air."

The sound of the *Languages* moves through the air and the nearby Atlantic, sending ripples across the surface of the water. Palmer's fleet is rocking violently as waves roll in and out underneath them.

At the auction, White people begin hearing the *Languages*. At first they look as if they're about to start dancing to an African drumbeat. Some of them look as though they're in a Second Line parade. But then, without warning, they are foaming from their mouths. Their eyes fill with blood. The *Languages* penetrate their brains like a poison. The entire trading post, the townspeople, and all the traders at that auction have been rendered *plum crazy*.

Like the old woman who killed Blue's daughter, Tsitra, and her boy.

The small boy who started the panic steps down from the tree stump, walks over to the group, lifts his little hand up into the blue streak circling them, touching Amanda's sound wave. "Mother. Mother. Where are we?"

"A place called North Carolina. How far did you travel?"

"A hundred and eighty-three sunrises and sunsets."

"Many days," Amanda says with heartbreak. "You have traveled to the other side of the flat world. West. Where did you come from?"

"Cameroon. In the hills."

"Who are the others?" Amanda wants to know. "Are they your family?"

"I don't know them. I couldn't even talk with them on the ship. They speak many different languages."

"Which ones helped you create the *Language* circle?"

"None of them," the boy says, tears streaming down his little face.

"How did you create the circle all by yourself?" Amanda asks.

"I just freed the ancient *Languages* into the wind. It affected the black-skinned people differently than the white-skinned people. They became allies. The Whites became mad."

"That's because the *Languages* created your shipmates but not the Others. The Others have different gods. Their gods created them out of the earth, not out of words," Amanda says.

"I thought everyone could hear the *Languages*," the boy says.

"Not everyone."

"How is that possible?" the boy asks.

"Only very special chosen people can hear the *Languages*. And even fewer can leverage them as you just did. How old are you?"

"Seven."

"Seven is the number of a new spiritual beginning. So young," Amanda whispers. "How did you get separated from your family?"

"My uncle wanted to rule my village. He sold my father, the chieftain, and me to the White people. We can't go back there. Where can we go?"

"The Gullah Isles can be seen from this shore. Just off this coast. Our fleet helped to overthrow the slave traders there. Or you can go north to Canada. There are sympathetic Whites there. Or you can go south to Haiti. It was captured by Francophone Africans."

"How do we get to Haiti? Where is it?" The boy doesn't want to live anywhere near this place, so the Gullah Islands are not an option in his mind. He also can't imagine sympathetic Whites. He has never met any. Haiti sounds like his only option.

"It is one thousand one hundred miles from here," Amanda says.

"How can we get there? Will you help us?" he asks.

"There is a ship in the harbor. It will take you there. Wait for me on the shore."

The commotion dies down. White people are spread out over the grounds, incapacitated. Some are dying. Black people stumble off the pedestals and the seven-year-old boy leads them to the port, where they will wait for Amanda to return.

Amanda rematerializes. She ignores the looks of confusion from her companions and leads them to Richard Mendenhall's house, located at the edge of the center of Old Jamestown, about a mile away from the slave auction. Amanda's family made a stopover there when they were running from Virginia. Richard's home exemplifies the community of Quakers who actively oppose slavery, promote education for all, and labor to create a life of peace and simplicity during troubled times.

"Richard!" says Amanda. "It's good to see you again."

"Oh my! Amanda. You survived. And you're all grown up!" They share a long embrace that betrays their weariness at the years of hiding and being hidden in underground pathways. "Your parents?"

"My mother died giving birth to my baby sister, who also died. My father, Dr. Coultoure, still lives in his manor."

Richard is surprised. He didn't know that Dr. Coultoure was Amanda's father.

"And who are your companions?" Richard asks.

"This is Palmer Rose. He captains our fleet of ten warships."

"Ten! That's wonderful," Richard says. "It is exactly what the movement needs."

"What's going on at the trading post?" Amanda asks.

"With the new revolts that have been traveling up the coast, new laws have been enacted. The government has turned our farm trading post into a slave-trading post. And soon it will be a military post."

"Then it will be the perfect location to execute our plan," Amanda says. "This is Father Mazenod. Xhosa. Kant. And Ismay Rigaud."

"Rigaud?" Richard asks warily.

"I am nothing like my father," Ismay says to reassure him.

"Ismay means," Father Mazenod interjects, "that she does not do her father's bidding." He adds this qualifier to Ismay's statement because he believes that Ismay is exactly like her father: single-minded and ambitious. "We will use the Rigaud name to set up a post for runaway purchased people."

"And we want to use your home as the stopover," Amanda adds.

"Of course!" Richard exclaims.

Richard invites the New Orleans Six into his home for an overnight stay. In the basement there is a tunnel that leads to the sea in one direction and to the woods in the other. People could hide in the last place law enforcement would think to look: a military outpost.

That night they map out nine stops along the Atlantic coast: through the Great Dismal Swamp. Then to Richmond, Virginia. Washington, D.C. Baltimore. Wilmington. Philadelphia. New York. New Bedford. Boston. Then over to Canada and back down the Great Lakes over to the Mississippi: Cleveland. Detroit. Chicago. St. Louis. Natchez. Then through the bayous to New Orleans. Down the Gulf coast to Texas. Then finally to Mexico. Other stops go south and east to the Bahamas, Cuba, Jamaica, and Haiti. They are also stops where prominent Quakers and/or free Black peoples have influence and resources.

When the Six leave Richard and go back to their ship, their fleet has added an additional five ships, formerly owned by the slave traders who were rendered insane. The boy and the other Africans are sitting on the beach, waiting for Amanda. One ship takes the newly freed Africans south to Haiti. The other four join the original ten and go north. Palmer sends a ship to each stop on the map they had drawn to drop off supplies of ammunition and letters of instructions from the Jamestown Quakers to prepare stops for the underground passageway to Canada.

"When this is over, then what?" Amanda asks Palmer. Amanda embarked on this journey with Palmer to satisfy his need for revenge, but also his need for adventure.

"Then Texas," Palmer says.

"Why Texas?" Amanda asks with a grimace. "Why would *I* want to live in Texas?"

"My family owns fourteen hundred acres of the richest Texas land in the region. Part of it sits on top of oil. The other part is the most fertile growing land in the state."

"And?" Amanda pushes.

"And. If you come with me, I will give you your own town."

The Six's next stop is Washington, D.C., to meet Mr. Samuel Morse. The Atlantic Sea is a deep black, so dark it swallows up the sky. As the fleet of ships glides over the top of the water, sound, too, is swallowed up by the vastness of blackness. They typically find a port masked by trees during the day, and when darkness falls, the ships come alive and memory overtakes thoughts. Amanda is thinking about Timbuktu, her maternal great-grandparents' home, when she is interrupted by the appearance of Kant and a question from Ismay.

"Why do you want to see Morse?"

"The scientists of my home nation believe the reason we don't remember much before we are two or four is because we haven't formed significant language yet. Our gods created everything out of words, so language is an important agent in the production and reproduction of who we are. That's why we call our gods *Languages*."

"And you believe that nonsense?" asks Ismay.

"You saw it for yourself in Jamestown," Amanda says.

"What did I see?"

"*Languages* re-*creating* the traders."

"Re-creating them into what?"

"As insane, of course. Colonial Europeans also believe in the power of language."

"What makes you say that?"

"Because they refused to let us use ours or to learn theirs. It was a ridiculous notion. But we understand. The kind of power language can engender will make you go *plum crazy*."

Recognition washes over Ismay's face. She remembers her father arguing for a law to ban reading for slaves and is beginning to understand why.

What Amanda didn't share with Ismay is that her real goal is to preserve *memory*. Slaveholding countries rewrite histories and wipe out languages to reconstruct memory. Amanda plans to co-opt Samuel Morse's telegraph machine for the underground railroad.

"Amanda, you know all about my family," Kant interjects, "but I know nothing of yours. I mean your biological family, not your *guardian*, Dr. Coultoure."

Amanda looks off into the black night. "How far back should I go?" she asks with the smile of a five-year-old bursting from her eyes.

"How far back *can* you go?" asks Kant.

Amanda thinks about that question and contemplates how much she wants to reveal about her relationship with time, deciding to start in 1069 BCE $(1 + 0 + 6 + 9 = 16 :: 1 + 6 = 7 :: Seven days of Creation)$. "My mother's family descends from Kush, an ancient empire along the Blue Nile that collapsed after only about fourteen hundred years."

"*Only* fourteen hundred!" Kant exclaims.

"Those who survive the wars with Kemet evolve and set up the kingdom of Sudan, and through a series of wars and marriages we push all the way west to birth the Songhai Empire."

"Today that empire would include which nations?" Kant asks.

"At the height of its prominence, from the Sudan to Mali."

She continues, "My mother's great ancestors, the Askia dynasty, established Timbuktu, where they build a series of astonishing libraries that hold the most sophisticated knowledge of the world—history, medicine, science, religion, culture, and time. The city grows to a population of more than one hundred thousand by 1450, many of whom are scholars who depend on and add to the libraries. There are more than twenty-five thousand academics in the city.

"The location is ideal for two things. It is on the edge of the constant war between the Songhai and Malian empires, serving as a neutral ground. Consequently, it survives the fall of the Songhai at the end of the fifteenth century, and the fall of the Malian empire by the seventeenth century. It also converges at the point where the desert and the river meet, so it's an ideal trading and learning center, also contributing to its survival. Travelers can get to it with great ease. My family has a strategic foothold on the western coast of the continent, mitigating trade and ideology between Africa and Europe.

"By the eighteenth century, its location is also its biggest weakness for my family. The trading not only includes gold and salt, but also human slaves."

Kant looks at Amanda with suspicion. "It is not like this transatlantic slave trading. The sale of peoples captured in war, for example, is a common practice that has been occurring since humans left their trees and caves for culture and societies and writing scripts. My family is unharmed in this trading of people, and profits from it, for more than three hundred years, until one morning, when my great-grandmother Princess Sunnia is captured by a Portuguese ship.

"That morning, she is on her way to her garden to plant seeds she had forged through manipulation of plants, something she had been studying in one of the libraries about how lightning affects plant growth. She is curious to know if the same science can be used to extend plant life. A few weeks earlier she had come across religious texts that seemed to be overlapping with the scientific ideas of nitrogen, oxygen, and electricity. However, the religious texts called the ideas heresy and labeled the activities as magic. Princess Sunnia reasoned that the authors were afraid of the science because they didn't understand it. She conducted experiments and accidently discovered a fertilizer that will extend plant life for decades.

"As she casually walks to her garden to do some further exploration, a horde of Malian men suddenly appear and grab her and anyone standing nearby. For a moment she is able to hold them off with the *Languages*."

"Is it the same *Languages* that we experienced in Jamestown?" Kant asks.

"Yes. The very same gods," Amanda says. "But one of the men covers her mouth and she becomes defenseless. And to surprise so great that she loses her grip on herself, she's handed over to Portuguese slave traders.

"The passage is so brutal that she nearly loses her mind—"

"Like the women on the rocky beach of St. James Parish," Kant interrupts.

"Indeed. But she uses her science/magic to protect herself. She travels inside herself and stays in a trance for the duration of the voyage. One of the crew almost throws her overboard, thinking she's dead. Though in a trance, she can still hear the chatter around her. She has chosen not to stop the man from throwing her overboard. But one of the fellow captured stops him. When the crewman looks down at Sunnia, her head looks like a bobcat's.

"The crewman, startled, drops her onto the floor. 'Fuckin' magic!' he exclaims. 'I told you not to take the royals. They're too powerful. Who knows what will happen to us on this sea with her on board,' he says to the captain.

" 'Her people said she was harmless. They just needed to get rid of her. Cut her out of the line.' Sunnia realizes at that moment that she had been sold by her husband's people.

" 'And what about her husband,' the crewman asks.

" 'They killed him and sold her to us.'

" '*Why not just kill her too?*'

" 'Something about snakes that can't be killed. That come back together, even when you chop off their heads.'

"Sunnia survives the voyage to the West World and is sold to Old Man Coultoure, and one year later, in 1770, she has her first child with Old Man Coultoure, Mali-a, my grandmother. Sunnia is broken by this Middle Passage and rape. But she raises her daughter to be fierce, and at nineteen years old Mali-a leads a group of enslaved peoples, many of whom are seasoned soldiers from their experience in their homes in Angola, where they had been trained in the use of weapons before they were captured and sold. They gather at Virginia Beach and raid a warehouse-like store and execute the White owners. They place their victims' heads on the store's front steps for all to see. They move on to other houses in the area, killing the occupants and burning buildings, marching through the colony toward the Atlantic and down the coast, where under Spanish law they would be free.

"As the march proceeds, not all the enslaved join the insurrection; in fact, some actually help hide their masters. But many are drawn to it, and the insurrectionists soon number about five hundred. They parade down the coast carrying banners and shouting, '*Lukango!*'—which means liberty, and perhaps salvation, in the native Kikongo of some of the warriors.

"They fight off the French and English for more than six months before the colonists rally and kill most of the revolutionaries. Mali-a is caught and returned to the Coultoure family in Virginia. As punishment, Old Man Coultoure separates her from her mother and gives her to his son, Dr. Coultoure. The next year, 1790, Mali-a leads another insurrection," Amanda continues, "but again she is sent back to the Coultoure family. As punishment this time, Dr. Coultoure rapes Mali-a every night for thirty nights. On the thirtieth night, Suna, my mother, is conceived."

"So. Wait. Your father is also your grandfather?" Kant questions in disbelief.

"Yes," Amanda says, "and his father, both my grandfather and my great-grandfather." The weight of the world lingers in those words. She clasps both hands on the ship's railing and looks out over the soundless, colorless sea. "Suna follows her mother's revolutionary path. Dr. Coultoure tries the same punishment on Suna as he had on her mother, but he is enchanted by Suna, who ran away to Hammond one summer when the Coultoure family summered in France and found a woman who could levitate people, among other things. Suna comes back to the plantation to check on her mother and to put a hex on Dr. Coultoure that would stop him from hurting her mother. Then she leaves the plantation again. This time Suna meets and marries Charles Deslondes—"

"From the Andry sugar plantation?" Kant interrupts. "On the German Coast area of Louisiana?" Kant is remembering the story Amanda told at Ismay's New Orleans salon about Deslondes, the night he met her. "*He* was your mother's husband?"

"Yes," Amanda says. "They lead the 1811 rebellion. But by the end of the month, Whites round up insurgents and summarily execute them, sever their heads, and place them along the road to New Orleans. Suna is caught and sent back to the Coultoure family."

"Good Lord," Kant says.

"Dr. Coultoure becomes besotted with Suna," Amanda continues. "One morning, out of the blue, he grabs Suna from behind, covers her mouth, and drags her behind a shed. She is defenseless without her voice and cannot recite her hex. The result of that rape was me."

Kant is quiet. Amanda looks behind her at dark shadows moving on the deck, and she realizes that Ismay has been listening the whole time. "Ten years after that rape, Suna takes me to Southampton County, Virginia, to join the rebellion led by Nathaniel Turner."

Kant thinks it is strange that Amanda uses the time marker *after the rape* rather than *after her birth*. He is taking notes in his journal as Amanda speaks.

"Suna is caught and executed. Before she dies, she instructs that I be taken to Hammond to meet the old woman who can levitate things, and then back to the Coultoure plantation."

"Really?" Kant asks, appalled. "Why there?"

"She knows that Dr. Coultoure loves me and by that time I have already begun making puzzles and increasing Dr. Coultoure's wealth and influence. She knows he will never hurt me.

"But before I go back, I go to Hammond, Louisiana. The old woman sees a gift in me. Unlike my mother, who had to use herbs and potions spoken with incantations, I can use my own spirit. I stay with her for three months, and I quickly learn how to see into the future; and, most importantly, how to shape-shift.

"When I return to Dr. Coultoure, I start with making puzzles, but I can also interact with spirit worlds through altered states of consciousness, like a trance or wind or fog. I can direct spirits and spiritual energies into the physical world. I can absorb energy waves, like sound."

Amanda stops talking. In that same moment, Kant and Ismay finally notice that although people are moving about on the ship around them, they have only been listening to Amanda's voice. As they travel to Washington, D.C., to learn more about the wires that can carry words across long distances of land, Amanda has consumed the sounds of the ship.

Kant's gaze returns to Amanda. He has grown extremely fond of her. He's astounded by her mind and overcome by her beauty: her dark hair, slender frame, and bright eyes the color of sea glass. But Kant is equally terrified of Palmer, so he hides his affection.

Ismay, who is also hearing this story for the first time, searches her own emotions for a way to respond to Amanda's family journey to these shores. To her surprise, and dismay, she can't find one. Aloof and ambivalent, she wanders off from their gathering to the head of the ship. She climbs a few feet up the mast and leans back onto it as if she were lying on a feather bed. Palmer orders Xhosa to watch her.

When they arrive in Washington, Ismay garners an invitation to Samuel Morse's home and office so the Six can view firsthand how the new telegraph machine works. Amanda is not as impressed with the telegraph machine as she had imagined she would be. But it is an interesting system. It might be good for emergencies, but it will work only in situations where the wires exist. *We need something in the sky that works to vibrate on air waves, the way sound does in the black space of a night ocean.*

While Ismay, Kant, and Mazenod are bedazzled by Morse playing with his machine, Amanda spots something else in the corner that she decides would be better for her plan: a rotary printing press. Amanda understands the role of memory in history and the role of language in memory. She has been studying the effects of the Atlantic slave trade and has seen how personal and public memories are manipulated and even become a source of legitimacy for slaveholders aware of their own fragile economic agenda. Amanda has concluded that language is a privileged source of knowledge transmission. And she intends to leverage it.

"What would convince you to give us your rotary printer?" Amanda asks Morse.

"Nothing I can imagine," Morse says.

"Oh, come on," Ismay interjects. "Of course you can." She looks at him with eyes that penetrate his senses so deeply that he starts to get a hard-on.

"I'm always amazed at how often and significantly men think with their dicks," Ismay says as she saunters down the road back to the ship with a rotary printing press. Four hours later, the New Orleans group leaves with a military escort pulling the printer on a wooden bed of eight wheels.

Ismay likes traveling with Amanda and doing these types of jobs, though not because of the cause. That horrifying night in St. James Parish changed her, but she continues to waver in her commitment. Still, she loves conning influential men out of the things they cherish. And she likes the feeling she gets when she makes peoples' dreams come true. Ismay was raised to please everyone—her mother, father, brother/sons, royal expectations—and she's become good at it. She likes it.

The group rejoins the crew on the ship, and they continue north to Canada and then back down the Mississippi. On their Chicago stop, Ismay's cousin John Kenedy has been waiting for her.

John owns seven hundred acres of South Texas land, and he wants to expand it to include another seven hundred acres— four hundred to the north for strategic gunrunning and three hundred to the south so that he can say that he lives in Mexico, a country more tolerant of his gunrunning activities. The business of running guns for the various European factions who are fighting over the newly "discovered" land in the West has rendered him broke (pardon me: he is overleveraged). At the Chicago port, John comes out to meet the crew. "Cousin," he says as he approaches Ismay, "it has been too long."

Ismay doesn't recognize John, but she recognizes the crescent. John's family are distant cousins on her maternal Irish great-great-grandfather's side of the family. She wonders if this cousin is the one she had been promised to by her father before her mother decided on different plans for her body. "I have a proposition for you," he tells her.

The Six accept John's invitation to go to a large boardinghouse, where they will stay while establishing underground railroad stops. Having sat down for the first proper meal they've had in some time, the Six are relaxed—as much as they can be, given their mission.

"And what is this proposal?" Ismay asks.

"Have you been to Mexico? In particular, South Texas?" John asks.

"No, but, coincidentally, we are heading that way."

Amanda listens keenly. They have been hoping to set up an underground railroad stop in Mexico, but Amanda also has a *knowing* that there is something special about the land.

"Despite the annexation, South Texas still functions as if it's a part of Mexico. Its strategic location is perfect for gunrunning. Are you interested?" John asks.

Palmer's previous disinterest shifts. "Say more," he says.

"I've been supplying arms to all factions. The French, British, Spanish, and Indians. If I can extend my land in both directions, I expand the business and monopolize it."

"What do you need?" Ismay asks.

"An investment," John says. "I need capital to expand the land."

"Perhaps," Ismay says with little interest.

Amanda and Palmer have amassed wealth while on their voyage. The dismantling of slave plantations, liberating all that wealth collected from the work of enslaved peoples, is profitable. Amanda says, "Palmer and I will back you, but it comes with conditions."

Ismay is surprised by Amanda's quick response, but honestly she doesn't care. She has no plans of living in Texas and she doesn't need the money. She's already the owner of half of northern France, where she plans to return after their stop on the Texas-Mexico border.

"What are the conditions?" John asks.

"I'll let you know when I see the land," Amanda says.

John runs his hand through his hair, weighing the risk against his desperation. "When can I expect the capital?"

"I'll wire it in the morning," Amanda says.

"And when can I expect you?" John says to Amanda.

"We have three more stops: St. Louis, Natchez, then through the Bayous to New Orleans. Afterward, we'll make our way to South Texas."

"Why New Orleans?" John asks. "Your father," he says to Ismay, "whose fleet you've stolen, is there. It seems too dangerous."

"My father is the reason for the stop." Ismay has one last mission before she heads to Texas.

"Then I shall wait for you and the Geechee Corridor in South Texas," John says. "Once you make the wire transfer, I will take my leave."

Ismay agreed to support Palmer's cause in exchange for Palmer assassinating her father. After two years of mayhem to his business and serious injury to his economic empire, the New Orleans Six are back and Rigaud has asked for a meeting with his daughter.

Ismay and Palmer go to the Rigaud mansion while Palmer's fleet and crew, including Amanda, Xhosa, and Mazenod, wait in the Gulf waters.

A greeting party meets them at the gate of Rigaud's estate, one of the six he has sprinkled up and down the East Coast. The butler takes Ismay and Palmer into the Roman Bath Room. Rigaud is waiting for them, naked in the bath.

"Join me," he invites them.

Ismay stands at the head of the bath near the window, where the sun is shining into the room and into her father's eyes. She looks more like a silhouette. She undresses, slowly, almost as if she were performing.

"Did you realize what Mother was doing to me?" she asks her father as she peels off pieces of her clothes.

"I was bewitched by your mother," he says.

"But that doesn't answer my question," she presses as she continues to remove bits of her clothing. "Did you know what it was doing to me?"

"Of course. That's why I took you across the Atlantic."

"But at what point did you realize it? Because you didn't take me to New Orleans until I was nineteen."

"What is the point of this now?" he asks in exasperation. "Look at you! You are beautiful, sensual, and formidable. Whatever your mother did, it only made you stronger."

"So you approve?"

Rigaud shifts to get a better look at his daughter, who is now nude as she steps down into the pool. When he shifts, he catches a glimmer of something shiny in Ismay's hand.

"Who is this?" Rigaud asks about Palmer.

"This is my friend Palmer."

"Join me," Rigaud says to Palmer, inviting him to come into the pool. *What kind of father fucks his daughter and invites another man to do the same while he watches?*

"Do I please you, Father?" Ismay interrupts their thoughts.

"You are destroying me. You and your friends have wrecked my East Coast business!"

"But my body pleases you?" she says coyly as she moves through the water toward Rigaud.

"This raiding can't go on," he says. "And yes. Of course. You know I have always loved you. And loved touching you."

"Did you not understand the brutality of Mother's plan?"

"Brutality?" Rigaud says dismissively. "Royal families have protected their bloodlines for hundreds of years in this way." Rigaud catches another glimpse of something shining, though he can't quite make it out because of the light in his eyes. "Who is this? This Palmer," he asks nervously.

"He's my friend."

"And why is he here?"

"You wanted to talk to us. We're here. So talk."

By now Ismay has reached her father and she slides her body against his. He relaxes in the pleasure of her touch and responds by pulling her closer to him. She lifts her right hand from the pool and plunges into Rigaud's neck with a twelve-inch knife.

Palmer, somewhat disappointed not to have delivered the blow himself, puts his own knife away and extends his hand toward Ismay. He pulls her out of the bloody pool (that Amanda had predicted when she and Ismay first met) and to the deck. She dresses. They leave the estate unencumbered by guards, who have no indication that anything has gone awry.

In 1851, four weeks after leaving New Orleans, the Six and their fleet of fourteen ships arrive in Kenedy County, off the Gulf coast of Texas. They are impatient to find the nearest hot bath and soft bed. The main house isn't built yet. To the disappointment of Ismay and Amanda, there are only a series of unimpressive wooden cottages peppered across the land. But the land is shimmering in the setting sunlight.

"How is it that the dirt is shimmering more than the water?" asks Xhosa.

No one has an answer. Amanda, with her umbrella in hand, kneels and scoops up handful after handful of sparkling ground, inspecting it both with eyes and magic. Ismay takes off her shoes and submerges her toes in the dirt, wiggling them around. Palmer climbs up three stories onto the mast of his ship to see as far as he can see. Mazenod takes out his cross and holy water and blesses the land with prayers of gratitude.

The land is laid out in concentric spirals, carved by the Coahuiltecan people hundreds of years ago, creating a golden ratio that mimics the spiral of a sunflower.

"After this, I looked, and, behold, a door was opened in heaven." Father Mazenod breaks the silence, quoting from the Book of Revelation.

"My line stops at the edge of those cabins. Your investment will allow me to expand north and south: north for economic logistics, and south because inside the golden ratio is the presence of zero-point energy." John Kenedy points to the spirals, and their eyes are drawn to a flickering, soft, slightly wavering light.

"What is zero-point energy?" asks Palmer.

"A potential fuel source," John says. "All of the European empires are looking for a way to harness and manipulate this energy. Apparently, the military applications alone are unlimited. But so is the possibility of space travel."

The crew stares at John in amazement.

"Traveling faster than the speed of light?" Kant asks.

"Apparently," John says. "If the energy can be manipulated, then, yes, it's possible."

"And the equation to manipulate it is coded within the spirals?" Amanda asks.

"Yes. If I can decipher the equation, then I can control the world's leaders."

"Why don't you already have it?" Amanda asks.

"Because the spirals extend four hundred acres in one

direction and three hundred in the other. Not my land. I can't get access long enough to study it."

Amanda thinks that if she can access the equation, then she can use it to teach others how to shape-shift. After all, that is how she shape-shifts, by creating and manipulating zero-point energy, but for her it happens naturally. Energy can neither be created nor be destroyed. But it can be converted from one form to another—which is exactly what shape-shifting is. Maybe that is something that can be taught. "How do you know about this equation planted in the land?" Amanda finally asks.

"The Coahuiltecan."

Amanda thinks carefully before she speaks. "These are my conditions for providing you with the funds to expand: the Coahuiltecan stay on the land as free people. I want an estate for my family. And a hundred acres for Father Mazenod, at the center of the sunflower, where he will build a small white chapel."

Three weeks later, Xhosa leaves with half the fleet on a journey to find Liberia and see it with his own eyes. Palmer keeps the other half of the fleet to run guns and bootleg liquor with John Kenedy. Xhosa promises that, should Palmer need him, he will not hesitate to return with the remainder of the fleet and render assistance. Amanda gives Xhosa a curved round disk the size of a small closet, made of copper, powered by an induction coil, and a monopole antenna that she developed after seeing the telegraph machine. She instructs him to climb to the top of the tallest structure near him and hold the disk in the direction of Kenedy County every day at sunrise and sunset. If Palmer needs to communicate with him, Xhosa should receive his signals over the airwaves.

Xhosa takes Kant and Ismay with him, taking Kant to Germany and Ismay to France. Ismay stops in Paris to shop before heading to northern France. Her brothers (who are actually her sons) hear of her return and send word to Paris that if she sets foot in northern France they will have her beheaded. And so two months later Ismay makes her way back to the United States and, having burned so many bridges in New Orleans, returns to South Texas to live on the land that shimmers like water.

Until the new estate is built, which will take a year, Amanda, Palmer, Mazenod, and Ismay live in the town of Rogio. Every day they travel to the estate in a black, no-glass-window, horse-drawn carriage from Rogio to The Ranch to spend their days on the land.

Seventeen years later, Amanda goes for her usual morning walk on the land, leaving Palmer and their three children with the nanny. She carries her journal to capture anything of importance, a habit she picked up from Kant. She is wearing a long, flowing white muslin dress that drapes her figure and has a flattering high Empire-style waistline. It is comfortable for these long treks. She carries a matching umbrella that sits in her gloved hand, slightly above her wide-brimmed, matching laced-enclosed hat—her signature look. One that most people think is silly. But this decision is the first she ever made on her own. When she paraded around that Virginia town with Mrs. Coultoure as her puppet, she thought the style would be less offensive and attract less attention. She thought she would blend in more. She was wrong, but she committed to the decision. And it was hers. As Amanda walks, she sees shadows zip past her in the bushes and stops to acknowledge them. Motionless, she closes her eyes and waits. The Coahuiltecan emerge from the brush and encircle her. "Sit with us. Please," they invite. She accepts. They sit for several minutes in silence. Amanda wonders, *Are you the Coahuiltecan people?*

And when she does, the chief breaks the silence as if he had heard her. "The term 'Coahuiltecan' is a geographic catchall that describes many groups as the native peoples of South Texas and northeastern Mexico. We are direct linear descendants of the Paleo-Indian peoples who came to the region more than thirteen thousand years ago. We have never left. And our name is our shield."

"What is your name?" Amanda asks reverently.

"Cotoname," he says.

They are shorter than Amanda. Their height reminds her of South Africans. They have strong, angular faces, and their arms and legs betray their skill as expert hunters. Although she has been living on The Ranch for seventeen years, this is the first time that Amanda has been allowed to see the Cotoname. She overheard some of their conversations and felt their presence, but it felt like she was separated from them by a curtain made of an invisible flesh. Amanda has been studying the time veil that sat on that land and how to cross over it to the particular place of the Cotoname. Today she has done it, without even trying. She simply has walked into the veil.

"Chief, can you tell me about the zero-point energy?"

"Yes, but you must not share it with the tall White man who runs guns. He will misuse it. The formula will take you many years to actuate, but here it is."

He picks up a stick and begins to write the equation in the dirt. As he writes, the chief also begins to translate a message from his wife, who sits beside him and uses a thirteen-thousand-year-old language. "She sees a young woman who will come to the little chapel and her mind will be wrecked by the grief of her life."

"That's my granddaughter," Amanda says.

"She will need help," he adds as he continues to write the formula in the dirt. "We will look after her when she comes. We will be here. Waiting for her."

Amanda sits very still. She honors their presence with her stillness. She wants to ask more questions, since she is certain she will never see them again, but she is unable to, sensing that it is more respectful to just sit still and accept what is offered. One by one, the Cotoname peel off from the group and disappear back into the brush.

Arrested by their presence, Amanda sits there alone another hour until finally Ismay approaches, releasing Amanda from her stillness. Amanda quickly transfers the formula into her journal and erases it from the dirt.

Ismay is wearing a long beige-and-brown dress with a drop waist and hundreds of small buttons running to the top of the neckline. The skirt sweeps the ground as she walks, and it opens to the front to reveal trousers and snakeskin cowboy boots. Her matching cowboy hat complements the outfit perfectly.

"Were you talking to someone?"

"You couldn't see them?" Amanda asks.

"See who?"

"The Cotoname of the Coahuiltecan. They've lived here for thousands of years."

"Their spirits still live here?" Ismay asks.

"*Spirits*?" Amanda often can't tell the difference between interacting with the spirit world and the physical. "Where are you going?"

"To the cliffs, to look out over the sea. Will you come with me?"

"Of course," Amanda answers.

They hike up the side of a cliff that is steep and rocky, with patches of greenery dispersed here and there. They stand on the edge of the rocks, taking in the twinkling valley and the adjacent ocean. Their faces are soft and mature, reflecting the admiration and trust they have developed for one another. When Ismay returned to South Texas, after her brothers/sons threatened to kill her if she went home, Amanda slept with her and held her the entire night. They have become friends over the years.

"Remember St. James Parish?" Ismay asks Amanda.

"How could I not?"

"That night changed me," Ismay says. "Before that night I had thought African peoples were the weakest people in the world. A curse from God at worst. A mistake by God at best. And I thought my father's weakness toward me was due to his Algerian blood. But that night I realized I had never met anyone stronger than people who could survive something like the Middle Passage. Since then, I've watched your mind match the cleverest scientists and surpass their inventiveness. I've watched Palmer develop strategic battle plans that would outmaneuver Robert E. Lee. And I've been amazed. But nothing has impressed me more than watching the women in St. James Parish throw themselves overboard onto those jagged rocks. The freedom of it . . . to just decide for yourself how you will use your own body."

"I have the formula for zero-point energy," Amanda says suddenly. "With it, I will teach my children how to shapeshift. Events have been set in motion. It is time for you to go," Amanda says.

"Where?" asks Ismay.

"The year two thousand and six."

Amanda brings Ismay to Automobile Industry Lane, Detroit. An axe-wielding Geechee woman is holding a baby and his mother hostage in a dilapidated two-story duplex. A man charging the house has to be restrained by three others standing in a crowd. Tall, lanky, skin the color of coal, wearing his doorman's uniform. "That's my daughter!" the man screams, hot liquid flowing from his eyes and spewing from his mouth. Inside the house are faint cries: "Please. Please. Somebody help me." The blood gurgles in the young woman's mouth and her breath snags in her throat as her spirit struggles to slip away. Amanda and Ismay stand near Tsitra, in proximity to Texas.

"Who is this?" asks Ismay. "What's going on?"

"This is my great-granddaughter."

"Why are we here?"

"This is where the breach occurs."

"What breach?"

"The one that we discussed at your party in the Red Room,

all those years ago. This is the proposal that you accepted. And it is coming due."

"So I come back as your great-granddaughter?"

"No. You will come back as her mother, Blue. But this tragedy will trigger your journey back to this land. Here. In South Texas. To The Ranch. To the zero-point energy field, where I, along with the Cotoname, will be able to guide Blue. And it is where you and I will reconnect."

Tsitra holds on to her life. Though faint, it is still seeping through her nostrils. Her flesh is still moving to the pulsating stream of blood running onto the floor. But she is alive, and she sees Amanda and Ismay. *She can see them.* Lying there, getting caked in her blood. *She can see them.* The axe-wielding woman is still holding Tsitra's son in one hand and the Georgia-made axe in the other. *She can see them.* The baby is not even crying at all. *She can see them.* The baby is looking up at his grandmother through the biggest, blackest, most innocent eyes one's ever seen. *She can see them.* Sitting on the floor next to her. *She can see them.* Comforting her. *She can see them.* Stroking her left cheek with the caress of a hand. *She can see them.* While the axe-wielding old woman rants and screams to the top of her lungs. *She can see them.*

"All is prepared," Amanda says to Ismay. "Do what you will."

Ismay is stunned. Amanda and Palmer have amassed riches beyond imagination. Palmer's family runs a fourteen-hundred-acre town. *It doesn't even feel logical how such depravity could live in the same family separated by only a century. What could have occurred that would cause such a rupture?*

Ismay is reluctant to reincarnate in such a wretched life, but there is also longing—for the freedom of releasing her own miserable history. The thought of her body submitting to her mother's will. The thought of her brothers/sons threatening to behead her if she returns home. She sees images of the African women at St. James Parish running up the stairs of the battered ship and so freely throwing themselves over.

So Ismay, without fanfare, walks over to the cliff, faces the clear blue water a hundred stories below, with the intention of giving it the purest kiss she has ever offered, and summarily throws herself over. *I want the impossible. I want to go back into my mother's womb. I want to float there. In that small universe made of past indulgences and anticipated futures. With no beginning, no end. Waiting for the new world to begin. I know I have been here before. And again I will be reborn.*

13

WHEN BLUE WENT TO SEE Father Kelley for their daily memory session, she brought two objects with her.

"What's that you have?" Father Kelley asked.

"A doorknob that I picked up on my last trip to Cuba. I had admired it and the owner gave it to me. I tucked it away in my luggage, but when I reached my next location and opened my luggage, there it was, sitting atop my clothes, just as big and shiny as you can imagine. And perfectly positioned. Like someone had placed it there."

Father Kelley smiled. "And the other thing?"

"My book. It was my dissertation."

Father Kelley opened the pages and thumbed through them. He read the "Acknowledgments" page, which included a note from one of Blue's students from when she taught middle school. At the bottom of that page, Blue had signed with this note: "To *my* teacher, Father Kelley."

Kelley got up from his chair, taking his time as a man

of a hundred and five years would. He slowly walked to his library and placed Blue's book on the shelf next to the Latin masters.

Blue reached past him and ran her fingers over her book and those next to it, wondering what it might have meant for her life if she had known earlier what she was meant to do. *What would it be like to be a writer?* In her mind, she put quotation marks around the word "writer." She had spent three years traveling around different nations in Africa, looking for meaning. She had found it in a sleepy South Texas town barely on a map.

Eleven years before that moment in Kenedy County on The Ranch, Blue stood on the New York City subway platform talking to her colleague, Maya, one of the teachers at the school Blue cofounded.

"What ails you, my darling?" Maya asked Blue. Maya talked like an old British queen without the British accent.

Blue's response was slow in coming. She didn't exactly know how to put words to what she was feeling. "Lost. I feel lost," Blue finally said.

"Lost? In what way? Professionally? Personally?"

"I feel . . . overwhelmingly sad."

"Sounds like melancholy."

"Melancholy?" Blue thought it was such a pretty word to describe a condition that left her feeling devoid of everything except these chaotic stirrings and desire to escape.

"Yes. Melancholy. But it has a root. Where is it rooted?" Maya asked.

"I feel trapped in my life. I spent so much money going to an Ivy League university and it got me no further than where I was before I went," Blue said.

"Where do you want to go, sweetness?"

"Somewhere where I fit in, where life makes sense, where *my* life makes sense."

"What about your life doesn't make sense?"

"I'm bored with work. I thought I had finally found something that would hold my attention forever. But it's not even been two years, and I already feel trapped."

"If you could do anything—anything—without considering any obstacles, what would it be?" Maya asked.

"Travel. I want to go around the world. I want to hear languages I've never heard before. I want to experience places I could not have imagined—something that is beyond anything that I could I imagine."

"Why something beyond what you can imagine?" Maya asked.

"Because . . . I just think my range of possibilities is too small. But how can I know if I only experience what I can imagine? The only way to imagine beyond the limitations of my life is to experience something beyond what I can imagine."

"Well, that's easy," Maya said, so nonchalantly. "If you're willing to travel without the comforts that you may be accustomed to, it can be done pretty cheaply."

"But I have kids." *So that's what happened to me. My kids. When they're with me, I don't make sense to myself. With them I'm overwhelmed by my life. My life, for all intents and purposes, shuts down. Goes into hiding. Hidden so well that even I can't see it.*

Blue's comment spurs Maya on. "My brother and I traveled with my mother, and we lived in the village when Mother conducted her anthropology research. It costs pennies on the dollar. And we had a world-class education. She homeschooled us. And the villagers would stand in as our teachers when we studied world history."

A train roared into the tunnel and came to a screeching stop. Blue and Maya looked to see if the oncoming train was either of theirs. It wasn't.

Blue looked back at Maya. "It sounds easy, but I just can't see it." The train doors opened, passengers rushing out as one small mass, moving like a ball made of people, rolling together until they reached the edge of the platform, and then they peeled off, going in many directions.

"Have you considered grad school?" Maya said.

"But I'm already in debt from my undergrad loans. And it doesn't seem to have done me much good. I mean, we only make thirty-five thousand a year."

Maya was currently in graduate school at NYU and paying for it with loans. It was a completely normal practice to her—so normal she didn't flinch at Blue's concern about money. "School provides an infrastructure for exploration. There are travel-abroad programs. There are grants that you might qualify for that allow you to work less. There are many options. And money is just money. You can always get it from somewhere."

Blue wanted to think that way about money, but money

completely and totally overwhelmed her. The need for it often paralyzed her ability to think or act.

"Listen," Maya said, "if you let money decide your path, you will never discover your passion. If you require loans to attend school, take as many as you need. Use them to help pay your expenses as well as your tuition. Use them to travel. It's the one place where people like you and me can easily get a loan. And the product that you buy with it can never be repossessed: once you have the knowledge and experience, it is yours forever."

Another train screeched into the tunnel as Blue mulled over the idea.

"It's the A train," Blue said. "That's mine."

The train stopped and another mass of passengers exited the sliding doors. Blue stepped to the side, waiting for the passengers to thin out. She looked at Maya, mouthed a goodbye, and stepped through the closing train doors.

On the train ride to Brooklyn, Blue turned over the idea of going back to school. *How could I afford it? The tuition. The books. Working full-time and going to graduate school.* Blue's thoughts shifted to argue both sides: *Teaching is the best possible full-time job I could have while going to school. Early days and summers off. Maya's doing it.* Possibility emerged in the conversation. *What would I study?* Blue began to feel excited about the idea of living in a village in Africa or South America and she remembered her eleven-year-old experience with the PBS documentary of European missionaries living in that village where they *created* a new language. She didn't want to be part of erasing a people's culture, their history, but she still loved the idea of being able to just *create* something. But fear of the cost crept back in, and she felt a pang in her belly as though a medieval torture tool were squeezing it. She considered giving up on the idea. Then she made a deal with God: *If you give me this gift, then I will know that you exist.*

Whenever Blue struggled with money, she also experienced a simultaneous struggle with the existence of God.

At two in the morning Blue heard a whisper inside her soul: *The New School.*

The New School for Social Research, the graduate social science school of the New School university, was started in the 1930s by a group of communist academics running from Hitler. The next day Blue called the New School and asked for the cultural studies department.

The woman who answered the phone said, "I'm sorry, we don't have a cultural studies department."

Blue was so disappointed and confused that she almost burst into tears.

The woman quickly followed her statement with "Tell me what you want to study."

Blue explained she wanted to study cultures and languages.

"Then you want anthropology," the woman said. "Hold on, I'll transfer you."

Only two weeks later, Blue was enrolled in the graduate program for anthropology with a scholarship to cover her full tuition and a generous offer of loans to cover her living expenses.

At the end of her second year of study, Guitar was released from prison early and Blue arranged for the kids to go to

Detroit for the summer while she traveled on a small grant. Her first stop: Cuba.

"*¡El pueblo unido jamás será vencido!*"
   "*¡El pueblo unido jamás será vencido!*"
   "*¡El pueblo unido jamás será vencido!*"
   "*¡El pueblo unido jamás será vencido!*"
   "The people united will never be defeated!"
   "The people united will never be defeated!"
   "The people united will never be defeated!"
   "The people united will never be defeated!"

The chant rose up and down in the voices of the audience of more than a thousand socialist revolutionaries. Flags from their countries swayed with the rhythm of the people's voices. A spontaneous cheer erupted unprovoked and a new chant erupted.

   "*¡Libertad!*"
   "Freedom!"
   "*¡Libertad!*"
   "Freedom!"
   "*¡Libertad!*"
   "Freedom!"

The crowd roared chants for more than an hour. Blue was seated in the middle of the auditorium, but she stood up when the chanting began, swept up by the wild energy. She turned haltingly in a three-hundred-and-sixty-degree circle, watching the flags sway. To her right were the flags of Venezuela, China, Algeria. She watched the young faces of college students, committed in a way she'd never seen at home. They were passionate and resolute about their freedom. She understood that hunger, but she wasn't sure what freedom really was.

She turned again as a burst of loud voices from Korea started another wave. The flags of India, Nepal, and Nicaragua followed suit. She turned another right and saw the flags of Portugal and Tanzania and the Sahrawi Arab Democratic Republic. In her last sweep right before making a full circle, Blue's eyes landed on the flag of Eritrea, held by a young man who looked as if he could be a distant relative. The man was waving his flag in rhythm with a South African woman who was wild and unrestrained, chanting and dancing, stirring up everyone around her.

Suddenly everything went eerily quiet. Blue turned full circle to face front again. The guest of honor walked out from behind the curtain. Greatness entered the room, and no one wanted to miss it. There was no pomp and circumstance, just a simple walk onto the stage under military guard. When at last he emerged, the crowd exploded with a roar that shook the building, the flags swaying and toppling over in a frenzy of anticipation.

Fidel Castro stepped onto the stage.

Blue had traveled to Cuba with a human rights organization, the only legal way to get there. The organization made all of the arrangements for food and lodging, as well as historical and political tours for their group of thirty people. The travelers were assigned to stay in three different private Cuban homes. It was a lot cheaper and more comfortable than the state-run hotels, and it provided Cubans with extra income. Blue was assigned to the old home of the poet Plácido.

She shared a room with two other travelers. Showers, cold water only, were a luxury. The water barely trickled, though the slow trickle made the cold hardly noticeable. It was also so hot in Cuba that the climate itself warmed the water. There was no water for flushing the toilet. Blue became accustomed to lifting the toilet seat and finding the excrement of a few people who had used it before her. There was no toilet paper, in fact almost no paper of any kind. There was, however, a doctor assigned to every four blocks of every neighborhood. The doctors wrote their prescriptions on the back of recycled, reused paper that Westerners brought to them as gifts. The food was tropical. Mangoes in everything. Juice. Pizza. Breakfast. Ripe, sweet, and juicy. But not plentiful. This was Cuba in 1999 during the Special Period, when the USSR had collapsed and Cuba no longer had a place to sell its sugar. The United States had placed an embargo on Cuba and they were starving to death.

The abysmal sanitation and contaminated raw fruits and vegetables overwhelmed Blue's immune system, and she developed a severe case of diarrhea. Unable to hold any food in her belly, she lost nine pounds in just a few days. The access to healthcare that Cuba offered was unmatched by anything Blue had experienced, but there was no actual medicine in the country. The host of the house, the great-niece of Plácido, who had grown fond of Blue for reasons she could not explain, moved Blue to a private separate room and called for an acupuncturist to come to the house and care for her.

In her new bedroom, which had been Plácido's master bedroom, Blue lay on the bed waiting for the acupuncturist to arrive. The bed had belonged to Plácido himself. The acupuncturist, a soft-spoken man with kind and wise eyes, took out his tools, long wooden needles, and for the next two hours told Blue the history of Cuba while he strategically placed the needles all over her body. Blue was so relaxed that as she lay there listening to the doctor, she noticed something shiny in the room, which was otherwise badly in need of cosmetic attention: peeling paint, exposed concrete walls, and distressed furniture from the 1800s adorned the large old room. Because of the lack of upkeep, the room was gray and brown and gray-blue, with the exception of this one shiny object: a crystal doorknob so lustrously bright that it looked like a giant blue diamond.

The acupuncturist finished his work and removed his needles, and Blue sat up. Her host asked her how she felt. Blue felt completely cured. No more queasiness. She felt hungry for the first time in days. But first she wanted to get a closer look at the doorknob.

At the rally on Blue's first day in Cuba, the Eritrean man had noticed Blue watching him. So he tracked her down. He found her the day after the acupuncture and called on Blue at Plácido's house. "I've been looking for you for seven days. My name is Saare."

Saare was the minister of youth culture and politics for the Eritrean government, and he was seven years younger than Blue. But everyone thought she was younger than him. With each year of separation from her kids, she grew another year younger.

Saare was just a couple of inches taller than Blue, who was

five foot seven. He was thin but strong. His skin was slightly lighter than Blue's and he had a head of wild, messy curly hair. Blue thought his smile could negotiate world peace.

The remainder of the trip—days that began with a morning walk along the Malecón, her hand in his, and ended with random dance parties full of rhythms of color and hues of music—flew by like the wind. Quickly and unexpectedly transient. When Saare had to go back to Eritrea, he made Blue promise she would come to Eritrea before going back to New York. She promised that she would.

Blue exchanged her return flight to New York for a new flight to Eritrea, with a layover in Cameroon. As she was packing, her host, Plácido's great-niece, saw Blue staring at the shiny doorknob.

"It is beautiful, isn't it?" she remarked to Blue.

"Magnificent. Especially in its randomness," Blue said.

"Random?" the host asked, almost insulted.

"Randomness is such a beautiful place of creativity! This doorknob feels like it was created in such a place," Blue said.

"Then you shall have it." Blue's host removed the knob from the door and handed it to her. "Please. Take it."

The next day, Saare met Blue at the Eritrean airport. When they arrived at his home, he offered her the guest room, or she could join him in his bedroom. She chose both. She would sleep with Saare in his room but keep her things in the guest room to have her own space.

Saare took Blue on a tour of the narrow northern highlands that ended in a system of hills where erosion had cut down to the basement rocks. They climbed up onto one of the rocky hills about five stories above the sea and had a picnic overlooking the Red Sea.

"Those ports over there," Saare pointed out, "used to be a gateway to a practice that was at first not thought to be that unusual." He paused as if to find the words to continue. "And when it was much too late, we realized that it was a horrific custom of stripping the humanity from a person's identity. It was a slavery that our people had never encountered and had no understanding of. But it was profitable, and we participated as aggressively as Europe." He stopped again.

Blue wasn't sure how to look at him. She certainly didn't blame him personally, but her family had been personally affected. She just had not thought about the transatlantic slave trade as such a nuanced experience before. She was intrigued by the way he spoke about the responsibility for the practice as something that he and his people owned. She had never heard Western nations speak about their role in the same way. She also felt shame. She wasn't exactly sure why, and as she continued to listen to him, she began to noodle at the shame.

"It was profitable," he said again. "We also sold gold and coffee."

Blue thought, *How strange . . . gold, coffee, and people . . . It sounds too strange for them to be in the same string of descriptive objects to be sold.* "And now," Saare continued, "we are the oppressed . . . It's as if the cycle is a pedagogy that the world learns . . . to . . ." His voice drifted off and Blue hoped he wouldn't continue. She wanted to hold on to his image as one of revolution and fierceness. She didn't want to see him as she had seen her own history—as devastated.

She looked to her right, and to her pleasant surprise she saw the freedom she had seen in the initial Cuban image of Saare. He was different than her. Even though he was fighting for his own definition of freedom. It was different than her fight. It came from a place of historic possibility. Blue leaned back onto the rock and let that look wash over her body. Her face softened. She gazed out onto the Red Sea. And for a long time the two sat in the silence of that look.

Finally, "What are you thinking?" Saare asked.

After a long pause Blue finally said, "I'm thinking . . . that for the first time in my life . . . I might be free."

"What is freedom to you?"

"This. The red dirt. The Red Sea. The desert. You?"

Blue stayed with Saare for a week, distracting him from his work every day of that week.

At the end of the week, Saare was sent to a conference in South Africa. He invited Blue to go with him.

"I can't afford to travel anywhere else but home," she said.

"All you need is a plane ticket. Everything else is covered. I can't ask my government to pay for my American lover's plane ticket. But the rest—lodging, food, entertainment within South Africa—can be easily covered."

"How much is the plane ticket?"

"It's only a few of your American dollars. You are rich here!" He laughed.

They left for South Africa and made a stop in Malawi to tour the newly established schools. Before this, the concept of school for Malawians was not a building where children went to learn but a time of day where people stopped their work in the fields, if they were so privileged, to learn with a traveling teacher. Saare had convinced his government to support the building of a new school.

After Malawi, Saare and Blue traveled south to South Africa, the only African nation that had won its independence without a war. South Africans were proud of that fact. Blue knew so because every South African government official she met repeated it to her.

Their first stop was Cape Town. Saare spent his days in meetings with government officials mapping out strategies to support more vulnerable African nations with education, irrigation techniques to prevent famine in drought, sanitation, and road infrastructure.

Blue spent her days in the township of Khayelitsha, which is alleged to be the largest shantytown in Africa. It is a city in itself. Its population is 99 percent Black, and a recent anthropological study revealed that twelve thousand households had no toilet. Blue had heard that there was a poverty even worse than her own. She wanted to see it for herself. She found it in Khayelitsha.

In the evening Blue and Saare met at their hotel, had dinner, and discussed their individual adventures. Before the day turned to night, they walked over to the beach to see the famous Cape Town sunset. The sun slowly descended before their eyes from high in the sky to the brink of the horizon, when it finally and abruptly dropped off the edge.

After South Africa, the summer ended for Blue. She had to go back to work at the middle school and back to her own studies. Saare returned to Eritrea and she to New York City with the promise to go back to Eritrea in the winter, during her school break.

Winter came and Saare was married. Blue was disappointed but she wasn't devastated. She knew that his family wanted him to marry the daughter of one of the richest men in Eritrea. Blue decided to go back to Cape Town and conduct her anthropological fieldwork in Khayelitsha. She went every summer and winter for two years.

One winter, she went to Cape Town early to participate in a New School program called the Democracy & Diversity Institute, held at the University of Cape Town. During the day students went to one workshop after the other with little breaks in between. At night the group partied. One night Blue went with them to a club she'd never heard of. They were mostly the only people in there. They thought it was strange but also cool to have a club to themselves. They all walked right onto the dance floor to dance and laugh and relax.

Ten minutes later, the South African SWAT team burst into the club with rifles drawn on the dancers.

"Get down on the floor! Get down on the floor! Get down on the floor!"

The Democracy & Diversity Institute students thought it was a prank at first, Blue included.

"Get down on the floor! Get down on the floor! Get down on the floor!"

The students dropped to the floor. The club was apparently a known drug den. The police separated the men from the women and sent female police offers to strip-search the women.

"I'm not stripping! Don't touch me! I have no drugs!" one student from Poland yelled. The police officer took her word for it and stopped the search, but the same police officer threatened Blue with violence when she pleaded her own innocence. After the searches, the students were released.

The institute's organizers took no responsibility for what happened. They blamed the students for going to a known drug den. None of the students were South African. How could they know? Blue was horrified that the institute's organizers, White professors from the New School, had no compassion for the brutality Blue had endured while her White counterparts were untouched.

The next day Blue decided to leave the conference and go north to Namibia.

Blue went to see a travel agent to book a flight to a small coastal city she'd heard about. Blue didn't even know if she was pronouncing the name correctly. She pushed her address book in front of the travel agent and pointed to the city and said, "I want to go here."

The travel agent said, "Oh, you want to go to Swakopmund. When do you want to leave?"

"Now," said Blue.

"It will take me about an hour to try to find connecting flights," the travel agent said. "There's a café next door. Wait there and come back in an hour."

Blue had learned about Swakopmund on a flight from South Africa to New York. An American woman sitting on the same row was crying because she didn't want to go home. She had been to a place so magical, it brought tears to her eyes.

At that time, South Africa was devastated by poverty and racial violence in the beginning stages of power transition from the White Afrikaans political system to the Black African National Congress. Blue couldn't imagine crying over leaving South Africa.

"Where were you?" Blue asked the woman.

"Swakopmund," the woman replied. She'd written the name down immediately.

Blue had to take a plane from South Africa to Botswana, then take a two-hour bus ride through the brush of Botswana to a dirt airstrip to get on a plane the size of a Cadillac that would fly her into the Namib Desert.

When her plane arrived in Botswana, there was supposed to be a bus that would take her to the next airport. The travel agent had made sure Blue knew the bus ride was not included in the package and that she would have to pay the driver when she arrived. Blue was pleasantly surprised to see the bus was actually waiting for her as planned.

She approached the bus. The driver, a dark-skinned man with a warm smile, greeted her wide-eyed curious face. "To the airport?" he asked her.

"Yes, please."

He took her luggage and put it on the bus. She was the only passenger.

"I need to stop at a cash machine and get money for the fare. I don't have any Botswana money."

"Sure. We'll stop along the way." He didn't seem concerned at all.

She wondered, *Is this what it's like to be White in America?*

Where you are always granted the benefit of doubt? Where people believe you because they have no reason not to?

They rode through the city and then stopped at a gas station that had an ATM.

"You can get money here." He pulled up to the machine so close that Blue stepped off the bus and three steps later she was in front of the machine. She inserted her bank card and out came Botswana pulas. Blue paid the driver and settled in the middle of the bus.

For two hours they rode along a tar road that cut through a bush area. About an hour into the ride, Blue saw two tall men holding rifles and wearing military uniforms emerge from the brush. The bus driver stopped the bus. The two men got onto the bus and talked to the driver in their own language, Setswana, visibly talking about Blue. They kept looking back at her. She looked at them with such a naïve, innocent smile that they finally just smiled back at her, tipped their hats, and left.

At the airport, a small plane sat on the dirt runway waiting for Blue. She took her luggage and ran for the plane. The plane was so small that the pilot asked one passenger to move to the other side of the plane to balance the weight. They lifted into the air and flew for two hours over the most magnificent scenery Blue had ever seen.

It was two hours of mesmerizing sand dunes streaked with blond, red, brown, and beige, taller than any mountain in America. The sky swirled in an assortment of blues that looked to Blue as if they held the incantations of witches. Looking down, she felt like she could be on another planet entirely. It looked like Jupiter.

The desert felt surely like the place Blue belonged.

Blue visualized her heart attaching itself to the land beneath her. She imagined the sand as breath but also the sand itself breathing in and out. She imagined touching it. Caressing it. She re-*membered* it to the space of her own memories. She re-appended it, like reattaching an arm back to her body. What Blue experienced felt like an evolutionary presence inside her soul, something too big for her body. It was a consciousness and the essence of who she was. It was as though her body were just tagging along. And it made her simultaneously tired and restless. As Blue glided along the tops of the sand mountains, she heard a whisper say, "Freedom is the highest form of worship." The whisper felt so distant that *it sounded like nickels dragging across the ocean floor*—like an ancient knowledge existing long before there were oceans or floors. As if it came from a land made of gingerbread or antiquities of rust.

Blue was one of only a few guests of the Namib Desert Resort Hotel and the only Black person who didn't work at the hotel. The entire staff knew her by name. She felt *rich*. When she'd first arrived in New York City, she'd moved through the world with the same audacity of possibility. She liked traveling with Saare, but traveling alone was more liberating than she ever thought possible. She had to figure out the world for herself, how to maneuver through it with grace and options. With Saare, she depended on him for his ideas about what they should do and where they should go. Alone, she depended only on herself. And that felt like how she might define freedom.

Blue went into her suite and unpacked her luggage. The giant diamond doorknob was tucked away in the corner. Blue had decided to travel with it on all her trips after Cuba. One day she might run into a door it opened.

She stayed in Swakopmund for a week. On her flight home to New York, Blue took out a map and drew a line over the nations in Africa where she had traveled. Cameroon. Eritrea. Malawi. South Africa. Namibia. Cameroon. Blue had begun to realize (*make real*) her eleven-year-old childhood dream of traveling around the world to experience other cultures, lands, peoples, and languages. The line on the map formed a shape that looked like a *Door*. Inside the *Door* she saw a vision of a South Texas ranch. Sixteen hours later, when Blue arrived in New York, she had come to an important decision. Blue decided that it was time for her to go home.

It took her a year to tie up loose ends and make the move back to Texas. Her kids were transitioning to high school. She gave them an option to come with her or go live with their dad in Detroit. Both Zion and Tsitra chose Detroit.

Blue left New York, a place where she thought she would live until she died. But instead of going back north to Dallas, she went south to Houston with the intention of eventually driving to the border where Texas and Mexico meet in the desert.

And morning passed.
Evening came.
Marking the sixth day.

14

WHEN PALMER LEAVES TEXAS IN 1843, it is a free state.
When he returns in 1851 it is a slave state. Nevertheless,
they run South Texas and are, consequently, untouched by the
oppression of slavery. And just as Palmer is about to join the
Union forces in the great Civil War, word comes from East Texas
that the Rose family's influence has been weakened. Severely.
They have been baited into a small private war with the governor, who dared George, Palmer's father, to do anything about
them infringing on the land that adjoins George's. And that war
has ended with the hanging of George. The mayor is hunting
down Palmer's siblings and killing them one by one. Leading
up to the famous forcible move of the Comanche people out of
Texas by the Texas Rangers and into Indian Territory, the Texas
Rangers are already disrupting First Land Peoples' customs
and destabilizing their history. The Rangers also, mistakenly,
round up some Mexican employees of the Rose family, because
the White redneck Rangers can't tell the difference between

First Land Peoples and Mexicans. The Rangers also round up some of the Rose family's purchased people, because the Rangers are bastard motherfuckers and don't see the difference between *slaves* and *Indians*.

The Rose family land sits above the richest oil wells in Texas and the governor has been looking for a way to use paper to seize it. The governor sent in the Texan Militia to take the land and hold it; they put in a puppet mayor to run it. All fourteen hundred acres of their land has been confiscated.

When Palmer, Amanda, their three boys, and Palmer's fleet of seven ships arrive in East Texas, Palmer's first job is to negotiate with the mayor to let the remaining members of his family live.

Palmer offers the new mayor his network of connections for gunrunning and bootleg liquor and his fleet and his skills as a military man to protect the mayor from the governor. In return, Palmer wants four hundred acres of their land back. The mayor agrees. Palmer puts his mother and his siblings on a hundred and fifty acres. He gives Amanda fifty acres for the town he promised her—a parcel of the East Texas land that is like the South Texas Ranch with a zero-point energy field in the center of it—and the remaining two hundred acres he leaves to be divided among his children upon his death.

Years later, Amanda is about eighty years old. At least, that's what her family thinks. Neither Amanda nor her family are really sure how old she is. After she lost her mother to a revolution, there was no one still around to know when she was born. There were no records with the Coultoures of her birth. And she moves across time so frequently that the lines of time often get tangled up. As her children get older, they openly joke that she looks younger than them. But secretly it's not a joke. She has pretty much stopped aging. Amanda's like Sarah. And Palmer's like Abraham. *Actually, a better analogy is like Methuselah. He lived to be nine hundred and sixty-nine years old. I've lived a lot longer than that.* She and Palmer, whom she has been using magic to keep as healthy as herself, now have six boys.

Palmer still runs guns and bootleg liquor, but he has been cleaning his money by investing in the construction of education, art, and public service centers.

Amanda has divided her fifty acres of land into four parcels and assigned each one to the study of some scientific breakthrough. The topic of research changes rapidly and seemingly erratically, though it all centers on zero-point energy fields and self-sustaining cell regeneration, allowing for both movement and life unbounded by time or space.

Every morning she awakens with the sun and, based on the hue of the light, she chooses a laboratory to work in. Today she is working in the plant life lab when she sees a vision inside the petals of a sunflower she's been grooming for the past six years. It's a fertility flower.

Inside is a staircase leading down, down, down into the flower. At the bottom is the basement floor of Ismay's New Orleans town house, which is also connected to the basement of the Big House on The Ranch in South Texas. And in that basement floor she sees her future granddaughter, Blue, talking to a priest. Amanda realizes (*makes real*) critical knowledge—the blue baby does not belong to any of her existing six boys. Blue's father hasn't been born yet. Amanda is delighted at this news because it means that her *cloud of witnesses* has worked out a deal in a *conversation* with their gods to allow her to birth a particular line that is only for this experiment.

Seven weeks later, in 1910, Amanda is pregnant with their seventh son.

Palmer names the boy Christopher Columbus Washington Rose, betraying Palmer's love for wandering on the open seas, exploring new places, and meeting new peoples. "This is the baby that we have been working to protect," Amanda says.

"Protect?" Palmer asks.

"The underground railroad stops. We set those up for him."

"Just him? Why?"

"Because your god made a deal with Lucifer the Angel. You call him Satan. But his real name is Lucifer. And he is your god's firstborn and favorite son. Lucifer made a bet with your god that if he could cut off a branch of your family, then your family would curse your god and turn their back on him."

"Why would God the Lord do such a horrible thing?"

"Because everything—things we can see, feel, touch, taste, hear—is simply an idea that a god had and wanted to see how it would unfold in experience." Amanda holds Christopher with such love in the bends of her arms.

"We are ideas in experience?" Palmer asks, trying to understand.

"Yes. But I made a different plan. Your god's plan was to doom your branch of your family to perpetual poverty and watch them worship him. I changed that deal, so we settled in South Texas instead of East Texas."

"But we're here now," Palmer says. "And there is still danger?"

"Yes. The arrangement to attack your line has shifted—away from you to one of your sons. My *cloud of witnesses* and I arranged to have the poverty end within the same generation, and they crafted this little one to bear the burden. And his last child, a blue baby girl, will be specially made to bring the experiment to an end."

"Ismay," Palmer says, remembering. "Ismay is your alternative plan?"

"She is. And she leaped into the space of re-creation at the exact moment of intersection: April 5, for the day of the defining moment; 4:44 p.m. for the time of birth; 1868 for the year. A hundred years later the blue baby will be born at 4:44 a.m.—one hundred and eighty degrees around—on April 5, 1968."

Ten years later, during one of Amanda's afternoon tea and entertaining sessions with a new patron who had come a long way from Mississippi to get some of Amanda's delicate sunflower medicine, Christopher walks into the red room, a grand room inspired by Ismay's New Orleans town house.

Christopher has darker skin than Amanda, and so her new patrons never recognize him as her son, because White people can see only similarity in skin color. They didn't see the very blatant resemblances in their light-colored eyes—one round and the other oval—their pug nose, their hair texture, or their facial shape.

Shoving a cup and saucer with thick, bright red lipstick stains around the rim of the cup toward Christopher, the new patron says to him, "Here, boy. Take this. And bring me another one." She doesn't even look at him. Christopher, who is not accustomed to such behavior, drops his chin and lifts his eyes to look at her and attempts to understand just exactly what is taking place. He knows he doesn't like it, but he wants to understand why. Is it race? Is it class? Or is it just bad manners?

Amanda and Palmer's children are not treated like the other colored children in the town. The first time Christopher experiences the difference is only a couple of days before. He and his best friend, TommyBoy, go into town to buy some candy at the restaurant. When they get there, they need to go to the bathroom. By now, bathrooms have moved inside, and they have designated races. Christopher and TommyBoy walk into the restaurant/store and speak, as they usually do, to the owner behind the counter.

"Howdy, Mr. Clay."

"Howdy there, Christopher. How's yo' folks?"

"They well enough."

Christopher waits for about five seconds, standing there in front of Mr. Clay with TommyBoy at his side. Then Christopher says: "TommyBoy's folks are well too." Mr. Clay looks at him like *Don't you know I don't give a damn about TommyBoy or his folks?* But Christopher doesn't understand the language of that look. So Christopher says: "Well. We'll be right back for some candy."

Christopher turns to go to the bathroom. There was one for

Coloreds and one for Whites. Christopher goes into the one he's always seen his parents go into. He knows they have labels, but he's never bothered reading them. Because his parents own so much of the county, they've mostly ignored race lines.

Christopher goes into the bathroom, uses it, and comes out. TommyBoy, waiting for Christopher to come out, starts walking into the same bathroom, when Mr. Clay grabs him up by his shirt collar and says: "Boy! What the hell do you think you doing? You take yo' little Black self in the right bathroom." And points him toward the "Coloreds" door, which actually opens to a long hallway that leads to a small outdoor woodshed with a door that opens to a hole in the ground that smells like death itself.

Christopher doesn't like it. But he has to figure out why he doesn't like it. When he gets home, he tells his mother what happened. He asks her, "Why couldn't TommyBoy use the same bathroom I used?"

This is a question that only Christopher would ask. His brothers understand and every day are thinking about how to leverage the privilege of their light skin, light eyes, and silky curls. Amanda has modeled this practice in all of her work as a scientist, as an abolitionist, as a mulatto who lived in the Big House of her father/grandfather/owner. She has seen how skin color is manipulated in the political arena and even become a source of legitimacy for Black people. But only Christopher would call her out on her participation in such a culture. The other boys thrive in it, and Amanda wishes that Christopher would learn to do the same, because as horrific as the practice is to her, she also knows it is the only way that he will survive.

So she answers Christopher's question with a bluntness that feels uncharacteristic. "Because he's a nigger," Amanda says, and she startles her own soul.

"He's the same as me."

"No. He is not. You are my son. And you must learn how to leverage that asset."

So when the Mississippi woman treats Christopher like a *nigger*, Christopher isn't sure if he should feel like TommyBoy felt with the bathroom or if he should leverage his asset and cut her throat.

While Christopher is deciding, Amanda looks at the Mississippi woman with a smile that almost breaks the woman in half. One of the servants, Joe, having a momma who practices the same kind of voodoo, understands Amanda's gift real well. He intervenes, immediately walking over and saying, "I'll take care of you, Madam."

The Mississippi woman quickly senses that she has committed a trespass and is overcome with a fear she can't explain.

"Let me introduce you to my son, Christopher," Amanda says. And as the woman continues to cringe in her discomfort, Amanda adds, "And now Joe will see you out."

The Mississippi woman, who wants to say, "But I'm not done yet," feels unable to speak. It is a pride that won't let her look like she cares about what a nigger does, and a pride that wants to say: *Who the hell do you think you are, nigger? You can't put me out of nothing!* Both feelings are so confusing to the woman that she loses her balance, and the disconnect gives her the most terrifying fear she's ever felt in her entire life. She thinks, *This must be what niggers feel when they're running blind through the woods at night and they hear the dogs coming up behind them.*

Two years later, while Amanda is entertaining a group of the mayor's friends with delicacies made from the petals of her genetically modified sunflowers, Christopher runs into the house, out of breath and panting.

"What's wrong?" Amanda asks with quiet dread. Christopher has inherited his father's restlessness and his mother's wit. The mixture has often proved to be deadly. "What is it, Christopher? Who's chasing you?" Fear begins to rise up her spine, causing her to sweat in an unnatural way and triggering her heart to pulse at a rapid irregular pace.

"What happened?" Amanda asks. "Who's chasing you?"

"White men," replies Christopher.

"Why?" asks Palmer. He's heard all the racket of the boy charging into the house, banging and falling through the front door, sending out a ring of panic. "What did you do?"

"Killed some."

"Some what?" Amanda and Palmer scream in unison.

"White men," Christopher says calmly.

"Why?" Amanda cries.

"Because I had to."

"We have to get you out of here. You can't stay here. They'll string you up," Palmer says.

"But, Palmer, he's just a boy." Although Black, Amanda has lived a privileged life. She has basically lived the life of a White woman. She cannot imagine that her boy could be hanged like a common nigger.

"He is not a boy. He's twelve. In this world, that makes him a man. And it wouldn't matter anyway," Palmer says grimly.

"But he's my boy. No one here will string up my boy."

"Are you out of your mind, woman? Those White folks don't care anything about you! They like what you do for them. You have to know that!" Palmer shouts. "They like the way you make them feel special and important. You think this shit makes them feel special? If niggers can just kill good White folks? You think they feel special then? You can do whatever else you want in this town. Use facilities reserved for White folks. Eat in places reserved for White folks. Walk around town with your umbrella like you're a French socialite. But you cannot kill White folks. That is reserved for them!"

Palmer's words bring Amanda to her senses. She stumbles and grabs the arm of a chair to catch herself. *Has my light-skin privilege blinded me? Have I been part of their formula that defines race all along? Have I been perpetuating this nonsense?*

Amanda re-collects herself. She knew this day would come. The passes she has been given by White society are not because of who she is, but because of what she does for them. And she has known for many years that one day she will have to send one of her children into the dark night to be cared for by the blue moonlight. But even though she has known all of this, she finds it nearly impossible to let Christopher go. She considers going with him. But she cannot imagine leaving her beloved Palmer and the other six children who are grown and have their own children now, her grandchildren. Given all of that, she decides that she will be more useful to Christopher if she simply manifests into his location in emergencies. Besides, she has already imbued him with the power to shape-shift with the sunflower tea that he drinks every morning.

"My boy will not hang from a tree," Palmer says, interrupting Amanda's thoughts. "Nor will he go through a trial. You are leaving. Now!"

"I've been rehearsing this moment for years. And now that it's here, I'm lost," Amanda says to Christopher.

"Leaving?" Christopher asks.

"Yes!" Palmer snaps.

"But my inheritance? What about my kids? You always said this land would stay in our family forever. It's for us and our kids and their kids." Strangely, Christopher is the calmest person among the three of them. He exhibits a confidence and audacity unmatched by his age.

"You forfeited that, son, when you broke the one rule we cannot break, creating a problem we cannot fix," Palmer says.

Amanda stands full of emotions and yet emotionless, holding on to herself as if she would fall apart if she let go. Her breath is heavy and loud, slow, then fast and irregular, and it mixes with her heartbeat to create a backdrop of irrationality, an eerie soundtrack, just hovering in the air. Christopher looks at both his parents, his eyes darting back and forth, trying to understand the language of their bodies.

Amanda takes deep breaths and for the first time she shape-shifts in front of Christopher with each breath, flickering in and out of visibility, like a hologram image with a bad connection. Christopher walks over to her and timidly reaches out to touch her. When his hand lands on her face, she shifts completely into a bobcat. Christopher remembers the bedtime stories that

Amanda used to tell him. He kneels next to Amanda and buries his face in her fur. "I've always suspected that the stories were true. I never imagined they were about you," he says.

Palmer goes into the wall safe, takes out two bundles of cash and gold, jewelry, a ruby necklace, and two ruby rings picked up on one of Amanda's trips to Egypt. Most importantly, he takes out the map of underground stops. Palmer places the things in a bag with food and water. He embraces his son for a long time and then releases him with a kiss. Amanda walks Christopher down to the river. Christopher already knew how to follow the river through the woods. When the other kids were learning book knowledge, he was learning survival knowledge from his father. Somehow, he had known this was what he would need.

Amanda takes Christopher along the coast through the thickets of woods. She delivers him to a pack of bobcats living in the mountainous woods along the water. She asks them to ensure her son makes it safely north. Christopher and Amanda kiss goodbye. Christopher disappears into the blackness of the night, never to see his parents or his home again.

It's 1922—and the breach has begun.

15

ON JULY 12, 2008, BLUE decided to move into the Big House. It was her seventh and last day at The Ranch. She chose the room at the end of the hallway with the banging door. Unlike the doors to the other rooms, it had been unlatched since Blue had arrived. The room was literally opening its door to her. When Blue pushed through it, she realized the doorknob was missing.

The room was massive. Bigger than Blue's first apartment in New York City. In fact, it was bigger than all of the apartments she had ever inhabited. There was a beautiful old stone fireplace against the wall, and a doorway that led to an additional room where two walls of windows provided two different views. Blue fell in love with the third room that led to the third-floor veranda, known to her as the Porch.

As they started their memory session, Father Kelley said, "I noticed you moved into a room upstairs. Will be you be comfortable? There's no air conditioner in the house."

"Yes, quite comfortable. I fell in love with the room at the end of the third floor. Do you know who it belonged to originally?"

"This house and the small chapel are the only original buildings still standing. There were once two other wings as large as this, making up three original wings. It was a large house indeed. One wing belonged to the owner, John Kenedy. Another belonged to a couple who invested the capital to purchase the land. This wing belonged to a French aristocrat, Kenedy's cousin. The room you chose was her bedroom."

Ironic, Blue thought, that she should be staying in the master bedroom of an 1800s tycoon, when Blue had come to The Ranch with the hopes of figuring out how she could keep her house and her car.

"It's your last day here. What's on your mind today?"

A single word, "failure," came to her. Blue had been thinking about failure as a concept all week.

"Fascinating," Father Kelley said softly. He had enjoyed his sessions with Blue that week. He would miss them when she left The Ranch. Although he suspected that his disappointment wouldn't last long. He suspected that he would be dead within weeks after she left. He could feel it in his soul. At a hundred and five, he was ready.

"How would you define failure?" Blue asked. "I mean, really, what do you think failure is?"

"Most people think it's the opposite of success," Father Kelley said. "But what if we thought of failure as a gap?"

"A gap?" Blue asked. "Like the space between one thing and another?"

"Yes. Like that. If you were to think of failure as a gap, how would you define it?"

"Then it could be a space where new invention could spontaneously occur."

"Yes, exactly," Father Kelley said. "Tell me about a failure you've experienced."

"Being a mother," Blue said without hesitation.

"What makes that a failure for you?"

"I often wondered why my life felt more worthless after I graduated from an Ivy League university than it was before I started. I often wondered why, after I graduated from Columbia University, I couldn't find the same decent jobs that I found when I enrolled in Columbia University. It made no sense to me. But one of the most critical things I've learned during this week's sessions with you is that there is a common denominator that underscores the misery of my life—and it's connected to my kids. When they're not with me, I am who I have always seen myself to be. Confident. Unmoved. Wise. Brave. Creative! But when they are with me, I become a completely different person. Insecure. Overwhelmed. And full of fear. Incredibly fearful. I failed my daughter, for sure. I can't imagine being any different for my son."

"How did you fail your daughter?"

"I don't understand," she replied.

"Was there a moment in time when you failed her? Or was it the lack of something that you should have provided?"

"So you're asking me if I define failure as a moment in time, or is failure a *thing* and is failure the lack of that thing?"

"Yes. That's what I'm asking. Can failure be achieved?"

"Achieved?" Blue asked.

"If it can be achieved, then is it not success?" Kelley posed.

"Failure is an elusive thing," Blue said.

"Yes. It flits and frets about our lives. Leaving traces of barbarity. Savagery. Even beauty. But mostly just unfinished business."

Blue had always thought of failure as something that sat atop the trees like an unseen wind, infiltrating every thought, every dream, every idea. It buried itself in the seed of a thing, becoming a seed-bearing failure, producing more failures. After her father's death, Blue experienced a string of events that she would describe as failures pinned to a clothesline, one after another, in perfect succession.

"Also, failure is temporary," Father Kelley said, interrupting her thought. "And it can only work within a set of parameters that are produced by the failure itself."

"Give me an example," Blue said.

"Let's take you as a mother. You only consider it a failure because your daughter lost her life. Would you still consider it a failure if she had lived?"

Blue shifted in her seat. "I think I would."

"Why?" Kelley asked.

"Whenever my kids were with me, when I was responsible for taking care of them, I could not succeed at anything that I set out to achieve."

"Okay. So if you had achieved the things you set out to attain *and* you had the kids with you, would it still be a failure?"

Blue rolled Father Kelley's words over in her head. "If I had achieved those things *and* I had the kids, would it still be a failure?" After a long pause, she finally said, "Yes."

"Why?"

"Because, like my parents, I feel tricked into wifedom and motherhood."

"So the parameters of this failure are that you did not want the traditional life that society expected of you, and that parameter defines your experiences when you have children. But if you remove that parameter, or consider how you could have kids but raise them in a nontraditional way, your failure no longer exists," he said. "Tell me about your daughter."

After a long, pregnant pause, she said, "As a baby, she almost never cried."

"And your son?"

"Almost never stopped crying," Blue said with a chuckle.

"Would you say your daughter was more independent?"

"I would say . . . that she was too big for the world she was born into. She seemed older also. Like she was somebody else. Somebody other than herself. She was meant for much bigger things. And she tried to reach outside of her grasp to grab hold of them. But she didn't really know how to do that."

The room was thick with apprehension. Blue could see hesitation and anxiety fidgeting inside the bodies of Tsitra's seventh-grade classmates and their parents at the prestigious New York City public art school for middle schoolers. The stage, lit by carefully designed stage lights that left lots of space for shadows to bounce around the room like children on a playground, held the uneasiness of the moment in full dramatic flair.

"We wanted to address the entire community, because the entire community is being hurt by these actions," the teacher and director of the play said to the group. "Things have come up missing. And we know who's doing it. And unfortunately we're going to have to ask you to leave the play," the director said to Tsitra.

A fellow Black parent turned to Blue. "We're with you. I mean, who do they think they are to blame one of the few Black kids for stealing! I mean, how stereotypically racist can they be? Do they have any proof?"

"We're not going to let them railroad your daughter," another Black parent told her. "We're with you."

The anger in Blue's stomach was made of confusion and resentment. It crept up through her chest, constricting it in ways that made her take involuntary deep breaths. The anger then moved up to her head. Its presence there disoriented her.

She opened her mouth to respond to the sympathetic support of the other Black parents, but nothing came out. Her words were tripping over themselves. "Don't bother," she would have said. "How dare they accuse my child of something in front of the whole group!" she would have added. *Why are you angry?* she asked herself. *Who are you angry with?* "She did it," Blue would have said. But then again, "What proof do you have?" she would have asked. *No, don't ask for proof!* she thought. "She's been stealing from me for months." The words were crisscrossing the internal mechanisms of survival in a way that made Blue unable to speak. Only a sigh moved past her lips as she simply turned and walked away. Tsitra turned to quickly follow Blue.

When Tsitra applied to the school, there had been little chance of her getting in. But she pulled it off. Her world shifted overnight as she went from attending elementary school with only Black and Brown classmates to entering sixth grade with classmates who were 95 percent White and well-off. The changes were most notably apparent in Tsitra's interactions with Blue.

That evening around the dinner table, the silence weighed down thought. Finally, Zion said, "Why did you let them kick Tsitra out of the play?"

"Because they were telling the truth," Blue responded.

"Did they offer any proof?"

"They didn't need to. Tsitra's been stealing money from the house for months. She's stolen money that was supposed to be for food for the house. For bills. I've had to borrow money to replace it."

"How do you know that?" he asked.

"I set up a test, a trap. She failed it—or passed it. She took the money."

"And what did you do with the money?" Zion asked Tsitra.

"She took her *friends* to lunch," Blue interjected. "While we didn't have enough food at home, she stole money to take her friends out!"

The look of shock on Zion's face made it heavier, too heavy for an eighth-grade student. Tsitra looked around the table with defiance stretched across her face like a mask and blurted out, "I wish I were never born!"

Tsitra had imagined it would work the way it did on television. The parent would take a deep breath and extend a physical gesture of love that would disarm the conversation. In that space, the child and the parent would express what they were really experiencing. And at the end of a thirty-minute episode, they would have solved the problem.

But instead of following the well-crafted social script of White America, Blue said with a cheekiness to match Tsitra's, "So do I."

The shock of Blue's statement rippled around the table on a wave that hit all three of them. Hard.

Tsitra, poised to play her role and argue why being born into this family was horror itself, was knocked over by the wave. Her breath literally shook and she became wobbly. She lost access to her own words.

Zion dropped his eyes and the shock wave began a slow implosion inside his spirit.

Blue felt the shock slamming into her kids and it upended her from her seat. She scanned the room because it felt as if they were not alone. She looked away from her kids because she couldn't bear to see them experiencing that moment. "But we're both here now. And every day we have the opportunity to make decisions, knowing that someone in the future will either thank us or wish we never existed. You need to make a decision about how you are going to be in this world. Only you can make that decision. Only you."

Zion's head dropped, and when she turned to attend to him, Blue saw Tsitra staring at her. Tsitra's eyes took on the look of another. She stared at Blue with her eyes wide open, the pupils rising to the top, her chin lowered, and her brows leveling off. Blue saw someone else *in* Tsitra's eyes. Inexplicably, Blue felt compelled to call the woman she could see *Mother*, and that terrified her.

Fear rose in the center of Blue's body, but before it had a chance to take over completely, she pushed away from the table and said with the most force she could muster, "Tsitra! I'm talking to you! Do you hear me? I am not talking to that person I see!" Blue screamed in order not to show the fear quickly overcoming her. "Do not let that person take over! *YOU* take control of your own life!"

Abruptly, Tsitra burst into dramatic tears and ran off to the bedroom she shared with her brother. "I want to go live with my father in Detroit!" she yelled through the door.

Blue thought again about the moments in her life that she would define as failure and began to see them as constructions that were merely reflective of the failures that produced them. She saw those moments only as a placeholder, but if she could just shift the parameters, a new definition of failure would arise, one that made it highly unlikely that failure could even exist at all.

"So failure is a dialogue between actions taken and actions to be taken. It's the gap between the two," she finally said to Father Kelley.

Blue left the memory session with Kelley's words about failure still untangling in her mind. *If he is correct, then failure is not something that should devastate me in the way that it has. It is easily manageable. I just need to shift the dialogue.*

She would miss her conversations with Father Kelley. She felt like a teenager leaving home for the first time.

Because she was only spending one night in the room before she left for Houston, Blue didn't unpack all of her things. But she did open her luggage to pull out all of her journals. She wanted to spread them over the bed. When she opened the luggage, the giant diamond-like doorknob greeted her. It sparkled in the sunlight. Blue meticulously took each journal from her bag and opened it to a page that corresponded with each day she had been at The Ranch. Then she laid her journals out on the bed, each one touching another one with words that Blue wanted to string together. Then she took her pen bag, which held more than twenty multicolored pens, and tossed the pens into the air, letting them drop down onto the bed.

It looked like a quilt stitched of journals and words and pens.

She picked up the doorknob and held it in her hand for a few long seconds. She looked back at the door with a missing doorknob.

She dropped the doorknob into her right hand and slid the door with her left hand into a position that allowed her to slip the doorknob into place.

It didn't fit.

She was relieved. Fear peeled back from her body, and she stumbled. She had been held up by her fear.

Blue decided to go up to the tower at the top of the Big House to look across the grounds of The Ranch once more before she did her morning run. It was only eight in the morning. She still had time to run three miles down to the beach and back before the sun got too hot at nine. A whisper in her spirit told her to take the doorknob with her. The door in the small atrium was so short that she had to bend over to get through it. She turned the knob, and the knob on the other side of the door fell off. When she stepped through, the knob was nowhere to be found. Sunlight flooded the small space, and two double glass doors led to the tower. She pushed through to the outside and walked around the outer edge, skimming the railing with her hand. She could see the tops of the trees all across the valley. Her insides felt strange. She had a loneliness she only remembered having when her father died, and then again when her mother died. She held on to her belly with both arms. Hot tears streamed down her face. She felt that if something or someone didn't grab hold of her right at that moment she might fall over the railing. She wanted so badly to be back in the moment that she could re-*member* like it was hers. She let out a languishing sigh: *God, I wanna come home.*

Suddenly, Blue saw herself arrive as a French aristocrat at the site where John Kenedy had wanted to build his Big House. She was an excessively beautiful woman. She rode in a sophisticated black carriage reserved for special visitors who occasionally came to the desert wilderness of South Texas. The land lined the coast of the Gulf of Mexico, and there was no city around for many, many miles, just a small town called Rogio with a general store, some other stores for ranchers, and one big white house on the corner of the two main streets that ran through the town. The French aristocrat had stayed at the white house while waiting for the estate to be built. She saw the three wings that Father Kelley had spoken of, one for John, one for herself, and one for two other people that Blue could see but didn't know who they were—a wife and husband who looked familiar. And, just as abruptly as the vision had started, it ended.

Blue ran back through the double glass doors. *She was re-membering*. Ran into the atrium and gripped the metal bolt, to turn the knob and open the door. But it wouldn't open. Without thinking about it, she placed her own doorknob on the metal bolt. It. Fit. Perfectly.

She had remembered.

She pulled the door toward her, stepped out of the atrium, ran down the black iron staircase—*she was remembering*—onto the third-floor landing, then down the hallway to the wide wooden staircase, down the stairs, two flights, taking two steps at a time, to Father Kelley's office. "*Her* bedroom?" Blue had assumed Father Kelley was talking about a man when he described the owner of the bedroom Blue had moved into.

"Yes," Father Kelley said, as he spun around in his swivel chair to face Blue. "Her name was Lady Ismay Lafayette Rigaud."

And morning passed.
Evening came.
Marking the seventh day.

16

BEFORE COMING TO THE RANCH, Blue has no memory beyond struggle.

But now she is starting to remember.

Every morning Blue runs down to the beach. This morning, after her monumental *memory session*, she is greeted by a two-ton bull sitting on the side of the dirt road under a tree. She stops when she catches sight of him. He lazily looks up at her. Blue isn't sure if she should just keep going or stop or turn around. The bull seems sleepy. But he's huge. His head moves slowly. A thin whistle escapes through his nose, along with a stringlike liquid. They stare at one another. Just as Blue decides to go back to The Ranch, the bull gets up and walks away from the road, farther into the greenery, and sits down under a different tree, clearing the path for Blue to go to the beach.

Blue thanks him with a nod. He nods back with a loud snort that slings liquid bubbles from his nostrils.

Sitting on the beach, Blue holds her legs up against her chest. She rocks back and forth in the wind blowing off the water. Her thoughts are layered on top of the rememberings of the past seven days, the past two years, the image of her daughter at the funeral home. When Blue first looked into the box that held her daughter's body, she flinched violently. She had not been prepared for what the body would look like. She refused to look at it again. She refused to sit with it in a wake. On the day of the actual service, she arrived late, consciously deciding to arrive after the box had been closed. She had let the Detroit family arrange the service because it seemed important to them. But only until they realized that Blue wasn't going to fight with them about it. Once they had that realization, they lost interest. Before they lost interest, they had decided on an open casket for a girl who had literally been hacked to death with an axe. "Dumbass motherfuckers!" Blue says aloud. Then she looks behind her at the bull sitting under the tree and he's staring at her like he's attentively listening.

Her thoughts continue to wander through the crevices of her life. She can't think of anyone in her family who has ever recovered from a tragic event. She went as far back as her maternal grandmother, who died in a nursing home where she had been sent after living for years in a mental institution. *I don't think I will recover.* Teardrops caked with blowing sand glisten on her face. She looks into the distance, hoping for a sign—something to tell her how to change her life. Along the line of the horizon, she sees an object shimmering in the water where the earth flattens.

What is that?

First, the crown of a head emerges from the waves, like the crowning of a baby pushing into the new world from the waters of its mother's womb. Then eyes that shine like green suns. Next, the entire head is visible and moving closer to the beach. Long black silky hair is revealed. Then shoulders. As the figure moves closer, Blue stands up and squints. Then arms and the upper body are visible. Blue continues to stare and try to make out if what she's seeing is what she thinks she's seeing: *A woman?* Then hips emerge and then legs and finally feet that are walking on the water.

As the figure continues to move closer, Blue starts walking backward slowly, still watching and rubbing her eyes to make sure she isn't seeing a mirage. Every time she closes her eyes, rubs them vigorously, and reopens them, the figure is closer. Blue backs up more quickly, as the figure seems to be moving more swiftly as it draws closer to Blue. Finally overcome with panic and fear, Blue turns and starts running back toward The Ranch.

Blue is a fast runner. She sprints past the old bull at a six-minute-mile pace. But she only gets a little way down the road when she is arrested by what she sees to her left: a red room with large glass windows, and on the other side of the windows there's a blue garden. There is a riotous feeling. Jubilant. Grinning faces laughing loudly. Clinking glasses. There is a sand-colored man in a tuxedo accompanied by a man with skin the color of a dark night who carries his hat in one hand while the other hand strokes a pearl railing. The weight of the world is etched in their faces. At the end of the block-long hallway is a sand-colored woman who looks like the water woman following Blue from the Gulf. She stands in a corner near the blue garden. Another woman, with skin the color of eggshells, emerges into the red room, wrapping a shimmering translucent red dress around her still wet body. Blue feels the dress wrapping around her own body.

Snatches of the past—images that she had been bumping into all week—are now full-on projections of present-moment reality. Even her own self is changing. The running shorts and top and sneakers that she is wearing are changing to the flowing red dress. She's now wearing the shimmering translucent red wraparound dress. Her hair is silky straight and wet and drops to the bottom of her back.

And now the watery figure from the Gulf is upon her, extending a greeting. "Old friend," the figure says with pity, because forty years in this life have been unkind to the once enchantingly beautiful woman. Her hands are rough and wrinkly. Worry lines contour across her forehead. Her body holds painful memories in the muscle. "Old friend," the water woman says. "As I promised. I have come."

On the fourth floor of Ismay's town house in 1848, Amanda defied the gods and changed everything. Amanda tinkered with God and Lucifer's experiment and cast her own spell in place of theirs, a seemingly impossible feat that she plotted and nurtured for decades. And like all good spells, only the sorcerer who threw the spell can break it. She has come to end the experiment.

Blue looks at Amanda with great confusion. There are clear memories now of coming into the town in a black carriage. She remembers the big white house on the corner where she stayed until the estate had been built. She remembers the shimmering ground they encountered as they embarked on this very beach. She remembers the Coahuiltecan. Xhosa. Mazenod. Palmer. Kant. And the voyage setting up underground railroad stops up the East Coast and back down the Mississippi. She remembers a wave so big it covered a mile of the shore, and so deep that small structures disappeared. She remembers the wave that scooped up Ismay's falling body.

"Who is Ismay?" Blue says in distress to the water woman as she struggles to regain her balance and catch herself from falling over the cliff. Blue remembers Ismay and is now embodying her memories.

In 2008, riding down the same road, looking simultaneously from the glass window of her luxury car and the no-glass window of her black horse-drawn carriage, IsmayBlue comes home.

Amanda extends her hands toward Blue. Ismay reciprocates and reaches back. Amanda takes both of Ismay's hands, takes three steps back, and pulls Ismay from Blue's body.

Blue looks down at the translucent figure separating from her body. Her eyes betray the panic creeping up the stem cells of her brain. Her face is contorted with anguish. Flashes of years layer one another: 1848, when they all met in the grand New Orleans town house, layered on top of 1968 during the thirty-six hours of labor when she dreamt of this life as a blue baby. The day after the 1848 party, when they rode into St. James Parish and were captured. The escape through the woods lit by blue moonlight, onto the rocky beach, and the ship where purchased people floated in a stew of their own urine, excrement, and seawater. Then 1986, when she was betrothed to a pitiful man with a more tragic history than her own. Three months after the rocky beach of St. James Parish, when they went on a magical voyage in a black sea inhabited by spirits, with a fleet of warships stolen from her father. And 1988, when Guitar dropped her off at the entrance of the emergency room to stumble into the hospital alone in labor with Tsitra. Twenty years after they all met, in 1868, when Ismay leaped into the Gulf. And 2006, when her daughter's murder sent her on this strange wonderland journey. All those memories sitting on top of one another, staggered and stair-stepping with an arrogance reserved for royalty.

Blue's body is convulsing from the fear. She is sweating. Her pulse is rapid. She feels faint. The ground is spinning beneath her feet. Her muscles are tense. Her stomach heaves, but nothing comes up.

Blue can feel the tearing starting at the tips of her fingers, a tingling sensation that spreads across her skin like ripples across the water that she can still hear behind her, goose bumps rising on the ripples. Every breath she takes begins to shallow into sharp and desperate gasps for an anchor of reality. The air in her lungs fills the widening void as the two bodies come unglued. Her mind and heart race against time continually bending back and forth from 1848 to 2008. The sound of a clock hand twitching echoes in the corner of her skull. Blue feels certain she is doomed. There is no hope of recovering from this earth-shattering surreality. Those are the last thoughts she can conceive before her mind succumbs to a complete breakdown and her body drops down onto the ground with a thud.

What is happening?

Am I dying?

Am I losing myself?

Am I losing my mind?

Is this real?

Who are these women?

Are they real?

Am I dreaming?

Am I awake?

Oh. God. What is happening?

Somebody.

Somebody. Please help me.

Blue looks around her. The surroundings still look normal.

What is happening?

The bull. Is he still there?

I need an anchor.

I feel like I'm falling over.

I'm losing myself!

He's still there.

Can you see these women, Mr. Bull?

Oh my God! I'm asking a bull if I've gone crazy!

"You're having a completely sane reaction to some fucked-up circumstances," Blue hears the water woman say. It sounds like it's coming from hundreds of years away. Since the first day on The Ranch, Blue has been afraid of this impending moment, when everything would collide and when reality would break down into new norms of insanity. But surprisingly, as Blue accepts what she takes as her fate, the panic begins to recede and the fear dwindles.

Staggering experiences overladen with experiments and agreements made by angels and gods and clever mulattoes.

The breach is collapsing.

Wallowing in the mud of wet sand. Blue light. Blue ceramics with white flowers. Made of sand and blue-green waters. A release occurs. Blue's memories start to unlock from alliances of degradation and degenerative histories. Blue light levitates her body slightly from the ground. She lies in a place called *Unconsciousness*. She sips on memories from cups made of fine china. She smells the silks of vibrant colors. She feels emptied out of horror and misery. Her skin is regenerating. Her hair is growing exponentially in time. Inconsequential people—people who want nothing from her nor can do anything for her; people whose only relevance is their humanity—surround her with joy in the crevices of their smiles and satisfaction piercing from their eyes. She sees struggle as self-imposed and made of her own undoing. Fear, ambivalence, and internal chaos sewn from rupture, social disconnection, large-scale trauma, and ritualized lies.

Amanda had a plan.

"The worst thing that slavery did for the more than nine million victims of it," Blue hears Amanda say, "was the rewrite of their story. Slaveholders only passed down stories of misery, ineptitude, and failure. This erasure wrecked us. Stripped us of our anchor. Made us fearful. Weaponized that fear and legalized the consequences. Put together, it left us without a *blueprint*."

Amanda continues, "But you're free now. The rupture that tore your father away from his inheritance was supposed to doom your branch of the family to eternal poverty. And it would have been the end of your family line, because the poverty strain attracted other strains. Your mother, bless her dear heart, was wrecked by her mother's insanity. Your husband and that wretched family doomed your daughter to grief and to misconceive the practical applications that life demands. We cannot always live in the clouds of our fantasies. A misconception of practicality framed all her decisions. It grieved my heart to watch her die so violently. No matter how hard you worked, you would never have escaped it. So I substituted Ismay into your body so that she would live that heartbroken life, and at the moment she died, at forty years old in 1868 at 4:44 p.m., you would return to this spot at forty. Born in 1968 at 4:44 a.m., you would return to the zero-point energy field of South Texas where I left a new energy constructed out of a new flesh in the gap of zero-point energy, a flesh for you to embody. You've been bumping into it all week. A flesh with the knowledge of your history and your possibility. A possibility embedded in a history without fear."

Blue's face softens as fear releases itself from her mind and brain.

"You have been so afraid of losing your mind," Amanda continues. "That's reasonable. But it wasn't *your* mind! Gods with too much time on their hands played a cruel experiment on you. They levied a war on your mind and body through an unjust institutional system of race designed to break you. Let it go.

"Your history does not control you. You control your history by taking control of who you are. Take control of who you are, and you can tell your own story."

As Blue lies on the ground, she experiences a feeling she has never felt before. It is pleasing and graceful, stylish and discerning, clever and inventive, nimble and dexterous. It feels empowering and connected to the fibers in her being. Like it can—like *she* can—*create*. She contemplates the feeling with earnest intention. She folds it over in her mind. She considers how the feeling is settling in her body. She resolves.

She feels free.

"Can you see now?" Amanda asks Blue. "Can you see that the other side of knowing is memory?"

Blue remembers hearing those words on her first day at The Ranch.

"Can you see that the loss of memory is insanity?"

Blue has wondered who spoke those words. She has wondered if she made them up in her own mind. As she listens to the water woman bending over her limp body, Blue re-*members* that the voice behind those words is the same voice that began interrogating her memory on July 12, 2006—the day it all started, the day when Tsitra was murdered, the day Blue was coerced across time so that she could know for certain that the water woman and her story are real.

"Can you see that the other side of insanity is sanity?"

Blue's eyes open to see the water woman standing over her and speaking the words from hundreds of years ago. Blue recognizes her from the vision that she had earlier that morning, and she remembers where she's seen the woman and her husband before. Their painted portraits stood on the bookcase in Blue's childhood home. It was Amanda and Palmer, her grandparents, who lived in the other wing of the South Texas ranch.

Amanda looks behind Blue's eyes, which are shaped just like Amanda's: one is round and one is oval. Amanda sees that Blue's eyes are still innocent and youthful. Inside is the girl Amanda planned more than a hundred years ago to protect.

"Can you see now," Amanda continues, "that the *blue* is where God lives?"

Blue squirms in the dirt. Sand sticks to her body. Her thoughts encircle Amanda's words, which feel like fingers caressing Blue's sense of possibility—possibilities of salvage and recovery. *I want the impossible. I want to go back into my mother's womb. I want to float there. In that small universe made of past indulgences and anticipated futures. With no beginning, no end. Waiting for the new world to begin. I know I have been here before. And again I have been reborn.*

By the seventh day, God has finished the work *She* has been doing; so on the seventh day, *She* rests from all her work, and the gap is emptied out. Ismay walks out of the gap—the space found between the last one and the next one. Ismay leaves Blue's body on the beach and walks with Amanda back into the Gulf of Mexico. They are both walking on the surface of the water and, as they move toward the horizon, their feet immerse into the ocean. Legs, hips, and buttocks follow suit. Arms and upper torsos plunge deeper. Their faces absorb the shimmering light that sits flat on the sea, as they are at eye level with the water. Finally, a lacy, frilly white umbrella submerges at the horizon, where the earth flattens, leaving Blue on the beach to alter her past, realized in the present and anticipating the future. A future that becomes present in a process of having been. Flashes of a rescripted history flicker before Blue's eyes: images of the New Orleans town house fourth-floor agreement, her own body hanging upside down and spinning into a shiny chrysalis and emerging as a swarm of tiny blue butterflies. *Blue kisses . . . raindrops . . . teardrops of sweet things. Smiling like pickles and chimera bells whispering words into her mouth; lickable words running shyly down her face like her own tears. Sweet smells of blue apples. Blue turkeys clapping blue wings. Bluegrass in Appalachian Mountains making music in the dew. Blue blessings in a desert place. Blue offerings of sweet fruit glittering from the ground, squeezing lines of tear-like water from its mouth. Soft feathers from cotton trees blowing stifling air. Blue spiders spinning blue webs catching sweet blue babies that no body wants.*

On July 12, 2008, a Friday, at 4:44 p.m., Blue is born again.

ACKNOWLEDGMENTS

First there was Halim.

But before that, there was Richard Peña. And Richard was the first person to tell me that what I was good at in my own mind was also good outside my own mind.

Then more than ten years after Richard, there was Lynn Love, who, when I said to her, "I really want to write novels, but I know that's not realistic," responded with, "Well. It *is* possible." And because she is a working writer, I began to become aware of something sweet and enchanting. I became aware of the thing that lives inside our souls, the thing that, every now and then, cajoles us toward the awareness of the probabilities of impossibility. Without that awareness, I could not have done this.

And then there was SARK (Susan Ariel Rainbow Kennedy), who, after I read her a paragraph of the first rough draft of *Blue*, spontaneously yelled out into the atmosphere of synchronistic manifestation, "Bestseller!" And because I didn't really believe in my own self, I didn't even hear the wonderful prediction that just suddenly overcame her emotions. But then she stopped me from moving on from that important creation moment and said, "Did you hear what I said?" And in case I hadn't, she repeated it.

And after SARK was Mona de Vestel, my developmental editor, who could see beauty tucked up inside a string of thoughts in no particular order of imagination but strung nonetheless in a particular succession of time misbehaving.

And after Mona, there was my agent, Mary Krienke, without whom *Blue* would not have seen the light of day. I love that phrase, *light of day*. I imagine *Blue* was hovering in the night space of a watery and formless place on the edge of creation, and suddenly the *light* made its appearance, and it became a *day*.

And after Mary, there was Chelsea Cutchens, whose brilliance shepherded *Blue* to the public, and who said she read the initial submission in two sittings, only because she had been interrupted by someone in the first sitting.

And at that moment, it occurred to me, and I hoped for the occurrence to be so, because it so easily slid into the space opened up by SARK, the space of synchronistic manifestation, and I dared to consider, to acknowledge, that with the community of creatives that had contributed to the making of me and this work, I dared to consider, to acknowledge, that *Blue* might be a page-turner. And in that daring space, I acknowledge each one of you, individually and collectively, as essential to this *light of day*.